She wouldn't climb out of the bed for her sister, but she had climbed into a crater. She wouldn't cross a room, but she had crossed a continent.

—*Anthony Marra*, A Constellation of Vital Phenomena

THE PROPHECY

"As the seas rise,
all will be crushed under a great revenge.
Even the Suffering Servant will not be able to stand against the
Cursed One.
Families will crumble as dust divides blood and
the betrayer unknowingly pulls the light to power.
If the Chosen One does not stand,
lands will be devoured by gnashing teeth, for the fate of all will
hinge on the bonds of one severed.

Carla, could you please make sure this gets emailed out?"

-*Thackeray Chadwick, famous prophet/womanizer*

PART I

SISTER OF THE CHOSEN ONE

1

VALORA

IT'S TIME TO SAVE THE WORLD. *AGAIN*.

From just above me comes a high-pitched wail, and the sustainable wood wall behind my head explodes into jagged shards. A Mistspawn, an abomination plucked from some underwater cave by Erys, Cursed One and ultimate pain-in-my-ass, pulls back its long tentacles and stares longingly my way. I can feel its breath on my face, can see the steaming black saliva dripping from its rotating rows of razor-sharp fangs. Its three eyeballs follow me as I dart behind a statue, its tentacles wriggling like manic snakes. I lean my head back against what remains of the wall and breathe. *This is what I do*, I remind myself. *This is what I train for*. Never mind that my heart is beating outside my chest and my hands are shaking. *Get it together, Chosen One*. The Mistspawn lurches forward but loses its balance in the process. It's hungry for me, for everyone inside the school, and that's its mistake. When you're hungry, you make dumb mistakes.

Just ask my sister.

I snicker at the thought and leap forward, rolling so that my knees absorb the impact, but it still hurts. I fight through the pain and look up. Above me, students and teachers watch from the windows of Proctor Moor, safe and protected behind the thick glass, watching Valora Rigmore do what she was prophesied to do: fight monsters. They will cry if I die. *Maybe.*

But not before they try to film the event live.

I hear it slouching up behind me, hear the wet smacking sounds of its tentacle feet. This one is faster than the other monsters have been. *They are always getting faster.* I watch as a tentacle begins to snake its way around the base of the statue in front of the school. I look up and see him: Everett Proctor in all his stone glory, his hands pushed out in front of him, his palms cracking with the telekinetic power that we share. I shake my head, my body hidden in his shadow.

The plaque at the base of the statue reads *All hail Everett Proctor, the most powerful Exceptional of all time.*

I hate him so much and could stew in that for a good long while, but this creature is now getting even closer to the school named after him and everyone is waiting on me to do something. I spin, but it's too late: I watch as tiny, wriggling creatures begin falling from its abdomen and slithering like mad towards the school. The last thing I want to do is find one of these monsters coming up the drain in my private bathroom, so I throw up my hands and focus on the doors and windows to the school. Those creatures can't get in; if that happens I won't see sleep for awhile and somehow I still have to take a math test tomorrow. I haven't studied. Um, ever.

I spread my fingers wide. All at once, I feel the rush of power leave through my palms, draining me as it goes, but all the doors and windows to the school slam shut. I hear the collective groan of hundreds of students as their entertainment for the day is abruptly ended for their own safety. What a bunch of whiners they are, especially considering that they'll all see it later. Videos of my fights will be broadcast everywhere at the school, on television networks, but most importantly, on the endless internet loop.

Using my fingers as though I'm opening a latch, I pull open just one single window, the one belonging to Miss Renata Flores, my mentor. Even in the middle of this chaos, I can already imagine the annoyance on her face and the admonitions that she will blast me with later. Another tentacle sneaks over the shoulder of the statue. Absentmindedly, I rub my throbbing hands, wrinkling up my nose in the way that my publicist has told me not to. The searing pain is back in my palms – it's particularly bad when I'm fighting. I'm jerked out of my pain by Renata madly screaming something from the window. I turn around two seconds too late.

Suddenly, the Mistspawn is upon me, wet tentacles all around as it heaves itself over the statue. Its fangs snap hungrily as the tiny little barbs in its arm dig into my right foot and drag me forward. My head hits the ground hard and I'm pulled toward it, sliding on my back through its nasty slime. I want to scream hysterically like any sane person would when being dragged into the mouth of a beast, but instead I flex my fingers and smile as the pain disappears.

One more time, I tell myself, *just one more time. One more fight.*

It's a lie. I know it. Renata Flores knows it. God, even this creature that looks like an angry rectum knows it. Instead of screaming I grab for the dagger in my boot, the one rigged with a laser edge that sparks when I open it. With a photogenic florish, I slice the Mistspawn's tentacle holding my other foot, and it flops to the ground. The creature lets out a scream that curdles my stomach.

I slowly climb to my feet, aware that every move I make will be analyzed, slow-motioned, and catalogued. "Valora Rigmore defeats Mistspawn," the papers will read tomorrow. My dad will frame it and give copies to everyone he knows. I know I should at least get a good picture out of this whole experience, so I turn my head, looking brazenly out over the green hills of Connecticut, hoping that there is a dramatic smear of blood on my cheek or something. The wind catches my jagged chin-length blonde hair (trimmed every other week!) and whips it around my head. I narrow my olive-green eyes into a stare of determination and slowly raise my hands.

CLICK. There it is, the money shot, and now it's time to actually fight, because I'm exhausted and this creature is gross and I'm going to have to take a thousand showers when I get back to my room. I dare to fantasize for a second that Grier won't be there and I'll have some peace and quiet. I almost laugh.

As if. *Grier's always there.*

The creature hurls itself towards me, tentacles outstretched in a death grip. I crouch down and lock eyes with the thing that wants to rip me limb from limb and wink. I press my hands outwards, feeling the power pool inside of them. I am careful, I am controlled. I'm not rushing because this is one of the fun parts. One of the *only* fun parts.

I maneuver around the monster, my feet quick, as it raises dozens of tentacles my way and hisses. When it gets close to me, I freeze its revolting jellied form in place. Technically, my Exceptional power is telekinesis, but what it really is is awesome. I begin to swirl my fingers, concentrating on the Mistspawn's tentacles – thicker than my head - as I make them wrap around its own body, tightening ever so slowly. This creature is going to be both the deer and the python and *I am going squeeze it to death.* I grin nastily as I wrap the last tentacle around its face, blocking its revolting mouth. Then I squeeze my hands together. Tighter. I twist my face as my knuckles go white. *Tighter.*

Once the Mistspawn is bound, I shoot out my other hand and swipe all the tiny monsters that are still running up the bridge and the walls of the school off into the moat. I don't need to worry; the nightmarish creatures that sleep in the foggy deep will take *good* care of them. Seconds later I hear their high-pitched screams followed by another sound: a disgusting gnashing, accompanied by whimpers of pain.

Oh, god. I roll my eyes. The Mistspawn is trying to eat through its own tentacle. It's time to finish this. With one forward hand motion, I fling back open the windows and the doors of Proctor Moor to let everyone see the big finish.

Eat it up, you sycophants.

Using the remnants of my power, I slowly raise both of my hands in front of me, lifting the monster up and off the ground. It's heavy, and it feels like the skin is being pulled from my palms. I shake the hair out of my face and focus on lifting it higher and higher until it's eye-level with Renata, who looks down at me with barely controlled fury. I can hear her now, the whip of her sharp Colombian accent: *Stop showing off! You are called to a serious vocation! You are the Chosen One!* I hear the delighted gasps of the younger students as they get to see the suffocating creature up close, black saliva dripping down onto the statue of Everett Proctor. I smile as an idea takes hold.

"Don't you dare," yells Renata from the balcony above me. "Valora. No. Stop!"

My left hand gives a tremble and I know what comes next; a searing pain that pierces and burns. Instead of feeling it, I throw my arms wide, pulling the power back within myself and the creature falls to earth, screaming as it goes. I step back as it falls and push my hand out in front of my face, creating a protective pocket of air in front of me. This is going to be gross, but one benefit to being Valora Rigmore is that you don't ever have clean-up duty. Ever.

The Mistspawn lands directly on top of the stone statue of Everett Proctor. The large statue splits its body down the center and it ends up a bloody, meaty donut at the bottom, a literal pile of steaming evil. I smile and drop my arm.

Take that, Erys. The crowd of students above me bursts into wild cheers and I raise my hands and wave at them with my golden nails flashing in the sunlight. (I really should have a sponsorship deals for these.) The modern metal drawbridge to the school unfolds itself and students come streaming out. I fight back the rising panic as everyone surges towards me, their waves crashing over my body.

"Let her through!" booms Renata's voice, and I'm incredibly grateful, because all I want to do now is take a nap and shower for eternity. My mentor takes my hand and moves me through the school, past the reading pods and the sustainable bamboo forest, past the line of teachers who are applauding me. No one stops her because she is Renata Flores and everyone is afraid of her.

We wind through the hallways until we make a right turn into the Rigmore Wing, the wing named after yours truly. Marking the hallway to my room are a number of framed posters on the wall which feature moments from different fights: one from when I defeated the Gallsoul in a graveyard outside of Mystic; another from when I lanced the Ash Golem through the forehead in Torrington, and finally, my headshot. As we hustle past, I stare at myself in wonder: Steely green eyes, sharp blond hair, my black military-esque uniform hugging all the right places: *who is that girl?*

Finally, my room appears on the right. Renata puts a hand on my back. "I'll save my lecture until tomorrow."

I nod weakly. "Thanks for that."

"You're getting reckless, Valora."

I ignore her and pull open the door. "Whatever you say, Renata."

She gives me a look that could freeze the sun before disappearing down the hallway. I slip into my room, but before I even take two steps forward, my blood starts to boil. There she is, my lovely twin sister Grier, sprawled in a chair and buried in a book, the only person in all of Proctor Moor who couldn't be bothered to watch me fight. She doesn't care. Familiar rage curls my fingers and her book slams shut before I fling it across the room. Grier sits up, her glasses askew on her face.

"What the hell, Valora?"

I smile meanly at her and sink onto my bed. I close my eyes and try to ignore the alarm bells ringing in my head, singing out troubling thoughts about monsters and prophecies and Erys.

Eventually, I hear my sister stomp out of our suite like a disgruntled troll and I give myself permission to fall into the deep sleep that follows a burst of telekinetic power.

But it's not an escape, even then.

The Chosen One does not dream good dreams.

2

GRIER

IN CASE YOU WERE WONDERING, IT SUCKS TO BE THE SISTER OF the Chosen One.

When most people think about sisters, they picture two girls laughing together, their heads bent in mutual conspiracy, bonded by their shared blood. This is not us. It has never been us. I don't even have a chance to glance up from my book before it's ripped from my hands and flung across the room.

"What the hell, Valora?" I squawk, scrambling to my feet as she stands there glowering down at me, one hand outstretched, fingers curled in menace. Even smeared with the blood of whatever now-dead creature lies rotting in the courtyard, my sister still looks amazing. She's the literal worst. Her royal highness lifts her chin and twists her mouth in a half-snarl before collapsing on her bed. Killing monsters must be exhausting.

Also exhausting? Being a total a-hole.

I consider saying something about the amount of blood she's going to leave on her ridiculous pile of throw pillows but decide against it. It won't be her problem to clean up, anyway.

Nothing is ever Valora's problem.

Instead, I say nothing and retreat to my side of the suite, the cozy little nook added as an afterthought to Valora's spacious private quarters. I grab everything off the beloved patchwork quilt my Nan gave me and sweep it neatly into my bag, mourning the loss of what was a wonderfully quiet moment. I love my room, especially when you-know-who isn't there.

With an annoyed frown, I toss my messenger bag over one shoulder and slip out without saying a word to my sister, who is lying on the bed with her eyes closed. She's probably replaying the battle, reveling in her fearless badassery. She never thinks about me; this I know for sure. I slam the door with a grunt and make my way to the cafeteria.

The halls of Proctor Moor are wide and full of natural light. Bucking the Connecticut trends of classic architecture, this school's buildings are sleek and contemporary, spacious structures of steel, glass, and sustainably-sourced wood. It's hard to mourn the lack of turrets when floor-to-ceiling glass walls show off green hills in the summer and an explosion of reds and golds in the fall. I stop and stare at the hills, wishing for the thousandth time that I could enjoy this school for what it is, and not who it was built for. I put my hand up against the glass, but no one can see me; for our safety, the glass in every building is mirrored, making it impossible for outsiders to see in. It's sort of a pathetic metaphor for my life really: the invisible girl standing in the wing that bears her family's name.

Exceptionals had schools before, but only in rinky-dink pockets in the U.S and the U.K. The government, originally very excited about the Exceptional gifts when they first emerged in the 1950's, made sure we were protected. Amongst their sock hops and blatant racism, a bunch of nervous old white men (who maybe thought we were witches for awhile) built a system to protect Exceptionals. The world knows about us, but they don't know many of us - we're kind of in our own world. They quickly learned that most of us were utterly useless and the funding ran low. Our schools were still funded by the taxes of normal folks, but they were pretty terrible. I get it. I mean, why build something cool for a guy whose gift is that he can inflate balloons just by thinking about it? But then...then came Everett Proctor and scary-as-hell Erys and the prophecy and Valora and *whoo boy, another weaponized telekinetic!* Hold the phone – this one is SUPER hot! Suddenly the government was wetting their pants to throw Department of Defense money at Exceptionals.

Thus, this school. These windows, that bamboo floor, those enormous framed posters of Valora that loom over me as I walk down the hall.

The first one is from the day our family went to Mystic Seaport for my dad's birthday. We'd been in the museum gift shop, Valora sighing loudly about how bored she was, when a Scaled Gallsoul began to slither in through a floor vent. I'd been flipping through a carousel of postcards when the black smoke billowed up and filled the room. I remember the burning, the thickness that made it impossible to breathe. I opened my eyes just in time to see Valora hurtling herself through the nearest window, somersaulting on the pavement outside before breaking into a dead sprint to lure the creature away from us. When the smoke cleared, my parents found me on the floor, shaking and red-eyed.

By the time Valora was found in a nearby cemetery surrounded by a black pool that was once the Gallsoul, our birthday plans were definitely wrecked. Instead of a dinner cruise, we had fast food in the back of a news van while Valora was interviewed. My parents didn't seem to mind, though. They never do. Especially my father, who basks in her glory like a snake in the sun.

I scan the next poster, my stomach churning slightly at the gory memory of Valora sending a parking sign flying through the air and straight through an Ash Ape's head as though she were stabbing a ripe melon. The image thankfully didn't include me off to the side, projectile barfing at the sight of it all. The final poster, which I know is secretly Valora's favorite since she stares at it all the damn time, was a gift from her official fan club. It depicts their hero as the world sees her: fierce, fearless, and beautiful. In the glass-covered poster, I see the reflection of my own frizzy brown hair, a stark contrast to Valora's razor-sharp locks. We have the same heavy brows, but hers are flawlessly arched, while mine are straight and unruly. Valora's cheeks are glowing; I blush easily, turning splotchy and red. I stare into her eyes, the same olive green as mine, then nervously pull at the hem of my long-sleeved t-shirt as I'm aware of my body shape in the glass. I'm sturdy and pear-shaped compared to my lithe, toned sister. Kind people would call me curvy; crueler people would call me...well, other things. We look nothing alike. This seems to be the one thing that surprises people the most when they find out we're twins.

"Oh!" they'll exclaim. "You're...twins! But you...you're not..." Yeah, that particular conversation that always ends up making me feeling small.

I give the Valoras in the posters a dirty look and head toward the cafeteria. As I pass the crowded foyer outside of the atrium, I catch snippets of excited conversation about the battle.

"Did you see how she strangled the thing with its own tentacles?" a bespectacled freshman boy squawks. "She made it kick its own ass!"

"The statue was SO gross!" a girl I recognize from my History of Exceptionals class groans. "I thought Miss Flores was going to freak!"

In the cafeteria I grab a tray, my eyes scanning the room for Agnes. We've known each other since fourth grade, when we were the last two to be picked for kickball at recess. By the time

I have chosen my lunch, I still haven't spotted her, so I take a seat at our usual spot along a wall of windows that faces a patch of evergreens. I'm watching a pair of squirrels chase each other among the tree branches when a deep, unfamiliar voice breaks my concentration.

"Excuse me, but is anyone sitting here?"

I startle and glance up, my heart thudding up into my throat. It's the new boy, Leo Something-or-other. I'd noticed him in the halls over the last few days, carrying a campus map like only new kids do. He looked lost, and he'd asked me for directions to the library. Now he's standing next to the table, tall and lean, his jet-black hair parted to one side and just the right amount of messy. I blink, running my tongue over my teeth, hoping there are no strawberry seeds stuck anywhere. He must be lost again. Maybe he's looking for my sister. What does he want? Does he know who I am?

"Um. Me. I am... sitting." I stammer. I groan inwardly. *Hi, my name is Grier and I know words.* "I mean," I shake my head, unable to keep from joining in as he breaks into a warm laughter. "Let me try that again. I'm sitting here; you may also sit here if you'd like."

"Excellent," he grins, settling his lanky frame into the seat next to me, his dark brown eyes crinkling at the corners. "I'm Leo Irsan. We sort of met the other day, remember?" He offers me his hand, his coppery skin warm and smooth against mine as I shake it. "Thanks for the help, by the way. What's your name?"

"Grier. Um, Grier Rigmore." I try not to wince at my last name. I watch the realization dawn on him and wait for the inevitable questions. He sits forward with fascination. Here we go.

"Rigmore? Like, as in, Valora Rigmore?"

I nod and look at the ground. "She's my sister. Twin sister, actually," I explain, prepared for the usual statements. No, I don't look like her. Yes, I can get you her autograph.

"Cool," Leo smiles, taking a huge bite of his sandwich.

"Yeah," I breathe out. That wasn't so bad.

He chews, swallows, then asks, "So, you see the fight today?"

My heart sinks, and I shake my head gently. "No, uh... No, I missed it. You?" I ask, though I'm certain of the answer.

"Oh, man, it was crazy. I'd never seen her fight in real life, only on TV, you know? There were all these nasty little baby monsters coming out of the thing's stomach, and she just, like, threw them in the moat like they were nothing, and then..."

I'm not really listening to what he's saying. Not because I've heard the same *awesome* story about my sister a hundred times, but because I can't help but focus on the way his face lights up when he talks, his black brows so expressive. His teeth are so perfectly straight. I wonder if he had braces as a kid. I wonder if...

"Grier?"

"Hmm?" I blink.

"I said, so if Valora's got the telekinesis thing going on, what's your Exceptional ability?" He grins, and I get distracted again. *Obviously not sparkling communication skills.*

"Portals. I mean, not portals to another dimension or anything cool like that. I can move stuff from here to there?" I shrug, feeling the blush creep up my neck.

Leo cocks his head, considering. "What kind of stuff?"

"Oh, very important stuff." I shake my head. "Watch."

I take a deep breath and focus my gaze on the banana sitting on his lunch tray. A shimmering whorl, like a slow-moving whirlpool, blooms under the fruit and expands, swallows the banana, then closes in on itself like water swirling down a drain before disappearing. I move my focus to the table next to my tray, where the whorl appears again, followed by Leo's banana. He grins, then laughs good-naturedly.

"Magic!" I intone, waving my fingers like a cheesy magician at a kid's birthday party. *Oh my God, WHY DID I DO THAT?*

"That's cool!" he marvels. "Can you send it to France, stick it in someone's drink?" he laughs.

I shake my head. "Only places I can see with my own eyes, unfortunately." *Otherwise I would portal myself the hell out of this school.* I'm about to ask about his own Exceptional abilities when Agnes appears, her brown curls windblown.

She stares at Leo for a moment, out of breath. "Well, you're a boy," she blurts, surprised. Leo chuckles.

"This is Leo Irsan, Agnes. He's new." I tell her, silently willing her to pull it together. "Leo? This is Agnes Brewster, my best friend." *Only friend, but that's not important right now.*

"Hi," she flushes, shaking Leo's outstretched hand, but he's already standing, having figured out that this table is not where he wants to be.

"Nice to meet you, Agnes. Hey, thanks for the lunchtime entertainment. I'm gonna get a closer look at the Mistspawn before they clean it up. I figured eating first was the way to go. See you around!"

Agnes and I watch him jog off, then she turns to me. "Sorry I'm late for lunch, I was...um." She pauses awkwardly.

"Looking at the monster my sister killed?" I finished for her.

"Yeah. She impaled it on the Everett Proctor statue. Serves him right, I think - the hero worship around that guy is out of control. So, in other news, you just had lunch with the new boy? That's something!" Agnes's eyes go wide behind her thick glasses, making her look even more like a surprised owl than usual.

"I have no idea what that was about. I mean, he probably wants to know how to get close to Valora, just like everybody else does," I shrug.

"He hasn't been here very long," Agnes offers. "Maybe he's just trying to make friends!"

"Maybe." A quiet glimmer of hope flickers inside of me.

"Are you going to eat that?" Agnes asked, pointing to Leo's banana, which still sits on the table next to my tray. "I didn't get lunch because I was looking at the monster, and we need to get to class."

"I portaled it, but in my experience, things still taste good afterwards. It's all yours."

We head out of the cafeteria and join the throng of students heading toward their afternoon classes in the science and technology wing. We enter the classroom through its double doors at nearly the same time as my sister, who shoves past us without so much as a glance, jostling Agnes, who trips over her own feet.

"Forget how to walk again, Agnes?" Valora snarks over her shoulder. It's amazing that she can be so exhausted and still make it to class with enough time to mock my friend.

I open my mouth to respond, mean words tasting salty and delicious on my tongue, but I'm interrupted by the cheerful voice of Mr. Allen Ferguson, Proctor Moor's beloved and newish physics teacher, joking with a group of students gathered around his podium at the front of the classroom. He's tall, slender, maybe in his early forties, and wearing a bow tie and suspenders. His hair, dark brown but greying at the temples, is wiry and perpetually messy. He's the one teacher here who treats everyone the same, and that includes my sister.

"Alright, everybody, it's new seating chart day!" Mr. Ferguson holds up a clipboard to a chorus of groans. He begins reading names off, gesturing to desks as he goes down the list. "Kelly, Daniel, over here; Agnes..." he points to a desk in the middle of the room, and Agnes turns to me with a shrug and a wave. "Gracie, Ben, Grier..."

It takes me a minute to fully realize that it was my name he read while pointing to the seat in the front, closest to the classroom door. The seat where, in every classroom she's in, Valora always gets to sit. After a second of pause, I decide to take it. The class watches in silent fascination as I walk across the classroom and slide into the seat. My heart is pounding, but I do it anyway.

Not everything belongs to my sister.

3

VALORA

As I stand in the bright classroom, sun glinting off our desks, it's obvious that Mr. Ferguson has no clue. It's not too much to ask to sit in the desk assigned specifically to *me*, the desk closest to the door in case I have to dash out and mutilate something in a big hurry. But no, Grier plops her round bottom down like she owns the place.

WHAT. THE. HELL.

Of all the teachers in the school, Mr. Ferguson is the least impressed by Valora Rigmore. He's not exactly mean, but he definitely doesn't like me.

I watch Grier settle into her new desk with a look of bewilderment. She's the same exact height as I am – 5'6" – but where I am all angles, she is soft and round. Her hair is untamable, always tangled up in a bun that she thinks looks cute but is really just messy. I watch as she dramatically drops her backpack – dark purple and plastered with old band stickers - on the floor before rooting through it.

I sigh, so tired that I can see pulses of light behind my eyeballs. *When does class begin again?* I glance at the clock and then frown in Grier's direction, where she is sitting forward like a damn beaver. With a smile, I let the tiniest bit of power flick out through my finger. Grier's pen flies off her desk and rolls under the teacher's feet. He looks at her with confusion.

"Oh crap, oh, so sorry!" She stumbles forward out of the desk, her cheeks flaming red. Mr. Ferguson gives her a kind smile and hands her back the pen.

"I think you dropped this, Grier." She gives a quick nod and heads back to MY desk, but not before shooting me a nasty look. Using your Exceptional gifts is forbidden inside of class-rooms, but no one would know it was me. *No one but Grier, which is all that matters.* I sit in a seat at the back of the room like some peasant, propping my dark leather boots onto the desk as my flock of girls arrives and descends around me.

"Valora!" Cicely swoops in loudly, making sure to attract the attention of everyone around us. I kind of want to smack her when she is like this. "You're okay! Thank God! I was so worried about you!"

She hugs me tight and I squirm until she releases me. *Of course you were worried,* I think. *Without me, how else would you keep your social status?* Cicely Nix has put a lot of effort into the Valora Rigmore legacy. I've known her since we were kids, and I know that somewhere inside of her is the funny, lighthearted girl I used to know. It's hard to see that girl now that she's been swallowed up being the resident Queen Bee of Proctor Moor. There is only one person in this school who doesn't fear the wrath of Cicely, and that's me, mostly because we both know I could throw her out a window. But sometimes she gets under my skin.

She gets under everyone's skin.

Still, I'm her most valuable currency; the fact that I'm the Chosen One and she's my chosen best friend, is something that she will tell anyone who's listening. She leans over and wraps her brown arms around my neck. "Ohh, you stink a little bit."

"Thanks," I mutter bitterly. *Sorry the blood of a monster who wanted to eat your face is offending you.*

She immediately changes the subject as the rest of the girls cluster around me, ignoring the new seating chart, my own little orbiting planets. Gillian Cline, Proctor Moor's soccer star, and quiet Anna Ng, who is honestly part of our group because of her insane amount of wealth. They sit around me, evicting the kids who were assigned to sit back here, and soon they are useless membranes bumping into each other, trying to find where they should sit. It's chaos. I stare hard at Mr. Ferguson. *That's what you get for moving me.*

Cicely leans over me and begins playing with her hair, and I can't help but stare. As her hands run over her hair, it changes color: what starts as white blond turns into pure silver strands, like moonlight on the water, and then it becomes a light lavender, spooled with strands of plum, then darkest navy dotted with white, like stars in the night sky. This is Cicely's Exceptional gift, and while it is completely useless, it is hypnotizing to watch. Especially considering that her eyes automatically change to accent the shade of her hair. She spins back around so her hands rest on my desk. Her hair stays navy, and her eyes are now a deep maroon, which makes her look like a vampire. "Why the hell is Grier sitting in your seat?" she asks.

I roll my eyes. "I don't know. Mr. Ferguson changed the seating chart."

Cicely doesn't even wait for me to finish. Her hand pops up in the air. Shit. "Umm..excuse me, Mr. Ferguson?"

"Yes, Cicely?"

"Mr. Ferguson, that seat up front is reserved for Valora. It's hers, not Grier's." He blinks at Cicely like he can't hear the words she is saying. Grier hangs her head.

"Actually, it's my job to make the seating chart, and not your concern, Cicely." The class snickers a little and Grier looks like she wants to die inside.

I feel the rare twinge of guilt and wave my hand. "It's fine."

Mr. Ferguson looks hard at me, and I see something in him that I haven't seen for a long time: disgust. "Well, Valora, if it's fine with your highness, then may I proceed with class?" He does an exaggerated bow in front of the class. *Is Mr. Ferguson mocking me?*

Cicely goes to speak, and my fingers twitch angrily under the desk, but nothing moves. "Let it go," I snap. "Seriously."

"But..if you let him do this..." Cicely's eyes narrow but she lets her sentence trail off. "Fine, Valora. Whatever."

"Thank you for your generosity," says Mr. Ferguson sarcastically. "Now, if everyone could open their textbooks to page 78, who can begin to tell me about the existence of space and genetic drift? You know, the existence of so called Portals? Tardis stuff."

Agnes, Grier's weird best friend, shoots her hand up in the air. Mr. Ferguson calls on her.

"Grier can make portals!" she says excitedly as my sister shoots daggers at her with her eyes. Mr. Ferguson sits on the desk. "Really?" he asks. "Let's talk about that!" Grier is beaming, but I lean back in the desk, fighting sleep. My sister's powers are pretty boring. He can make me sit back here, but he can't make me listen, and my day is about to get even more draining because I can see an ominous form lurking outside the classroom door.

Anna leans forward. "Valora, your boyfriend is here..."

I smile because that's what I'm supposed to do, before I close my eyes. Here's something my friends don't know: I fantasize about one thing and one thing only. My bed.

An hour passes and finally class ends. I don't remember a thing, but I make sure to shove Mr. Ferguson's coat off the chair as I walk out with a twist of my wrist. I give him a smirk. *What is he going to do, tell the principal?*

News flash for Mr. Ferguson, they would fire a thousand

teachers before they gave Valora Rigmore detention. I leave the classroom and there in the hallway, standing in front of my locker, is Julian North. When he sees me, he stops speaking with his little group of minions, each of them mirroring his silence before dispersing without command.

If Cicely is the Queen of Proctor Moor, Julian is undoubtedly the King. His hands are shoved casually in his pockets, his jeans the kind that never slouch. His straight blond hair is cut diagonally so that half of it hangs shaggily over his face. When he sees me, I feel the heat of that famous Julian North grin, the one that promises vacations in the Bahamas, flights to Norway to see the museum of the Exceptionals, kisses on a sleigh in Telluride. He tosses his hair out of his mischievous blue eyes, eyes that I once found fathomless. Now I find them smothering. He smooths out his grey jacket sitting comfortably atop a tight t-shirt.

"Hey! Can I walk to you Flores's office, Val?"

"Don't call me Val, Julian." He knows I hate it and that's why he persists. I forgive it because he's my boyfriend and I should love him. I should *like* him. I sigh. "Sure, but you can't stay. You know how she gets."

Julian reaches out and I let him take my arm but not my hand. I don't know exactly where Julian and I are in our relationship, but we aren't where he would like us to be: practically engaged, an airplane writing our names across the sky as we declare this world our kingdom.

As we walk through the open hallways, I feel the lingering stares as both girls and boys lust after him with hungry eyes. I feel guilty, so I squeeze his arm, a tiny reassurance that we're fine. Someday we'll get married and inherit his parents' huge beach house and we'll have beautiful little Exceptionals. Our future rolls along like a glorious train of destiny, and I'm tied to the tracks.

I may be the Chosen One, but I have no idea how to stop this.

Julian has just started walking me up the winding staircase to Renata's office when I hear applause below me. My classmates are clapping for me. *Oh, that's right, I killed something today.* I try to smile and wave, but it's a fake smile and a half-hearted pageant wave. For a second I love the sound of the applause, but then I hear a familiar sound underneath it. It's the sound that means I'm crazy, a menacing whisper that pulses underneath it all, a fear that I don't dare name. I see Julian's beautiful mouth moving, telling me to enjoy the moment, but I can only hear the whisper, faint as the wind: *You aren't enough, Valora.*

Then it's gone, and the clapping returns. I pull away from Julian and go to knock on Renata's door, but she yanks it open before I can do it. Renata gives Julian an exasperated look and then glares at the students below me. "Mr. North, I'm sure you know Valora is capable of walking places alone." Julian bows dramatically to her before reaching over and kisses my lips right in front of her. It's loaded with expectations. "Get to class!" she thunders, and my classmates scatter like cockroaches. My mentor pulls me inside her classroom.

Unlike the rest of Proctor Moor, Renata's classroom feels neither new nor clean. Her walls are mostly blackboards covered with scrawled formulas. One time I saw a recipe up there, and another time the number of a gentleman named "James from the Drinkery." I wisely chose not to comment on any of it.

She bustles around the room now, clearing papers so that I can sit. Her black wavy hair is pulling out of her braid, her white shirt tucked halfway into high-waisted maroon pants. When my butt hits the seat, I sag forward. I love being in this room, because it's one of the few places that I can be myself. I don't have to hold my head high, I don't have to act like I'm not exhausted. I'm not the Chosen One in this room. I'm just me. Renata bends over, hands on her hips. Her thick black eyebrows are like furry caterpillars dancing across her face as she looks into my eyes with equal parts love and fury. My parents love Renata. My Nan doesn't.

"What did it cost you, Valora? Huh? Lifting the monster?" I shake my head, not wanting to admit that it took a lot out of me. She steps back and continues to blast me. "Quite the show-man, aren't we? You endangered yourself, Valora, and even worse, others! What if you had lost control of it and it had careened into the side of the school? There is no need for you to take such risks! People look up to you, Valora..."

"I know, I know, I KNOW!" I snap, burying my face in my hands. I knew this lecture was coming, but it still feels terrible. There is nothing worse than the disappointment of the woman who has been my teacher since I was ten years old.

"Let me see your hands!" I turn over my palms and she inspects them with care. She grabs ahold of a lamp with a single glowing Edison bulb and traces her hands over my sore palms. I feel warmth flowing over my skin. Renata's gift is that she can transfer energy. While she can't create energy from within herself, she can transfer it from one thing to another, either from a socket to a lightbulb or from a person to another person, but only in small amounts. This is how most Excep-tional gifts are in our world; small and mostly useless, though practical when put to use in relatable fields. I feel my energy perk up, nothing crazy, but like drinking a cup of coffee. My back straightens. I feel better. She sits back and looks at me as a long sigh escapes her lips. "Valora. You cannot keep pushing yourself past your limit for no reason."

"But I wanted to," I answer. "And after all, it was just me out there. Me, who has to make the right decisions at the perfect moment or else my face will get sucked off by tentacles with hooks on them!"

"Valora, Valora, Valora..." She says my name like it's her business.

It is, technically, I guess, her business.

My mentor stands and begins pacing. I can see the worry etched in the wrinkled corners of her eyes. "Eleven attacks in the last three months. That's more monsters than we've seen in the last seven years." She stops moving and tugs at her braid, something she does when she is on the verge of a frenzied thought. She turns to the blackboard and I lean back, stretching out my spine, which feels tight and hot.

"Hold!" she shouts suddenly and tosses a peach into the air, arcing it above my head. I weakly raise my hand up and the peach stops in mid-air. Renata turns back to the blackboard. "Spin!" she orders, and with a turn of my wrist, the peach begins to rotate as I turn it around in my mind. "Counterclockwise now." My wrists ache and my palms are sweating, but I change its direction. I'll be holding this damn peach the whole time, no doubt. It doesn't matter that earlier today I defeated a manic sea-monster.

I can see her thinking about the monster now, her mind cleaving its way through their facts and history. Monsters are rare, and usually lurk in only certain parts of the earth: desolate, wet parts where they can slink around unnoticed or in total isolation: in thick jungles, or freezing cold corners of Siberia where a glacier seal can serve as a tasty snack. We don't see them often, though we know they're out there. Seeing a monster in Connecticut, or really anywhere in society, is like running into a lion at the grocery store. It just doesn't happen. I mean, if you go hunting after a Rangibeest pack, you're probably going to die a horrible death. But if you're a regular person living in a city or suburb, chances are you will only see monsters on nature documentaries. At least, that's how it was before Erys came along. And now...the monsters are lots of places they shouldn't be, and the ones that come out are hell-bent on attacking humans.

A Kongamato in San Diego. A couple of Clouded Succubi slithering out of a ride at Disney World. A Mistspawn at Proctor Moor. The horror of it is always shocking, but the more it happens, the more people become immune to the breaking news cycle, the more desperate they become for a permanent solution. We all know why it's happening, but no one wants to say it. The whispers in the street of her return are growing louder. Because there is only one Exceptional in the world who can control monsters. Erys.

And the pressure mounts for the Chosen One to do something.

"Valora! Where are you? I was saying that the only conclusion we can draw from these escalating attacks is that Erys is testing you. She's sending increasingly aggressive monsters, in both size and intellect, to gauge your strength...and your will to fight."

"Fantastic," I sigh "Great news all around."

Renata shakes her head and sets down her chalk. "We have to increase your training. She will strike fast and hard when she comes, without warning. No more silly classes to distract you."

"No more classes?" My head jerks up. I don't particularly love classes, but that doesn't mean that I want to be cut out of life at Proctor Moor completely. "No. I mean, okay, if you have to cut class, cut physics. Mr. Ferguson is terrible. That's an extra hour I can be here training with you, but can you just leave the rest alone? I want...." I'm not sure how to phrase it. "I want my life."

Renata sits beside me and takes my face in her hands. "I know that sometimes being the Chosen One comes with a high cost."

You don't know anything, I want to say, but I don't. My

patience is worn thin with her fretting, my body exhausted, but I'll do what she wants. I'll stay. I'll train.

Hours later, I am dismissed and walk out into the empty hallways. It feels like I am being chased by something invisible and so I begin running. My legs love the challenge and soon I am flying through the halls of Proctor Moor, in and out of the golden autumn light. I run to the furthest reaches of the school where the windows look out over the green hills, and I stop at the drinking fountain. I drink and then lean my sweaty head against the windows, watching as the cleaning crew packs up their mops and pulls away from the school, leaving the statue of Everett Proctor gleaming.

"Here stands Everett Proctor...." I mutter, rolling my forehead back and forth across the glass, probably looking like a crazy person. *Who knows, maybe Valora Rigmore is crazy; wouldn't that be fun?* I watch the sun slowly set over the horizon, watch the statue sink into darkness until the ring of solar lights around him kicks on. The glowing inscription around the statue reads: "Here stands Everett Proctor, the greatest Exceptional ever to live."

What it should read is: *Here stands Everett Proctor, who was much stronger than I am, and who was still ripped into pieces by Erys.*

4

GRIER

"READ AHEAD TWO CHAPTERS AND BE PREPARED FOR A QUIZ NEXT time!" Miss Hanson, our literature teacher, calls out over the chaos of chairs being pushed away from tables.

"Ahhhh, freedom!" Leo sighs happily, stretching his arms up over his head and yawning. The hem of his shirt lifts high enough to display a few inches of smooth, brown skin. Two weeks ago, I had assumed the one lunch conversation would be it, and he'd get absorbed into Valora's merry band of admirers, but he keeps showing up. It turns out that it's sort of easy to forget to be intimidated when someone is so likeable. We follow Agnes through the door and into the hallway over-looking the atrium, which is teeming with students excited to be off for the weekend.

Leo turns to me and all I can think about is his mouth. "Wanna go wander? I haven't seen the orchards yet. It's too nice out to stay in." He playfully elbows me and nods in the direc-tion of the three-story floor-to-ceiling bank of windows. He's not wrong; the sky is a startling deep blue, and the Connecticut hills are putting on an autumnal fireworks display. But really...*he wants to go for a walk with me in the orchard?* He probably doesn't know it, but "going to the orchard" is slang for making out at Proctor Moor, especially because you can get all sorts of handsy out of the view of the adults...or so I've heard. Maybe they read sonnets out there, I wouldn't know. But Leo, he can't know that, right? My breathing becomes shorter.

"Aw, that sounds fun," Agnes answers. "Eager minds await, though – I'm tutoring today. Bring me some apples!"

I suspiciously watch my friend go and take a deep breath. Leo touches my shoulder and I jump. He laughs, this deep, beautiful chuckle. I feel it in my toes, a warm sensation spreading upward. "Grier - you got something better to do? If I go alone, I may wander into the forest, never be heard from again. No pressure, though."

Against my better judgment, I nod. "Well, if it's your safety at risk ..." We laugh as we head towards the grounds behind the school, and I wonder if it will always be this way.

"Grier?" I stop short, and turn to see Renata, Valora's mentor, examining me carefully. My God, she's terrifying. I avoid her at all costs. "Where are you going?"

"We're just going to the orchards, Miss Flores," Leo responds.

She exhales and pats me brusquely on the shoulder, giving me a small smile. "Be vigilant and please do not stay out past dusk. Enjoy your *walk*." She says the word walk like it's the last thing she thinks we'll do. *Oh joy, a teacher thinks I am kissing someone!*

"Thank you, Miss Flores," I mumble as she turns and strides away.

Leo pushes open the doors and inhales deeply as we step outside. I do the same, filling my lungs with fall air so crisp and clean, it almost hurts. "I love Los Angeles, but this," Leo gestures at the sloping hills, the trees bursting with vibrant autumn hues, "is something spectacular. Sometimes I think the reason my parents let me go to school so far from home is so they could come visit during the fall. They lived in New York when I was born, before my dad's job took them to California, and my mom misses having four seasons."

"What's your dad's job?"

"He's a clinical psychologist. He's Exceptional; he can sense peoples' emotions below the surface, stuff they aren't necessarily tuned into yet themselves."

"Whoa. That's intense."

"Yeah, it's not at all weird growing up with a parent who senses all your unspoken feelings," he laughs. "Has its perks, though, I guess."

It's not at all weird growing up the sister of the most amazing hero in the whole world, I think. *Except there are no perks.*

"Do you miss your family, living so far away from them?" We follow the smooth stone path along one side of Proctor Moor's kitchen gardens. A handful of students are out tending the autumn crops. A pair of girls a year behind me look up as we walk past. There's a comfortable silence for a few moments before he speaks softly.

"I've actually never been this far from home by myself. My parents studied in this country while their families lived back in Indonesia. I guess I should be glad they're only across the country instead of across the world, but it still seems really far sometimes, you know?" The thought strikes me: Leo's homesick. I nod, though I don't really know what that is like. Home for me is close enough to make a day trip, and I've been a student here so long, it's just normal to be away from my parents all the time. And home...home isn't always a comfortable place.

"Do you ever go there to visit? Indonesia?"

"Once a year! It's beautiful. You'd love it there. We should go." His voice is warm and low, and he's walking close enough to me that I feel his breath on my cheek when he turns toward me.

My voice seems unnecessarily loud as I blurt, "Okay!" I wince immediately. *God, why do I not know how to be around a boy? Why am I shouting at him?*

Leo chuckles. "Alright! It's a date. I mean, are you sure you can't create a portal strong enough to drop us across the planet?" He claps his hands together and bounces on the balls of his feet. "Worth a shot!"

I can't help but laugh, my nerves dissipating a little. "I wish! Hey, what about you?" I poke at him with one finger.

"Me?"

"Yeah! You've never told me what your gift was! What's your deal?"

"Aha!" He looks kind of ashamed. "My gift is temperature changes. It's really not that great."

"Like giving yourself a fever to get out of school?"

"If only. No." He stops and turns to me. "Here, hold still." He presses his fingertips together, palms a few inches apart, and closes his eyes. I examine his face closely, the way his soot-black lashes brush his cheekbones, the way he furrows his brow while he concentrates. I'm suddenly aware that the air around me has a chill to it, and I feel goosebumps prickle up on my arms.

"Did you just make it colder outside?!" I exclaim, and Leo's dark brown eyes open, twinkling.

"I did! Well, in about a ten-foot radius. Not all of outside."

"Can you make it freeze?"

"Only if it's already pretty close to freezing." He shakes his head. "I can manage about fifty degrees one way or the other, and only in small spaces. It's more effective indoors, in smaller rooms, but it has its uses."

We've reached the orchard, and I lead Leo to the small pile of wooden baskets nestled at the base of a tree. "We have to each take a basket of apples back to the school," I tell him. "Orchard rules."

"Child labor, always a great idea for the establishment." Leo grabs two baskets and tosses one to me. "Sorry. Sometimes I like to make jokes about child labor to impress girls." He grimaces. I smile, seeing I'm not the only one making a fool of myself. Also, he wants to impress me? I'm going to die right here.

The orchard, just far enough removed from the imposing modern school to feel like real New England countryside, is quiet. Late afternoon sunlight filters down through the leaves, dappling the soft grass and warming the earth. I drop my basket at my feet and take a deep breath, closing my eyes, wrapping my arms around myself. When Valora and I were little, we loved apple picking with our parents. I was always the brave one, shimmying up trees to reach the best apples, so proud of myself, until the day Valora reached up with her palm and brought the apple down to herself while my parents exploded with pride.

That's when everything changed.

I exhale and open my eyes, noticing Leo watching me, his head tilted slightly, an easy smile spreading over his face. "Penny for your thoughts?"

I smile and shake my head. "Just reminiscing, I guess."

We make our way into the trees, stopping occasionally to pluck rosy fruit. I use the sleeve of my long cardigan sweater to shine a pretty pink and green mottled apple, and take a bite. The flesh is the perfect balance of sweet and tart.

"So what about your parents?" Leo asks. "Are they both gifted, too?"

I chew and swallow, then wipe the apple juice from my face. "No, just my dad. He has really mild telekinetic abilities, but he can't really do much with them anymore. Mostly he just runs the Valora circus." I shrug.

"I figured with Valora in your family, at least someone else would have some sort of kickass gifts!"

I feel my heart drop to my feet. There it is. The true prize: Valora, the Chosen One. I grimace, trying to keep my tone light. "Nope."

"Was that crazy, then? Growing up with someone like her in the family?"

"I guess." *Please, can we talk about something, anything, else?*

"Did you always know she was the Chosen One?"

"Yep." I give a curt nod, silently willing him to drop it.

He grins. "Only room for one exceptional Exceptional in the family, I suppose. One girl moves bananas, the other one saves the world." He raises one arm, palm open, jazz-hand style.

His words pass through me like a cold, cruel dagger. I'm silent, unsure if I can speak without choking up. He's not wrong, after all. I offer a weak smile and turn away, my eyes trained on the leaf-carpeted ground before me. "Grier?"

I don't answer, and focus on twisting and pulling an apple from a nearby branch. It's weird...one side of it is blackened.

"Grier? What's the matter? Did I say something? Oh God, I did, didn't I?"

I stop, letting the apple fall from my hand and land on the ground beside me. There is ash on my hand. I meet his eyes with a steely gaze. "I know where I fall on the food chain, Leo. You don't need to remind me."

"Grier." His hand is on my shoulder. "Shit. That was...that came out wrong. That's not what I meant. I don't know what I meant. I was trying to be funny. It wasn't funny." He's leaning in, trying to make eye contact. I'm afraid if I look at him, I'll cry. When I finally look at him, his brow is furrowed with intensity. Are we both just fumbling through this? Is it possible I'm not the only awkward one here?

I take a deep breath. "Okay. Can we just pick apples now?"

One corner of his mouth lifts into a smile, and he bends over to retrieve the apple I dropped. He steps closer, so close we're almost touching, and takes one of my hands and places the apple in it. He smells like the woods, like mint and soap and...and...he leans forward. I lean in to meet him. "Peace offering?" he says softly, nodding toward the apple. His other hand is still under mine, warm and smooth. I swallow hard, trying to calm my nerves. *What is happening? Is this real life right now?*

I concede with a small smile and a nod. "I accept this particularly hideous bruised apple."

He chuckles softly and leans in when a brief, deafening whoosh startles us. Jumping apart, we both glance around the orchard for the source of the sound. My heart pounds in my chest. It sounded foreign. Animalistic.

"What the hell was that?" I whisper.

WHOOOOOSH. A plume of fire shoots past us, blasting leaves off the tree we are standing under. Leo jerks me backwards toward him and we both fall to the ground. The blast is followed by a sizzle and a low grumbling. Leo's gaze focuses somewhere behind me, and his eyes go wide. All the color drains from his face.

"Turn. Around. Slowly," he breathes. "Don't make a sound."

Shaking, I slowly pivot as burning leaves fall all around me. There, on the outer edge of the orchard closest to the moor, stands an enormous, hunched beast. Deep crimson and black shaggy fur covers its body. It is perched on all fours, solid and muscled like a great ape. Around its feet, smoke rises from its claws. I can't make out much of its face besides the two tusk-like fangs curving upward, razor sharp and clear as day. Huge black horns rise and curl away from its massive head.

The creature lets out a low bellow, and jets of flame shoot from its feet with a tremendous whoosh. I yank Leo behind the nearest tree, pressing him against the rough bark. He's shaking, pale, eyes wide. "It's a Russet Flame. It..." he gulps, trying to steady himself. "It's a *monster*, Grier. It smells us. I'm sure it smells us. It has to know we're here. It could burn us alive."

It *smells* us? "Can it see us?" I whisper.

Leo shakes his head slightly. "I don't know. Maybe. They don't see very well. But their sense of smell. It's...it can smell us. It knows we're here."

My mind races and I take a deep breath, letting it out slowly. We need a plan, or we're going to die here in the orchard, incinerated under the apple trees. And I will Never. Get. Kissed.

Hell no to this. "What about its hearing?"

"Um..." Leo squeezes his eyes closed and nods. "I think they can hear okay. I think. I'm not sure. I..." He's frantic.

"Okay. Leo. Listen to me." I'm surprised by how calm my voice sounds. "We're going to throw the apples as hard as we can that way and then we're going to run to that tree." I point out a wide maple about fifty yards from us, halfway between where we are and the edge of the orchard closest to Proctor Moor. I press the apple I'm holding into his hands. "Lick it, bite it, and then throw it as hard as you can, and then...run."

His fingers curl around the apple and he takes a loud bite, licks the outside, winds up, and hurls it into the orchard, sending the potent scent of his saliva with it. I do the same. They thud against a low-hanging branch. The beast bellows again, flames whooshing, but we don't wait to see any more. We sprint, scrambling through apple trees. I peek cautiously around the tree, half certain the beast will be closer, seeking us out. I breathe a shaky sigh of relief when I see that it hasn't moved much but has turned toward our thrown apples, its head lifted high as though it's sniffing the air.

I turn to Leo. "Okay. One more time. Throw it that way." I nod in the direction of the first apples. "Then we're going to make a break for it. Once we get to the edge of the orchard, we sprint. Got it?"

He nods mutely, his face pale. He steps slowly away from

the maple tree and aims. The second the apple flies from his fingers, he grabs my hand and we run. I'm too scared to even process his hand wrapping around my own.

I feel heat at my back as the monster bellows again, but I don't look back. I run, I run until I can't breathe anymore. We reach the edge of the orchard, and Leo drops my hand. I'm no runner, but somehow I'm keeping up with him, my legs pumping as though my life depends on it. My life does depend on it.

A surprising wave of empathy for my sister washes over me. *It's real. That thing was real.* My sides are aching and I can hardly breathe as we reach the wide doors leading back into the school. Leo yanks open the door and turns to me, grabbing my hand again and shoving me into the building first before yanking the door closed behind us. We're safe, for now. We're safe, but I can't stop shaking, can't stop feeling the flames at my back.

5

VALORA

It's midday Thursday, and someone is pounding on my bedroom door. I don't want to leave my dream, don't want to leave this warm, safe bed. The knocking continues. *Dammit*. I pry my eyes open, staring at the ceiling for a moment as my body screams at me to go back to sleep.

Someone is going to die for this.

"What. The. Hell. Is. It?" My mouth is dry as I fumble to my feet. "Hold on." I wave my hand at the door to unlock it and open it, but the surge is too much; my power is always strongest after I sleep. The door flies open, almost pulling off its hinges.

With an uncomfortable smile, my PR agent Marnie pokes her head inside the door, her eyes growing concerned when she spots me rocking greasy hair and pajamas. "Valora?"

"Yeah?" I rub my eyes sleepily.

Marnie rocks back on her stiletto heel. "Um. Sorry. Did you forget that you have a photo shoot and interview this afternoon?" she asks gently.

Shit. "Yeah, I did. I...crap." I'm having trouble thinking. Marnie purses her lips together. "Should I shower real quick?" She shakes her head, her bun bouncing a little.

"You know what...I think we can work with this." She raises her hands up like a camera, framing me between her two thumbs. "The real cost of heroism."

I fight the temptation to roll my eyes.

"We'll do the makeup lightly and fix the hair a bit., but... I like this look. That shirt is just tight enough. Yeah. You've got a Starbucks from Battlestar Galactica thing happening and I love it."

I glance down at my black sweatpants and grey tank top. This?

"Okay..." She yanks a granola bar and a thermos of coffee out of her bag and gets to work. After a second I reach over and grab the necklace that Nan sent me last year. It's three silver hexagons, each smaller than the last, the last which has silver rays of sun shooting across it. It's my favorite thing. I meet Marnie's eyes.

"I'm wearing this."

After a quick fix of my face and hair, Marnie hurries me into a vacant classroom. The room is dark, and all around me are people setting up cameras and speaking in hushed whispers. Only one person actually approaches me – the interviewer – a disarmingly attractive British man.

"Hello! I'm Hugh." He pumps my hand up and down violently while Renata eyes him suspiciously from the corner. I love that she's always here, even after my outburst the other day. She's my constant, in a way that no one else is. I'll never tell her.

I am led over to the interviewer, who seats me in an uncomfortable chair and takes the comfy one across from me. I am somehow both exhausted and highly caffeinated. Inside, I'm telling my brain to wake up, trying to remember the formulaic yet charming answers for these questions that I've memorized over the years. The lights flick on, uncomfortably bright.

He sits forward in his chair. "So, Valora, what's it like to be the Chosen One?" I blink, unprepared. I do get asked this, but never out of the gate. For a moment, my mind fumbles and I briefly entertain the idea of telling him the truth. Instead, I keep grinning politely and my mouth forms the words without my brain even telling it to.

"It's an honor. I've known from the time I was very young that this was my destiny. The prophecy was a guidebook for the future, and I'm blessed to be the recipient of Thackeray Chadwick's words. I really consider myself just a keeper of the telekinetic legacy that Everett Proctor left behind, nothing more. I owe everything to my family and friends, and those supporters who have helped me get where I am." *Bullshit, bullshit, bullshit.*

The interview proceeds as normal for the next ten minutes, until I see Hugh shift in his seat. "There are rumors that you are getting very serious with Julian North. What would you say about that?"

I laugh lightly as if the question doesn't bother me, but inside I cringe. "I don't think anyone is honestly interested in my dating life."

He smiles. "On the contrary, I think everyone in the world would love to know about your love life, Valora."

"Then I hate to disappoint, but I'm not really in a place to talk about that. I *can* confirm that Julian North is just as handsome as he is rumored to be." This will be enough, a kernel of information to whip those who care into a frenzy. And Julian will be thrilled.

The interview lasts for about another five minutes, and I signal Renata by scratching my nose that I'm ready to stop. She steps forward, her voice firm. "One last question Hugh; Valora has training to attend to, and we've already given you much more time than the last interviewer." She always says this.

Hugh straightens his shoulders and looks down at his paper and then back at me. His flinty eyes meet mine and I see defiance. He asks his last question. "Valora, what would you say to those who wonder if you are strong enough to defeat Erys? How can someone as young and inexperienced as you defeat someone like her when she defeated Everett Proctor in just a matter of minutes? There are quiet murmurings that you are not, in fact, up to the task."

I am not enough.

"You're done!" growls Renata, pushing past him. "Hugh, you know better than that. We were very clear in our form what was and was not appropriate for this line of questioning."

"It's an honest question, Miss Flores, and I think our readers deserve to know the truth." He looks back at me, but I'm already climbing out of my chair. "Valora! Can you answer?"

"You may call me Miss Rigmore," I say coldly. "And this interview is over." I shift my hand, and his ceramic coffee mug tips in his hand, sending hot liquid splashing over his crotch. He yelps and jumps up. "The wind is strong in here," I say coldly, before turning my back on him. I stalk toward the stool in the corner, shaking with anger.

"Four shots," I snap at the photographer, who hops to the ready. She trains the lens on me and I sit on the stool, pull my legs up to my chest, and put my chin on my knees, making eye contact with the person behind the lens. I don't fix my hair or jut my chin forward or puff my chest out like normal. I just sit.

"Smile?" she asks, and I shake my head. I don't feel like smiling right now. Instead, I just stare at the lens, my mind and body exhausted.

She takes a few pictures and stands back. "Wow. I like it. Come see." I decide not to hate her and step forward to look at the display. *My god, I love them.* Instead of the overly made-up, smiling Valora, I see strong Valora, someone whose face matches her powers. I look raw and real. The light catches my necklace. Even my untrained eye can tell this is a great shot. I thank the photographer and walk out with Renata into the bright hallways.

"That was awful," I snap, rubbing my hands together. "No more interviews for a while. I'm serious, Renata. I'm not feeling up to them lately."

Renata nods. "I'll talk to the Board, but I agree." I love how I don't get to decide what I want; instead it's a room of old men who fight nothing.

"Miss Flores!" A shout echoes up the corridor and we both turn. It's Grier, and she's all out of breath and red-faced. That new boy is running next to her – what's his name again? Liam? When they reach us, the boy puts his hand on Grier's shoulder. The way he looks at her makes me smile a bit; this boy likes her, I can tell. I have no idea why, seeing how she is dressed like someone's depressed mom, but he does. I feel a strange mixture of jealousy and pride stir in me, but I try to push it down. Good for her.

My sister takes a deep breath. "We just came in from the orchard, and there was..." She can't even quite bring herself to say it. I watch her struggle with the word, and I know why: because if she says it, it's real. What I do is real, and what threatens us is real. My eyes meet hers.

"Say it, Grier."

She swallows. "There was a monster in the orchard. We saw it, and it saw us. Then we ran."

The boy speaks up. "It was a Russet Flame. I'm sure of it."

Renata turns to him. "That's a very specific monster, are you sure? What's your name?"

"Leo Irsan, and I'm positive. I know my monsters, Miss Flores."

"So it seems. Valora, with me." She's already walking.

I'm still wearing only a tank top and sweats. I motion to Grier. "Give me your sweater!" After a moment's hesitation, Grier rips off her cardigan and hands it to me. Leo tries not to notice Grier's tight shirt underneath it. I wrap it around myself. It smells like our home and for a moment I am there, relaxing on the couch while Mom plays with my hair.

Renata spins towards the intercom that sits at the end of each hallway and punches in an access code. "All students to your dorm rooms. This is not a drill. All students return to your dorm room and take precautionary measures." All around me I hear groans. Renata clears her throat. "Also, Pike Paskell, please report to the orchard. Pike Paskell, report to the orchard immediately."

My heart freezes, and I look quizzically at Renata. She shrugs. "If we are dealing with fire, we might as well have some help." She turns back to Grier and Leo. "Head to your dorm."

"Can we help?" It's the first time I've heard Grier ask that.

"No Grier, thank you." My sister looks at me for a long moment, like she wants to say something. But she doesn't, and as she has done our entire lives, turns her back on me and heads up the hallway.

I follow Renata toward the doors. She presses her hand into the fingerprint scanner. Then she closes her eyes and reaches for my hand. I slip mine into hers and immediately feel a surge of power passing through her palm from the electronic keypad. She waits a second while the power builds and then slumps forward. A surge like that takes a lot out of her. I feel power rushing through my veins: energy and heat. There it is, the voice again, like someone whispering from underneath a river: *you aren't enough.*

"Hey!" I turn around and he's right there. I try my best not to meet Pike Paskell's gaze, but it's almost impossible. Pike used to be Julian's friend, but that was before they had a falling out two summers ago. Pike's brown skin is warm in this light and his impossibly dark eyes are fixed curiously on my face. Above them a curly black mohawk arches dramatically away from his forehead. I can't look at him for too long, because I start to think strange things. Pike has always looked at me in a way that no one else does, with a naked intensity that makes me very uncomfortable. Pike's trouble for the Valora brand, and I know it. Instead of looking at him, I lift my eyes to Renata. She nods, and we walk out of the school into the orchard.

Outside, nothing appears amiss. The leaves in the trees rustle in the wind as we pass beneath them. Pike lifts his nose. "I smell sulfur." He sniffs. "And smoke, but not flame. This way."

We head to the rear of the orchard, where a handful of trees are nothing but smoking black husks. I'm looking for a monster and my defenses are ready, but I'm also thinking about how Grier had a boy out here. *Do I know nothing about her anymore? How is it that my weird sister is getting action while I can barely even think about that right now?*

Pike steps up behind me. "Pretty exciting, eh? Monster hunting." I stare at him for a long moment, taking in his perfectly arched eyebrow and the hint of sarcasm in his voice. "Wait. Look there!" I look behind me. At first I see nothing, but then I notice the black grooves in the dirt at my feet. Pike crouches with Renata as they inspect the tracks. "See, he dragged his knuckles here." Pike does his own marking, but his hands are flaming now and where he trails his fingers, black earth follows. "He made his way over here, to this corner."

He points us to the end of the orchard, where apple trees meet the impassive Connecticut woods. The rivets in the earth get longer and wider, more than two feet across. My heartbeat speeds up. *This guy was big.* The thought stops me cold: Grier could have easily died out here. I blink in the light, temporarily taken aback by this reality. I shake my head as Renata steps up to inspect the trees. "It ate some of the apples."

Pike appears before me. "And it burned down the shed. But then it left. " Remnants of burned ash trails out from the orchard and into the woods. I step forward, but Renata pulls me back.

"No, Valora. Never outside the boundaries of the school. That's exactly what Erys wants, for you to wander off the protected grounds of the school, alone." She narrows her eyes. "In fact, I would say that's exactly what this is. A trap. Let's not fall into it. Back inside the school."

I point to the woods, where in the distance I spot something smoking. "We're just going to let it stay there?"

Renata shakes her head. "Russet Flames are shy and they have no interest in being around humans. They aren't carnivores. It's true they can do great damage if angered, but in my opinion, we should leave him be. If Erys wanted him to attack us, he would have."

Pike nods. "My parents had one when I was young. We had to let it go when it was six months old, but they are basically the yellow labs of the monster world." The shock on my face makes him burst into laughter. He has a nice laugh. "Yes, I know. Having a monster for a pet is illegal, but my parents have never really been into the rules."

Renata snaps her fingers at us and we both hop to the ready, trailing behind her. "Would you have followed it if I wasn't here, Valora?" Renata asks me.

I think about it. "Maybe."

"You know very well that you can't tell where Everett Proctor's school defenses end and start, so you are more likely to wander outside of them."

Ah, the legendary chemical defenses of Proctor Moor. Only scientists really understand how they work, except that I know this: Erys's actual DNA cannot be on the grounds around the school or she will be vaporized. Besides being the greatest Exceptional of all time, Everett Proctor was also a chemist. It was the only defense he left us before his untimely demise.

"What's her deal, anyway?" asks Pike, stopping to sniff a

trail of burned leaves. God, why am I so distracted in his presence?

Renata steps over an overturned bucket of apples as we walk back to the school. "Do you know anything about Erys, Pike?"

"Only what I've read online."

She shakes her head with a sigh. "I am officially assigning you to be better informed. Most of her life remains a mystery, but what we know now is that she was born and raised in the darkest parts of the Everglades, kept tucked away from kindness for far too long. The Everglades, as you know, are a perfect host to monsters of every shape, be it giant pythons or Fanged Chilopoda. At some point when she was young, Erys learned that she was the first Exceptional in history whose gift was that she could control monsters. All of them. And that was before the Baleful – a dark creature who has never been studied or captured – attached itself to her." I try not to listen in on the story I've heard a thousand times.

"Enemies of her poor, abusive family were quickly extinguished, and the monsters that should have stayed in the darkest parts of the swamp began emerging into normal society. Her particular madness made it hard to track, since we never knew what she would do next. One day it was a Golden Scorpion burying itself in the neck of a politician, and the next it was a Spiralkin let loose in a daycare." Her hands clutched nervously, looking like she wants to say more. "She has no compassion, no rules of morality. Erys brings out the worst natural instincts of monsters. She wanted power, but more than that she wanted attention, recognition. She was jealous of the focus of the entire Exceptional world on Everett Proctor, and made him her enemy." She raises her eyebrows at Pike and I see a glimpse of tears in her eyes. "You've seen the video, I assume, of their final battle."

Pike nods. "Only about a hundred times." I focus my eyes

on the ground. I've watched it only once, when I first arrived at Proctor Moor and Renata had forced me to. I only made it through the first minute before I had passed out cold on the ground. What Erys did haunts my dreams. "Everett Proctor was such a badass," grins Pike, shaking me out of my fog.

"And yet he died." I retort, coming over the hill. He looks at me with surprise.

Renata turns to us both. "Thanks for coming out with us Pike. Valora, shall we? We'll stop by the office and report what we found in the orchard."

I nod and follow dutifully behind her, at once relieved and sad to leave Pike Paskell behind. He watches me go and I can feel his eyes on me like a slow burning ember.

6

GRIER

Conversation buzzes around me in the cafeteria as I sit at my usual table and eagerly open my latest letter from Nan, who makes it a point to send both me and my sister a handwritten note every single week. She's the best. Valora never says so, but I know she looks forward to them as much as I do. Our grandmother is the one person in our family I can talk to about anything, and last week, in my letter back to her, I'd poured out my soul about Leo. Truthfully: the best advice always comes from old ladies who don't give a shit.

"*Dearest Grier,*

This Leo boy sounds absolutely wonderful! He certainly—"

"Calling this risotto has to be false advertising," Leo's voice startles me as he drops his tray onto the table next to me and groans, gesturing at the gluey puddle on his plate.

I hastily shove the letter into my pocket and laugh.

"They tell you those are mushrooms, but I'm pretty sure it's recycled Mistspawn," Agnes chimes in, sliding into the seat across from me. "Waste not, want not."

I groan and stifle a bitter grin. "Valora has saved us from being eaten by monsters, so that we may eat them, instead." I take a forkful of my mushroom risotto and chew. "Amen. May the glory be to her holy name."

"Amen, amen." Leo and Agnes cross themselves as I force down the bite of gray rice and wipe my mouth with a napkin.

"Ugh. If I can't eat it, that's saying something," Out of the corner of my eye, I see Agnes shoot me a disapproving glance. She's always chiding me that I'm way meaner to myself than anyone else is, but she doesn't understand that it's a deflection. When I say it first, I'm taking the power of the words away.

There's a brief lull in the conversation. Agnes fidgets with her glasses. Leo looks like he is completely unsure what to say, but he keeps stealing glances my direction. Finally, he breaks the silence. "You guys up for movie night in the auditorium?" I almost drop my fork. Sitting in the dark with this boy? Suddenly I'm finding it a little hard to breathe. *It's not a date. It's not a date,* I tell myself.

Proctor Moor shows movies on a massive projection screen in the auditorium every Friday evening, complete with popcorn and snacks. It's not a bad way to spend an evening, but it gets a little old when most of the movies are action films featuring a smoking-hot heroine, who *definitely* doesn't remind me of anyone I know.

"I'm in!" Agnes agrees, turning hopefully toward me with her blue eyes magnified behind her thick lenses. "I think a light-hearted movie sounds like a great way to wrap up this strange week. Also...sour gummies."

Leo raises his eyebrows at me. "Grier, you coming?" His tone is hopeful.

I feel it again, this warm, fluttering sensation that starts in my belly and spreads outwards every time he looks at me like that. Agnes and I almost always skip movie night, but..."Yeah, sure," I try to keep my voice relaxed, like attractive foreign boys want to see movies with me all the time. "You had me at sour gummies."

After dinner, the three of us head in the direction of the auditorium, and I hang back a little as Leo and Agnes fall into discussion about which Ivy League schools are best for those with Exceptional gifts.

"Grier! So glad I ran into you before the weekend!" A male voice behind me takes me by surprise and I startle, whirling around. Mr. Ferguson is leaning casually against the polished wood panels of the hallway, hands in the pockets of his jeans. He smiles warmly at me, eyes crinkling.

Leo and Agnes have stopped and turned, curious. "Hey, Mr. Ferguson!"

"Agnes. Leo," he acknowledges them kindly.

"Go on without me," I tell them, gesturing towards the auditorium. "Save me a seat, and some gummies!" Leo grins and Agnes waves as they head off.

Mr. Ferguson steps toward me, still smiling. "Grier, sorry to disrupt your evening, but I have a book you might find interesting. It's sort of a more in-depth look into what we talked about with portals in class the other day. Of course, we didn't have class today..." he trails off, his tone slightly annoyed.

"Yeah," I shrug. "Another medal ceremony for Valora. Whoopee."

Mr. Ferguson glances around and leans in conspiratorially. "Just between you and me, I skipped the ceremony. I figured there were already enough fans," he murmurs with a smirk. An involuntary laugh escapes my lips. Nobody skips out on mandatory Valora-admiration time. "I trust you'll keep my secret." He smiles. "Now. Care to step into my office?" He gestures to a nearby doorway and I follow him.

Allen Ferguson's office is, like most faculty offices, small and narrow. Built-in bookshelves full to the point of bursting line both sides of the room, and a worn but cheerful woven kilim covers most of the polished bamboo floor. A high-backed black leather chair sits behind the uncluttered desk, and two plush armchairs upholstered in a shocking orange velvet sit facing it.

"Whoa," I laugh. "I almost didn't notice those ridiculous chairs."

Allen chuckles. "Subtle, aren't they? I think you'll find them to be extraordinarily comfortable, though."

I glance around me at the bookshelves, stretching to the ceiling, a rolling ladder propped along one side. "These bookshelves, though..." I shake my head. "These are amazing."

"Would you believe I've memorized every word of every book on these shelves?"

"Are you serious?!" My eyes widen.

Allen nods. "It's my gift," he explains. "Everything I've ever seen or read, every conversation I've ever had, every memory," he taps his forehead with one finger, "is locked up here in perfect detail."

I could drool. The ability to keep books inside yourself forever? I'm rarely jealous of another Exceptional gift, but that would be incredible. He hands me a heavy tome bound in crimson leather: *Electron Diffusion Regions: The Manipulation of X-Points.*

"I promise the book itself isn't as unreadable as the title. It's about portals."

I forget to breathe as my fingers trace over the embossed title. I feel a warmth spreading through me. No teacher has ever even cared to know more about my gift, let alone given me a book about it. *He found this book just for me?* It's an unfamiliar but not unpleasant feeling.

"I can't wait to read it. I'm going to start tonight." I can't stop smiling.

"Excellent. You have an extremely interesting gift, Grier. I'm a physics guy, so of course I'm fascinated by it. I look forward to hearing what you think of the book!"

I can feel my face flushing, and I stammer out a thank you.

He looks at me kindly.

"Don't doubt yourself or your gift, Grier. I know that's probably easier said than done, living in Valora's shadow."

"Thank you, Mr. Ferguson."

"Please. Call me Allen."

"Thank you...Allen." The first name will take some getting used to. "I better go. My friends are waiting."

"Ah, yes, movie night awaits. Enjoy *Superteam: Return of the Viper!*" He walks me to the door.

"I'll try," I roll my eyes. "Thanks again for the book!"

"You're most welcome, Grier," he smiles as he shuts the door.

The auditorium lights are just beginning to dim when I find Leo and Agnes.

"What'd Mr. Ferguson want?" Agnes asks, moving her sweater from the empty seat between her and Leo. She made it so I would sit by him. I don't deserve her.

"He had a book he wanted to lend me. I think he's fascinated by my portals – thanks for bringing that up, by the way. Did you get snacks?"

"Popcorn and sour gummies, duh," Leo tips the bag of neon worms toward me. I pluck a few from the bag and pop them in my mouth, relishing the pleasant stinging at the back of my cheeks as the sugar dissolves from the sour candy. The movie begins.

About an hour in, as the lithe, redheaded heroine scales the walls of an alien spaceship, I stifle a yawn and reach down for another handful of popcorn. As my fingers close over the kernels, Leo's hand gently comes down over mine. A jolt runs through my entire body, and I freeze as his fingers curl slightly, fingertips brushing my palm. My heart thuds wildly, as a rushing sound fills my ears. I stare straight ahead. *Is he...?* He can't be. I twitch my fingers and his wrap tighter around my own. I'm still thinking I'm going to die of happiness, when suddenly the entire auditorium goes black. Leo's hand yanks away from mine. A chorus of groans goes up from the crowd. I hear Proctor Moor's generators hum to life, and dim lighting along the aisles click on, followed by a giant power surge that sends all the lights in the room blazing.

"What the hell is going on?" Agnes mumbles as the room flickers again to a weak glow.

Ms. Stein, one of the dormitory supervisors, makes her way to the front of the auditorium and nervously claps her hands for attention over the dull roar of student conversation.

"Ladies and gentlemen! Quiet down, please!" For a petite woman, she's surprisingly loud. "If we're going to be relying on generators until we get this power issue figured out, we'll have to postpone movie night." She claps her hands again over the grumbling. "I know, I know. I'm sorry. If it makes you feel any better, I'm sure that the hero and the heroine end up together and no one actually dies."

A voice behind me boos. "That's enough, Julian! Off you go." She dismisses us with a flick of her wrists.

"Damn," Leo sighs. "Wanna go play cards or something?" Agnes nods, and they both turn to me.

"I think I'm actually gonna go read a while." I offer up the book Mr. Ferguson had given me, hoping it provides a decent excuse so I don't have to figure out what holding hands with Leo means. My head is swirling and I don't trust myself right now. I need to retreat, read Nan's letter, make sense of every-thing. I yawn for good measure. "I'm pretty tired."

Agnes raises a skeptical brow at me, and Leo looks disap-pointed, but smiles. "Sure. Can we walk you to Rigmore?"

I agree, and we join the throng of students carefully shuf-fling out of the dim auditorium. The lights keep sporadically dimming and brightening as we make our way across the school. "See you at breakfast tomorrow?" Leo asks eagerly when we reach the Rigmore wing, and I feel that little seedling of hope perk up again.

"I'm not a girl who misses a meal," I tell him, ignoring Agnes' frown. I take a moment and center myself, trying not to be the girl who makes jokes about her own weight. "I mean, yes."

Leo laughs. I love the way it sounds. "'Night, Grier."

I push open one of the heavy doors. "Night."

I hug my book to my chest and make my way past the enormous framed posters of my sister, when a buzzing sound, low but steadily increasing in volume, stops me again. The light from the wall sconces grows brighter, but when I turn to glance at the dimmer switches, I'm still alone. The skin on the back of my neck prickles, and the hairs on my arms stand up as the lights blaze brighter, blinding me. A deafening crack drops me to the ground as several light bulbs pop and the hall is cloaked in darkness. I let out a shout and scoot backwards, hitting the floor as a sizzling shower of sparks erupts. Something steps past me in the darkness.

My heart thuds wildly in my chest, and I try to catch my breath in the darkness as a few of the sconces flicker back to life. Shaking, I reach for my book and pull myself to my feet in the dim light. The hall is empty; I must have been imagining things.

I'm about to reach for the door when I see it: The poster of Valora is cracked and splintered, as though someone had taken a pickaxe to it with surgical precision. Her face is untouched, the shiny blond hair intact...but someone has attacked her hands. Printed pieces of them curl on the ground in a shower of glass shards. Her palms; her power. Destroyed. I hear a whisper, but when I turn there is no one there. For the second time this week, I run.

7

VALORA

CICELY AND THE GIRLS ARE ALL CLUSTERED ON MY BED AND WE'RE laughing about Anna's hopeless crush on Kristopher Tagg, a boy who definitely prefers other boys. There is a sound of rattling locks. Grier. She steps through the door breathless, her cheeks flushed.

"Valora!" When she sees the girls on my bed, her momentum is lost. "Oh, right, your squad is here." She turns and walks towards her side of the room with a sigh. *Could Grier just not be exasperated for once in her life?* She plops on her bed and begins fiddling with our dad's old guitar. She's always wanted to play but has never learned, and now she's just making noise in hopes that my friends will leave.

"Hey!" I snap back to attention at Cicely's voice. Gillian is leaning over her, stroking her pale grey hair patiently. Sometimes our little group reminds me of a pile of puppies, all hungry for approval and warmth. Other days, it's a den of snakes.

"So..." Cicely's eyebrows raise. "When are you and Julian going to make it official and go to the mat?" *The mat* is short for the place behind the gym where they store the wrestling mats.

It's also where kids at Proctor Moor go to have sex. I've never been there and I have no desire to take Julian there, though I'm sure he would love to go.

Julian. I groan and lean back onto Cicely. "I don't know. Maybe never." I pretend to be interested in my fingernails.

"What do you mean, maybe never?" Cicely sits up. "What is going on with you guys, anyway?"

I won't meet her eyes. "Nothing. I'm just not feeling that excited about him lately."

Her eyes narrow. "Dude. Why not? He's the hottest guy in school and he's crazy about you!" I think I see a flicker of jealousy in her sea-glass eyes.

Anna sits up, resting her pretty face in her hand. "Maybe it's that Valora likes someone else. Maybe like, I don't know...Pike Paskell? I heard you went to the orchard with him." Heat floods my face and I feel tiny pricks of light in my palm. When I look across the room, Grier is looking at me, surprised. I shoot Anna a cool glance.

"Yeah, because we were hunting a monster. You honestly think I would be into someone like Pike Paskell?" Cicely is looking at me, her eyes now ballerina pink, and I can see the gears turning in her mind; I decide to deflect their attention onto my sister. It's not my proudest moment.

"Grier, what are you staring at?" I bite. "Don't you have your own life to worry about?" My sister jerks away from us and heads back to the enormous book in her hands.

"Yeah, Grier, what are you reading?" Cicely rises from the bed like an uncoiling snake. I start to raise my voice in protest but it falls away. Instead I silently watch the Queen Bee of Proctor Moor advance on Grier. "Where did you get that huge book? From Agnes? It's too bad she can't read a book on how not to be a freak."

Grier tucks the book protectively against her chest. "Agnes isn't a freak," she snaps, and I'm immediately ashamed that while I was too afraid to speak, my timid sister isn't. "And Mr. Ferguson lent me the book. He has a fantastic collection, not that you would be interested."

"Hmmm." Cicely isn't even listening to her. "He likes you, Mr. Ferguson, doesn't he?" Grier says nothing. Cicely runs a hand through her hair, making it ice white, and then her eyes turn a gleaming silver. She looks like a wolf. My sister's silence is the only opening Cicely needs. "Have you ever wondered, Grier, why you're here?"

"Any time I'm in a room with you."

Stop her, stop her, my brain says, but for some reason I don't. I just stand there watching while Cicely perches on the edge of Grier's bed, hissing her words. "No really, why are you here? In this world. Do you wonder why?"

Grier's face hardens and I can almost read her mind. *Every day of my life.*

Cicely sneers. "It's so Valora can have your organs someday. I mean, what else could you possibly be good for?" Grier sighs, as if she is put out by this conversation. Cicely makes another attempt: "Also, I saw you talking to Leo Irsan today."

Bullseye. Grier flinches. "So?"

"So, he's pretty cute, and for a while I couldn't understand why he was talking to you – like, maybe he has a thing for chubby girls? Or maybe he needs a tutor."

"I heard you need a tutor," deadpans Grier. "In like every subject."

I want to cheer for my sister, but instead I watch Cicely tear at her. And I don't know why. *What's wrong with me? I can fight monsters but not my best friend?*

"No. It's even more basic than that." She leans forward towards Grier, who is now looking more cornered.

I find my voice. "Cicely..." She shushes me with one hand, and I feel my fingers curl a bit.

"It's simple. He's using you to get close to Valora. Proximity to power. First you, the sad misfit no one understands, and then step by step, he'll inch closer to her until..." She snaps her fingers in Grier's face. "He breaks your heart and then you have only your big book to cry into."

Grier holds her gaze steady, but I can tell she's shaken; Cicely's hit a nerve.

I stand. "Alright, alright. Cicely...enough." I sigh. "I need to go to bed." Grier holds my gaze before shaking her head, but I see her eyes are filled with tears.

"See you later, loser!" Cicely murmurs at Grier, and on her way out, she reaches under Grier's record player and with a flick of her wrist sends it tumbling. She sails out of the room trailed by Anna and Gillian, like little ducklings following their mama. Grier lunges for her record player, but she doesn't need to; it stops about an inch from the floor, floating in mid-air. I turn my hand and it comes to rests gently on the rug. Grier doesn't say anything as she picks up the player and sets it back on the shelf.

"You're welcome," I swallow, not knowing what else to say.

She whirls on me and the anger I see in her eyes is unmatched by anything I've seen there before. I step back.

"Thank you? Is that what you want right now, Valora? A thank you? Do you know what I was coming in to tell you?" She points to the door. "I was coming to tell you that someone destroyed your picture out there and you know what's crazy? I was actually worried about you for a second. But then I remember, oh that's right, silly Grier...your sister doesn't care about you *at all!* So why bother?" Tears are streaming down her face now. "You let Cicely do whatever she wants because you are so worried that for a second someone might actually see you. But I know the truth; that when everyone sees the real you, they'll see you're as shallow as your poster. All image and no substance. You want to be the hero, but heroes are usually *good.*"

Her words spark something in me. "You're worried about me, Grier? *Really?* Then how come you never come to any of my fights?"

Grier won't meet my eyes. "I don't... I know you'll be fine."

"Oh really? How would you know, considering that you don't watch them?"

My sister slams her book down on her bed. "Because you're always fine, Valora! Because how could you not be? Your whole life is everyone bending over to worship the ground you walk on. *What did Valora have for lunch?* I'll have that. *What did Valora do yesterday?* Oh, you can read about that in a magazine. *What is Valora wearing? What is Valora fighting? Who is Valora dating?* How can you not be fine when every single thing in the world is already about you? VALORA, WE ARE STANDING IN THE RIGMORE WING!"

I shake my head. Grier has never understood me and she's never wanted to. To Grier, my life is one big walk through a candy shop, rather than a graveyard. How do I explain to her that I can't worry about her feelings when I am always worried about the next fight and the next? My voice catches in my throat. "You don't get it."

Grier sneers. "I get that you throw me to the wolves when it suits you. I get that you can't just let me have *one tiny thing.*" Her voice shakes with anger.. "Not one thing, Valora. Not one seat at the front of the class. Not one boy who might like me for me. Not one peaceful moment where your friends can just leave me alone."

Her face is all pinched now, and I feel a cold pang of guilt. It hurts my chest, the same way it does when my power runs out, foreign and sharp. How can I explain this to her? "School doesn't matter, Grier. Those girls, they are nothing in the grand scheme of things. Proctor Moor...it's nothing. Erys..."

"It matters to me," she mutters. "It all matters to me. Your friends and their cruelty, the new boy. But you wouldn't care about that. You've never cared about me. I'm nothing, I'm dust, I'm....the sister of the Chosen One."

I'm not sure how to say I'm sorry. I'm not sure I want to. She's not even trying to understand what this feels like: the pressure, the expectations, the fear that pumps through my veins. So I say nothing. But she does speak, and her words punch through my chest.

"I hate being your sister."

Tears spring to my eyes at her words, but Grier doesn't see because she immediately bends over and pulls out her headphones. I know this conversation is coming to an end and I desperately don't want to it to. I want to tell her what it's really like. I want to tell her about the whispering doubt. I need someone – anyone – to understand me. But the sister that I shared a womb with might as well be a thousand miles away as she plops on her bed and shuts me out again. Loneliness curls inside of me and I take a step towards her. I have just reached out my hand when the lights give a flicker and stop my momentum.

"Well, that's not creepy," I whisper, but she doesn't hear me.

The lights stop flickering and I walk back to my bed, looking for something to do in a room crackling with tension. I dump out my backpack, shuffling through the homework that I'll half-heartedly look at tonight. Let Grier be the straight-A student.

I reach for the letter that arrived from my Nan today, when a fancy green envelope with gold lettering falls out of my publicity folder. I groan at the sight of it. *It can't be that time of year again – can it?*

"Green Hills is here," I mutter out loud, though Grier doesn't even look up. Gold confetti falls into my hand as I rip open the envelope.

The Regents & the Board of Directors of Proctor Moor

are proud to announce that you,
Valora Rigmore, have been selected to perform in
the Green Hills Invitational on November 26.
Students must be inside Canterbury Pavilion at 9 a.m. for their
scheduling.
"Let those with gifts show their mirth,
On cool green hills of sacred earth" - *Everett Proctor*

November 26...why does that sound familiar? I glance at my calendar hanging on the wall; Grier's lame Christmas present from the year before. There, on the date, is a big note: Mom and Dad in Greece! That's right, I remind myself, it's their anniversary trip. Well, at least I won't have Dad's expectations to worry about. One less thing. I crumple up the invitation and turn just in time to see Grier staring at me from her bed, before she quickly returns to her book. She doesn't say anything, but I know that Grier has always dreamed about participating in the Green Hills Invitational. It's a chance to show your powers, to become Exceptional among the Exceptional. It can land you future jobs, or even a free ride to college. But moving a chocolate bar from the kitchen to where you sit on the couch isn't impressive.

I leave the invitation crumpled on the bed, stuff Nan's letter into my pocket, and head out the door. I feel suffocated by Grier's judgmental gaze and so any place is better than where she is. I'm not sure where I'm going, but it feels good to be quiet in this empty hall until... I stop.

In front of me is the mutilated poster that Grier mentioned. Two circular cracks rest over my palms, the glass exploding outwards from the puncture marks. My hands are trembling, clenching as I reach for the picture, my fingers trailing over cracks, my mind reeling.

Someone hit this hard. Someone who was just a few steps from our door.

8

GRIER

"I HAVE A NEW THEORY," AGNES WHISPERS. "CICELY IS ERYS'S most dangerous monster, but nobody notices because of the skin suit she's wearing. Think about it. What better way to get close to Valora..." She lowers her voice to a demonic growl, "Than to be her best friend.."

I want to laugh, but I bite my cheek instead. Agnes and I are tucked away in the atrium where enormous floor pillows make a nook between decorative planter boxes.

"Could be. Could be." I close my eyes and stretch out. "If she's a monster, she's the one we should be worried about, not Erys. She's too convincing." Cicely's words have been playing on a loop in my brain in the days since the confrontation in Valora's room a few days ago. "But maybe she's right."

He's using you to get to Valora. Close proximity to power.

Agnes turns over, her thick chestnut hair catching the light, the filtered rays of the sun lighting her from behind. She's radiant. I don't tell her because I know she'd never believe me. Not that it matters much. Agnes doesn't seem to be interested in boys *or* girls.

"Grier, no she is NOT. I know what you're doing." I say

nothing. She presses on. "You only ever believe the worst things about yourself, and it makes me sad, because none of it's true. You've let other people define you for a long time." Agnes's cheeks are pink, her fists clenched. My sweet, loyal friend.

I shake my head. "Agnes, Cicely can't be the only person wondering why Leo would want to be hanging out with us. He looks like he was express-shipped here from California to round out Valora's posse of genetic perfection."

"So? So because he's super attractive, he automatically has to be an asshole? You really believe there's no possible way a guy who's funny and smart, enjoys the company of other funny, smart people?"

I press my palms to my eyes and exhale. "Yeah, but..."

"Yeah, but nothing, Grier. How is that fair?"

"Yeah, you're right. It's not fair."

She blows on her bangs – it's what she does when she's mad. "You know, he hangs out with me, too, Grier. You think he's just pretending to like me, too, just to get to Valora? Is that really the only reason anybody would want to hang out with us?"

I finally make eye contact with her. She's hurt. My heart sinks. "I'm sorry I'm so crazy right now." My apology is wrenched out of me. "But I like him, Agnes. When we were in the orchard, before we saw the Russet Flame, I thought he was going to kiss me... In that moment, I wasn't afraid of anything, I just really wanted him to. Then later when I thought about it, it all seemed so stupid."

"Except it's not," Agnes interrupts. "It's not stupid. I definitely get the feeling that he's into you. It's kind of obvious, in fact, and honestly, Grier, I wish you could just understand that that isn't the craziest thing to ever happen." She crosses her spindly arms over her chest, daring me to argue.

I fiddle with the frayed cuffs of my long-sleeved t-shirt for a long time, then nod. "I know."

"Just let things be how they are. Stop being so weird around him; you know he notices." Agnes nudges my leg with the toe of her sneakers. "I mean, just be your normal weird. He's into your normal weird, I promise."

"When'd you get so wise?"

"Oh, you know," she shrugs, standing up and stretching. "Comes with age and experience. Seriously, though. Just..."

I nod. "I know. Just let it be. Hey, I'm gonna go see if Mr. Ferguson is in his office so I can return his book. See you later?"

"See you later, normal weird."

When I reach his office, Mr. Ferg...*uh, Allen's* door is cracked open, but I knock anyway.

"Come on in!"

I peek my head around the door to find him behind his desk, reading. He peers up over his glasses at me, and his face breaks into a smile.

"Are you busy?" I ask tentatively, not wanting to interrupt him.

"Not at all, Grier! Please come in. What a nice surprise." He rises from behind his desk and gestures to one of those vivid orange chairs. "Have a seat!" I enter his bright, airy office and settle into a chair, clutching the book he lent me across my midsection. "What brings you here on this fine morning?" he nods toward the book. "Have you already finished it?"

"Last night. I wanted to return it to you."

"Excellent! Am I correct in assuming you enjoyed it, since you read it so quickly?"

"I did. I really appreciated the section on conserving momentum relative to the portal normal and the rules of absolute speed. Good stuff." I nod, feeling myself relaxing a bit, settling into the chair. I'm telling the truth. I did enjoy it, even if there were some parts I barely understood.

"Fantastic. It's heavy, and I want to hear all about your thoughts on it. But first, I have something I'd like to discuss."

He leans forward, long fingers laced together. "The Green Hills Showcase is coming up, as I'm sure you know."

Of course I know. I'm Valora's sister. I roll my eyes. "Oh, you mean the talent show for a bunch of kids with moderately cool gifts serving as the opening act for the Chosen One?"

Allen bursts out laughing. "That's the one. It's meant to be a chance for Proctor Moor's most uniquely gifted students to demonstrate their abilities, even if now it's become something...else. Which is why, Grier, I think you should consider participating."

There's a pause, then I snort. "Oh, sure. I'm assuming my invitation just got lost in the mail."

"Grier. I'm serious."

"So am I! I haven't been invited. Besides, what am I going to do, portal a sandwich from one hand to the other?" I try to keep my tone light, but I'm in disbelief.

"Have you ever done anything intensive to hone your gift?" he asks, leaning forward. "Any special training, any exercises to improve or grow your ability?"

"No." I'd never even thought about it, because it seemed unnecessary.

"Grier, there's a world of possibilities. I don't think you realize what you could do with your abilities if you truly applied yourself."

My heart is pounding unexpectedly. "You really think so?"

"I know so. I've been deemed master of ceremonies for this event – probably because they couldn't sucker anyone else into it - and I think an unexpected encore after the main event would be a fantastic surprise." I blink. He's proposing that I perform at the end, after my sister?! "I could train you, Grier. Think of how exciting this would be! Think of how delighted people would be to see that you, too, have amazing gifts."

His idea is completely crazy, but his excitement is contagious. *Could I really do this?* I slowly mull it over. "My parents will be out of town that week; they'll be in Greece."

"One might see that as a sign."

The words escape my lips before I can stop it. "Okay, I'll do it."

Allen's eyes twinkle with delight. He emphatically slaps an open palm on my leg. "Fantastic! You will be the highlight of the event, Grier. You'll see." I'm blushing, I'm sure of it, but I can't stop myself from grinning.

He pops up. "Okay then. So, we begin training. Right now."

"Right now." Okay...

"Portal the book you returned as far as you can, Grier. Let's see what you can do."

I stand, take a deep breath to steady myself, and focus in on the book, reaching my right hand toward it and flexing my fingers. I concentrate my energy and feel the familiar tingling flow down my forearm like the beginning stages of pins and needles. And there it is. My sparkling blue vortex forms under the book, swallowing it whole.

"Open the portal across the hallway, Grier." His voice is steady, calm.

"I don't think..." I protest.

"Try."

I stand and focus on a spot out the door and into the hallway, a good ten feet further than I remember ever being able to portal anything, and extend my hand toward it, bearing down. The tingling sensation grows stronger, and the tips of my fingers begin to ache. The ache deepens into a burn, which spreads slowly up my palm and into my wrist. It's not unbearable yet, but it's far from pleasant. I grit my teeth and concentrate, and suddenly I see it: the tiniest, quarter-sized glimmer of light in the hallway, slowly spinning outward.

"Stay focused!" Allen's voice seems muffled, as though he's calling to me from another room.

The book appears, and I yelp, both from surprise and from the searing pain that shoots up my forearm and into my heart. The portal disappears as the book thuds to the floor in front of the lockers. Stunned, I collapse into the orange chair. "Oh my God." I'm breathless.

I turn to see Allen, leaning back in his chair, eyes on me. "How did it feel?" he asks softly.

"It hurt a little," I admit. "It usually only tingles. This time it burned, especially right at the end, all the way into my chest."

"I won't lie to you, Grier. It may hurt at times, but no more than your muscles would after a strenuous workout. Much like exercise, the harder you work and the more you practice, it will hurt less and get easier. It'll be like you're building muscle memory." *Oh, sure. I work out all the time, so I totally know what you mean,* I think.

"Now. This time I want you to try to move the book all the way from the hallway..." he gestures toward his office door on the opposite side of the room, "back to where it was."

I'm tired, but I don't want to stop. "Okay," I say, resolutely, flexing my fingers.

"Good. And I want you to take your time. Don't worry about how quickly you can get the portal to grow; focus on concentrating a steady energy to the portal instead. This time we we're focusing on strength, not size or speed. Understood?"

I take a breath. "Yes."

We work for hours, moving items from place to place in his office, the hallway, and even on the ceiling. I even move a heavy glass paperweight from his desk to the console table outside his office door, then move it back with the same portal, dropping it carefully. It lands cleanly on the narrow ledge, and I can't keep myself from grinning. "What's next?"

Allen chuckles as he looks at his watch. "I think that's enough formal training for today. We can start working on larger objects next time. The more you do this, the easier it becomes. Practice when you're in your room, when you're hanging out with your friends. Others know about your gift, right?"

"Yeah, people know about it. I just don't use it very often, because I never had any reason to."

"Well, now you do. But let's keep your training a surprise for the time being. That way no one will see it coming, and you'll stun them all!"

A thrill of excitement rushes through my veins. *I will stun them. Me.* "My lips are sealed.'

"Great." He smiles. "Now, you haven't moved the hands on the clock, but they've moved themselves. It's late."

My stomach chooses that moment to growl audibly and I want to die inside. "It's..." I stutter.

"Time for dinner," he finishes for me, amused. "See you tomorrow, after classes are done for the day?"

"I can't wait."

I reach the cafeteria just before the peak dinner rush hits and spot Leo and Agnes settling in at our usual table as I pick up my tray. Leo catches my eye and grins at me, that quick, easy flash of a smile that makes my heart rate jump. I return the smile and head toward them, feeling lighter and happier than I have in a long time.

Leo pulls out the chair next to him. Something – relief, maybe? – flickers across his face. I feel a pang of guilt for being so standoffish lately. "Hey!" he greets me. "I wondered if you were going to join us!" I sit beside him, and my stomach goes all fluttery as our shoulders touch.

"Ugh, damn it, I forgot to get a drink," Agnes grumbles. "I'm going to get a soda. Anybody else want anything?"

I'm about to shake my head when I spot something across the room: a chilled, unopened bottle of Agnes' favorite soda sitting on Cicely's tray. *Practice makes perfect.* "I'll get it for you, Agnes."

"Oh! Okay, thanks!" She gives me a quizzical look when I stay seated and extend my arm slightly, fingers flexed. Agnes turns in her chair to look in the direction of Cicely's table, and Leo cranes his head to see. When Cicely turns to talk to Anna, I open the portal underneath her soda, and just like that, the bottle is gone. Agnes gasps and turns back to me, just in time to see the bottle appear a few inches above my tray before dropping and rolling onto its side. Calmly, I pick up the bottle and hand it to her. "Wait a few minutes to open it so it doesn't spray everywhere," I tell her, then nod back toward Cicely, who has just realized her bottle is gone.

"What the HELL?" we hear her squawk. "Who took my drink?" The three of us, unable to contain ourselves, burst into quiet laughter.

9

VALORA

I FEEL THE EXHAUSTION SLOWLY SEEPING INTO MY BONES. Training is over, thankfully, and Renata locks the gym door behind me with a grimace. About an hour ago, I impaled the scoreboard with a spear that was meant for a target below. It'll be quietly fixed tomorrow. Through the sweat dripping down my face, I watch her fumble nervously with the lock. She's so edgy these days...and she's not alone.

It's been three weeks since we saw the monster in the orchard and somehow the story around it has grown from a non-incident involving a lazy creature into a full-out confrontation, with Pike and me at the center. I hear whispers about it everywhere I go. The rumors aren't just about the fight; it's about Pike and me and how we went "missing" afterward, which isn't true at all. I don't exactly understand what happened, but one minute I was indestructible and now... suddenly there is a crack in the armor, like people were waiting for it. Renata has always taught me that people live vicariously through their idols, but even more than that, they want to see their idols fall.

Cicely isn't currently speaking to me because she thinks I've kept a secret from her – which is bullshit - and is wounded by *the very idea* that I might not share every inch of my feelings with her. Julian is acting bizarre, showing up everywhere I go, strutting around like a peacock and flinging his arm roughly around me like some goon marking his territory. Pike seems as equally bewildered as I am; he's been inundated lately with guys who want to hang with him and girls who want to date him. It's amazing what the "ol' Rigmore boost" can do for a person's social status. I just want to hide, but instead I've focused on my training with Renata, which has been exhausting and therapeutic all at once. Every day between classes and after school, I am lifting and throwing things while I'm running. I'm wielding weapons and working on my aim. She pushes me past my limits and while I scream at her and curse her name, I'm getting stronger; I can feel it. My power is growing. *It's still not enough.*

I grimace. There it is again, the whisper.

I throw my gym bag over my shoulder and rub my burning hands together as I walk down the hallway. Renata has procured for me a set of ever-cold hand wraps, courtesy of a skilled Exceptional in New York. They are fantastic for cooling the burning sensation in my hands during trainings – and later, for actual confrontations. The pain still pulls at my wrists like a sharp piano wire, but at least I can function. I slap the sides of my face as I try to keep awake. I have to get back to my room so I can sleep for at least an hour. Tomorrow is the Green Hills Invitational, and I am supposed to do my normal big demonstration at the end of it. Renata has pared it down to a few very simple tricks; exhausting, sure, but easy nonetheless. The crowd will probably be disappointed.

I don't care.

There is a sea of students ahead and they part like water as I pass. "Valora! How was training today?" One eager female student, probably a freshman, tries to engage me at risk to herself. It's pretty brave, and in return I give her a dazzling smile.

"It was good! Thanks for asking." She turns to her friends with open mouths and they squeal. *See, I can be nice.* I cringe when I think about how I probably don't look great right now; my hair is soaked with sweat and pulled back from my face in a tight bun. I'm wearing black leggings and a loose Proctor Moor sweatshirt. I wonder what all these people are waiting for as I turn the corner to head back to my room.

I stop short when I see a line of pink carnations bordering the edge of the Rigmore Wing. *Ummm...what the hell?* I step forward into a break in the crowd, kicking one of the carnations with my foot before I start to turn. *Maybe I'll take the back staircases, just in case...*but that's when I hear some familiar lyrics:

Remember when we were dancing on the waves
That was us, in that moment
And I knew that you would love me
As the sun set in our shadow

Oh shit. I know this song.

It was playing the first time Julian and I ever hung out together. It's called "Love Me" and it was on the radio in the background when we met the summer before my ninth grade year; the year we started at Proctor Moor. My family had been invited to Julian's family's infamous Summer Bash –totally because of who I am - and we made a trip of it. My parents were thrilled with the idea that we had reached some new social echelon. I was excited at the thought of showing off my new bikini and possibly meeting some cute boys that already went to Proctor Moor. Grier was excited for nothing, as always, and

slumped unhappily in the backseat when my parents refused to leave her at home. I remember pressing my nose to the window as we drove up, taking in this enormous white beach house, all angles and windows, landscaped with white drifts of sand and black rocks.

"Could it be any more amazing?" I whispered.

"Could you be any more superficial?" sneered Grier, but I could tell even she was a bit impressed. She waited a second and then turned back to me. "That was mean, I'm sorry. It's a cool house. But..." She fidgeted. "Will you stay with me? At the party. You know I get shy."

I roll my eyes, but I nod. "Yeah sure, I'll stay with you – but we are talking to people, okay? We need to get in on the ground floor at Proctor Moor before we start next year.."

Grier shook her head. "Valora...there is no ground floor for you. You're the penthouse." But I was already jumping out of the car as it pulled up, leaving her far behind. I didn't keep my promise to her, and a few hours in I found myself outside on the patio with sophomore Julian North, the most gorgeous boy I had ever seen.

As he handed me a stolen Mimosa that tasted like fizzy dreams, he took my hand and kissed my cheek. "Love Me" was playing as he leaned in, his mouth brushing my ear. "Someday, I'm going to marry the Chosen One." Then his hand found its way up my shirt.

T hinking of it now, the memory makes me an'
myself and at Julian - but I don't have time tc
on that because lined up on either side of me in the
a dozen of my friends, all silently holding pink c'
hallway floor is covered with them, sprinkled l'
for a good twenty feet, and right in the middl

display is Julian, looking like a god. He reaches out his hand for me.

"This is our song, Val." Half the girls around us sigh.

"What is this?" I'm trying to look pleased, trying to smile, but it's incredibly difficult. I can't seem to hold onto it. Julian steps forward. He's wearing a tuxedo, and I'm pretty sure that no one has ever looked as good as he does right now, and yet... it's not him I'm thinking about. Then he gets down on one knee and fear rushes over me. "Stop!" I blurt, not understanding but not wanting this to continue. "What are you doing?" *Please don't let this be what I think it is.*

"Valora Rigmore, I knew that I loved you from the first moment I saw you standing on the beach that night, and I've only grown to love you more since." His stare is intense, as is the silence around me. My heart is pounding in my chest, and I feel something dangerous rising inside of me. He produces a pink carnation from behind his back. "Valora, will you go to prom with me?"

Relief washes over me. But then to my horror, I can't help the laughter that follows. Prom. PROM. "All this for prom? Julian, isn't that like...in the spring?"

Julian swallows angrily, trying to hide his annoyance. "Yeah, I just wanted to ask you early." I shake my head as laughter continues to explode. I can't help it. There are monsters edging closer to the school every day and the entire world is depending on me to live up to my destiny as the Chosen One and he's talking about *fucking PROM*?

I can feel everything inside of me crumpling like a piece of metal, one break and then another, wrenching into sharp corners. There is a buzzing in my ears and I twist my head in an ttempt to shake the migraine that is rapidly approaching. I am ᐟtired.

Cicely steps out from the crowd, a frown on her face.

"Valora...we planned this big surprise, say something!" Her

eyes drop to Julian and back to me. I look down at him and for a moment I feel pity, for his doomed public display of affection. Only, I know it's not affection. Prom is five months away, and he's wanting to make sure that everyone knows that Valora Rigmore belongs to him. Only him.

The gym bag drops from my arm. "No."

Julian's eyes meet mine. "What do you mean no?"

I step forward, anger roiling off me now. "I mean no, I don't want to go with you, Julian. I mean no, I am not even thinking about prom right now. Really, Julian? A stupid dance? Is that what you care about?"

Julian's face changes. "Valora...maybe we should..." But I'm in it now and I can't stop what's happening inside of me. The Valora veneer is breaking.

"What do you want from me?" I snap at him, and then at the crowd. "It's not enough that I'm saving you? All of you?" There is a sharp intake of breath around me, followed by an awkward silence. Then I hear a giggle near the back. "You think this is funny? Are you going to think it's funny when Erys shows up with her army of monsters and rips your head from your body?"

I thrust my hands out angrily in front of me and all the pink carnations rise simultaneously into the air. Julian looks up at me, terrified but also ashamed of my behavior. God, I hate him. *I hate him.*

"We're done." I say to him as he sputters beside me. Then I spell it out for him again in short, loud words. "We. Are. Done."

I'm losing control. The carnations continue to float at eye level as the lockers on either side of us begin rattling and pulling out from the wall. With a mean smile, I push my hands forward. The carnation heads begin flying at students, a delightful game of dodgeball where I have the only weapon. The girls scream as if they are being shot at by actual bullets. The boys dive for cover. I send a flurry of them at Julian, who kneels on the floor, covering his head as they pound him. But I'm not done. *Oh yes, I'm not even close to done.* I smile as the lockers start crumpling at the end of the hallway and fluorescent lights begin swinging when I hear a voice behind me.

"Valora?" The voice is deep, tinged with authority. Mr. Ferguson emerges from the crowd. "Valora. Stop. Right now."

His voice cuts through the loud humming in my brain and my arms drop to my side. The carnations fall to the floor as Julian is stares at me angrily. I watch him as he climbs to his feet and drops his own flower to the ground. "You're going to regret this, you psycho." he hisses, his shoulder bumping mine as he storms past. Cicely meets my eyes and shakes her head.

Mr. Ferguson walks up behind me and puts his hand on my shoulder. I shake it free. "You okay, Valora?" he asks cautiously.

"Yeah." I take a deep breath.

He turns to the rest of the students. "Go to class or you will all be banned from Green Hills," he commands, and they immediately scatter. My friend Tony passes by me with a smile. "Bad ass, Valora!"

"Don't cuss in front of a teacher, Mr. London," Mr. Ferguson growls.

"Sorry." He is the last one to leave the hallway.

My shoulders shrug forward as they exit. "Uh, yeah, so I think I kind of lost control? I'm just really exhausted. I'm sorry about the lockers."

He raises an eyebrow. "You're more powerful than you think, but don't worry. No one is hurt. Man, you almost went full-on Carrie there. Be careful with that." But then he looks at the carnations on the ground and the flameless candles lining the walls. "But also, who does this in high school? Was he proposing marriage?"

"Prom."

He tilts his head. "It's been awhile since I've attended one, but isn't prom in the spring?"

"It's not about prom," I mutter and he nods slowly.

"I can see that. You know, I've never wanted to pry into your business..." I laugh because he is making me uncomfortable. "But Julian North has never seemed to be the right choice for you."

"Uh, thanks, Mr. Ferguson, I'll keep that in mind." I look over the scattered mess of the hallway. "Though, I'm pretty sure it's over, by the looks of it." I'm not sure how I should feel, but I'm pretty sure that I shouldn't feel nothing.

He bends over and picks up my gym bag. I take it from him, ignoring the wide smile he gives me. "Best of luck tomorrow. The showcase always makes quite an impression." The way he says it implies that he means something else.

"Thanks." I leave him behind, crushing carnations under my feet as I make my way to my room. I clap my hands together angrily, feeling the warm glow of power I just used. I know I should feel bad that I hurt Julian, but what I feel is the complete opposite: I feel free, like a giant weight has physically been taken off my shoulders. I can't keep the smile off my face as I unlock my bedroom door. The bed is waiting for me.

Finally, rest. Finally, home. I take a breath. *Finally, free.*

I take the first peaceful nap I've had in years.

The next day, I am standing behind a curtain at Canterbury Pavilion, about to be ushered out to the Green Hills Showcase and listening to Mr. Ferguson recite my accomplishments. "Prophesied from birth, possessing the greatest power Exceptionals have seen since Everett Proctor, gifted student and fashion icon...You know her name and now you will know her power!" *Ugh, he's really pouring it on.* I take a deep breath and exhale the way Renata has taught me. My tricks are nothing but fodder for the crowd. I could do them in my sleep. I have nothing to worry about. And yet...

"Please help me welcome our star performer..." Something is prodding at my brain, a whispering dread that I can't name. I try to get a handle on it. *Stage fright? It can't be.* I run my fingers through my hair, pressing my fingertips against my temples.

"You know her as the Chosen One..." It's time. I straighten my back and lift my chin. My black uniform is snug and tight, the cape draping just above the floor. The crowd is roaring now, on their feet, and the sound washes over me and raises the hair on my arms. "Give it up for the pride of Proctor Moor...Miss Valora Rigmore!" I step out from behind the curtain. The spotlight finds me and the crowd goes wild. I scan the arena for my parent's proud faces – a force of habit- before I remember that they are in Greece.

I am even more alone than I thought.

As I plant my feet, I feel that same dread, like a cold finger at the base of my neck. It's like someone is watching me...which is stupid, because everyone IS watching me. The feeling remains, but instead of worrying about it, I flex my fingers and give my hair a shake. I turn and face the nameless thousands, raising my palms slowly and dramatically.

If it's the Chosen One they want, that's who I'll give them.

10

GRIER

THUNDEROUS APPLAUSE RINGS OUT, NEARLY DEAFENING DESPITE the open-air stadium. I peer out from behind a panel, my stomach churning at the sight of thousands of people standing on their feet and cheering for my sister. Canterbury Pavilion, Proctor Moor's outdoor amphitheater, is packed to capacity. Valora stands confidently at the center of the stage, beaming, her arms stretched above her head in triumph as her cape flutters and twists around her.

Yeah, hell no. I turn to Allen. "I can't follow that!"

He chuckles calmly and places his hands on my shoulders, leveling with me. "You *can* follow that, Grier, and you're going to. Valora gave them just what they were expecting to see; parlor tricks. You're going to give them the unexpected." His eyes sparkle with intensity behind his tortoiseshell glasses.

I glance down at my long-agonized-over outfit: maroon leggings, black ankle boots stolen from Valora's closet, and a long-sleeved grey tunic sweater. In my room, I'd felt some semblance of satisfaction with my appearance; I'd gone digging in my sister's makeup and found a rosy lip stain and some mascara promising an Orgasmic Blast. However, the second

Valora stepped onto the stage, my confidence began rapidly depleting.

Allen reaches out and lets his hand rest on my shoulder. "Grier. Take a deep breath. This is it." He strides past me to center stage where Valora had stood only seconds before. He holds up his hands to quiet the crowd, and waits as the rapturous applause dies down.

"Students, colleagues, families, esteemed members of our community," he begins, his voice ringing out into the air. "You've witnessed a spectacular display of abilities here today. This, of course, is what the Green Hills Showcase is intended to do: to give you a glimpse into the Exceptional gifts of our best and brightest students." He's charismatic, and has the crowd's rapt attention. From across the stage, I see Valora in the wings. Her arms are folded tightly across her slumped body, a faint look of annoyance on her face. *My sister looks tired.*

Allen continues. "Today it gives me great pleasure to announce just one more surprise exhibition. Ladies and gentlemen, please welcome to the stage Miss Grier Rigmore."

There's a momentary stunned silence before the crowd breaks into polite applause. Out of the corner of my eye, I see Valora's jaw drop, and it gives me a sudden surge of confidence I wasn't expecting. I take a deep breath and force my feet to take me out onto the stage.

Allen claps me on one shoulder and groans into his microphone. "Grier, I can't believe it. I'd planned to take notes on your performance for you to review later, and I seem to have forgotten my notepad and pen backstage. Would you be so kind as to help me out?"

"Of course!" I smile broadly and hold out one hand toward the direction I'd just entered, and wait a beat.

"Grier, could you please get my notepad and paper?" Allen taps his foot impatiently.

"What do you think I'm doing?!" I chide him, and I hear a

few faint snickers in the audience as I focus my energy offstage to where I can barely see the props in the dim light, my fingers tingling. I turn to Allen, gently raise my other hand between us, and concentrate until my portal appears and his leather-bound folio and pen drop neatly onto the ground in front of him.

"Thank you, Grier. Now, I had a podium I'd planned to use..."

"No trouble at all!" I assure him, lacing my fingers together in front of me, stretching, and cracking my knuckles theatrically. I take a deep breath and turn again to face offstage. This takes more effort, and is no small feat on my part. A slow burn creeps from my fingers, through my palm and up to my wrist. *Please let me get the portal large enough*, I will myself silently. I see the silhouette of the podium disappear, and exhale in relief before turning my aim to the far opposite side of the stage and flexing my fingers. I hear a few gasps from the audience as it widens, swirling, a few feet above the stage floor. The podium appears suddenly, landing with a solid thunk, and the crowd roars with delight. I'm unable to keep myself from grinning, my cheeks hot and flushed. *Is this what it feels like to be Valora every day?*

"Wonderful! Just wonderful. Now, one more thing. A stool, perhaps?"

I gave an exaggerated sigh, and a ripple of laughter rises from the crowd. "One more thing," I agree, and close my eyes to center myself.

This is happening.

My fingers and palms burn as the tall, simple stool appears out of my portal and drops neatly in place. Allen strides toward it as the crowd cheers. Aiming carefully, I wait until he turns to sit down, then bare down, fingers flexed. Timing is everything. The stool disappears right as he sits down, sending him sprawling onto the stage floor. The audience screams with laughter, and as Allen scrambles to stand and brush himself off,

I am easily able to make the stool reappear right next to me. I sit on it, raise my arms over my head triumphantly, and grin. *Thhheeaaaatttteeerrr!*

Allen addresses the crowd. "Miss *Grier* Rigmore is a student of remarkable abilities. Will you allow her a few more moments of your time?" I hear enthusiastic cheering in response.

Allen brings out a bow, arrows, and small target. The audience gasps, and I stand, flexing my fingers in anticipation. He leaves the target on the front edge of the stage, selects a few arrows, and drops the rest through the open trapdoor in the stage. The arrowhead is wrapped in flammable, kerosene-dampened cloth. Allen produces a silver lighter from his pocket and ignites the end of the arrow, which flickers with a bright blue flame. He picks up the bow and takes precise aim at the target across the stage. The audience is so silent that I can hear a faint chirping sound from somewhere outside the stadium.

Allen draws the arrow back, pauses, then suddenly spins and shoots it straight out over the sea of spectators. The crowd gasps in shock as the flaming arrow arcs up over the crowd before curving downward... straight toward the spectators. As they scream, I throw my hand up and my blue shimmering portal appears about ten yards above the heads of startled audience members and swallows the flaming arrow before it lands. I spin and shoot my other hand toward the target, my arm burning as the flaming arrow explodes out from my portal buries itself squarely in the bullseye with a satisfying thud.

There's a second of utter silence and then a deafening roar of wild applause.

"Ready for the fun part?" Allen's voice is in my ear, and I nod excitedly. From offstage, he retrieves half a dozen confetti cannons, packed full of enough rainbow-colored confetti to cover half a football field. Stepping back, he hoists a cannon to his shoulder and pulls the ripcord. I'm ready and waiting, and the confetti shoots directly into my portal. Aiming carefully, I create another above the heads of the people I'd saved just moments ago and watch with delight as a cheerful shower of rainbow confetti begins to flutter out over their heads. Allen fires another canon, then another and each time, I move the confetti, sending it raining down on different areas of the stadium. In under a minute the entirety of Canterbury Pavilion is swirling like the inside of a rainbow snow globe. I stand utterly still for a moment and let the sound of an ecstatic crowd wash over me.

It's the best moment of my life so far.

Offstage, the dim lighting backstage flickers momentarily, but before I can say something, Allen turns to me. "How are you feeling?" he asks. I grin and shake my head, unable to find the right words. "Grier. I'm proud of you!" he tells me, and I feel tears prick my eyes. He leans in to say something, but I hear familiar voices and spin to greet them.

"Grier!" Leo's voice shakes me out of my haze, and I turn to find him and Agnes rushing toward me. I run to meet them. Agnes tackle-hugs me first, her spindly frame nearly sending me tumbling over.

"Oh my god! You were amazing! Grier! I didn't even know you could do that!" Her eyes are shining as she steps back and squeezes my hands. "I need to know everything! You have so much to tell me!"

I laugh. "I know! I'm sorry, I have gone crazy keeping this a surprise."

"You were..." Leo steps forward, his coppery skin warm against a navy wool coat, bits of confetti in his hair, his dark brown eyes wide. "Grier."

He says my name and it's as though everything around me goes blurry, except for him. He lifts one hand and gently brushes a fleck of bright pink confetti from my hair, his fingertips settling lightly at the nape of my neck as his thumb grazes my cheek.

This is happening. I am about to have my first kiss.

He leans in closer, so close I can feel his breath, the warmth from his skin even before his forehead gently touches mine. I'm so wrapped up in this magical, color-drenched moment that I almost don't even hear the screaming when it begins.

As Leo leans in, Agnes's panicked cries jolt us back into reality. When I look back, her face has gone ghostly white. I follow her horrified gaze out further into the stadium, where the people in the top rows are running and screaming. I look back at Leo, and that's when I see them just over his head: the shadows of creatures wheeling overhead on veined wings, black as a moonless night. Their horrifying skeletal bodies are easily ten feet long, hairless and covered in black skin stretched taut. Bat-like wings twice the length of their bodies end in razor-sharp claws. The creatures circle once above the crowd before the largest one dives down into the stadium with a murderous scream, its sunken eyes blood red. We watch in horror as it rakes its claws over a woman running toward the stage for shelter. It picks her up, flies upwards about fifty feet, and drops her. She falls screaming as blood pours from her torn shoulder, but she lands on a group of Proctor Moor soccer players with outstretched arms. Before we can even react, two more creatures dive into the stands as the rest circle overhead. Terror fills the stadium.

Leo grabs my hand. "*Mantharas.* We have to get out of the open. Now."

We run, dodging abandoned coats and bags. Bits of confetti still drift lazily, now a stark contrast to a stadium engulfed in chaos. I nearly trip over a little girl in a red coat who darts in front of me, racing back out into the arena. What is she doing? Instinctively, I stop and turn to see her duck into an aisle and reach for something under a seat. She pulls out a stuffed Valora doll, clutching it to her chest. Overhead, I hear the screeching of Mantharas. My heart stops. *Where the hell is my sister?*

Leo tugs my hand. "Grier! Come ON!"

I turn to follow but stop again when I hear the little girl cry out, "Mommy!"

"Janie!" A frantic cry comes the floor of the auditorium, and I see a woman, searching for her daughter. "Janie!"

"Go. I'll be right behind you!" I yell, running toward the little girl as I hear her mother screaming at the top of her lungs, her fear so real it pierces straight through me.

"Janie, get down!"

One of the Mantharas has zeroed in on its tiny target, its sunken eyes glinting as it rights itself and dives straight for her. Without thinking, I thrust my hand forward toward her, a searing pain surging up my arm and though my heart as I focus my portal. Just as the beast's lethal claws close in on her, Janie disappears a shimmering blue light. Confused by the portal, the creature crashes into the stands before it screams in anger and wheels around. Sweating and shaking, I stumble toward the stage, hand outstretched. I feel a surge of energy, followed by a fresh wave of excruciating pain, as my second portal appears above the floor of the auditorium. I see the little girl tumble down safely out of the portal into her mother's arms, and then there is only blackness that swallows me whole.

11

VALORA

MY SISTER IS GOING TO GET KISSED. IN ALL MY LIFE, NO BOY HAS ever looked at me the way that Leo is looking at Grier now. He doesn't want anything from her; he just wants her. *What must that feel like?* I watch them through rainbow whirlwind of confetti as Leo slowly leans in toward Grier. *I'm even more alone than I thought,* I think, the idea hard and bitter.

And that's when I hear it: an inhuman screech, like nails running down metal. It raises the hair on my arms and suddenly everything inside me is attuned to the sound. In the stands, people are still laughing as confetti falls around them. Some have turned to look at the stage, wondering if this is another showcase piece, but they are wrong: only one thing makes that kind of noise. I, of all people, should know.

The screech echoes again, and this time the crowd stops, all eyes turning to the sky. I see a monstrous shadow above the parapets of the arena, hear the whoosh of leathery wings. I push back the black velvet curtain and slowly walk onto the floor of Canterbury Pavilion, my cape fluttering behind me. My feet feel like I am slogging through water, and there is a strange buzzing in my ears. The roar of the crowd I know so well pitches into a scream, and their fear holds me down like a heavy stone.

That's when I see them. Mantharas.

Everything fades into slow motion as the first hideous creature looks hungrily over the crowd. After a second, it tips its head back and screams as the shadows of maybe a dozen more pass over my face. Mantharas are supposed to live only near the temperate deserts in India. They emerge at night and occasionally swipe a child from remote desert settlements. But now they are here, at the Green Hills showcase. *In Connecticut.*

My brain is spinning. All around me, I hear screams, hear Renata yelling my name, but I'm too far gone to listen to her. I watch in horror as the Mantharas swoop over the edges of the crowd. They pluck people up out of their seats and soar across the arena, talons digging into shoulders, chests. I watch a sophomore get dragged over a snack concession cart before his friend grabs his legs and the Mantharas releases with a screech. Out of the corner of my eye, I see Julian and his entourage trying to make their way down to the floor of the stadium as a Manthara swoops down, raking its mouth over the shoulder of a pretty girl named Stephanie. Julian doesn't even look back as he sprints away. Cicely and Gillian are crouched down in their seats in the front row, tears running down their faces as they clutch each other. Cicely's hair has gone white with fear.

I know I should do something, but I'm frozen - I don't know what's happening. It's like my limbs aren't working, like my body is made of stone and I'm screaming from somewhere deep inside of it. All the expectations of the Chosen One crash over me like a tidal wave. I feel the air pressing in around me as the ground seems to shift under my feet. *I'm afraid. Oh God, I'm afraid.*

They are waiting for you, I hear myself whisper. Move! Move! But I can't move. I can't....

My hair is blown back from my face by a blast of fetid wind, and the largest Mantharas lands directly in front of me, shaking the ground as it does. Slowly it shakes its head at me and I hear the rattle of old, creaking bones. The mutant bat folds up its wings and falls onto all fours, crooked legs and claws raking that infamous Canterbury Pavilion grass. I've never seen a Mantharas so huge, so it must be the Queen. It hisses at me as black liquid oozes out from red eyes, black talons slick with the blood of others. I smell it as it nears; the sickly-sweet carrion of death.

The Mantharas tilts its head my direction and begins crawling quickly toward me, huge wings jutting out behind it like mountain peaks. I can't breathe, can't move, because my panic has frozen me to the spot. The bat screams in my face, its steaming mouth wide and cavernous. I can see fangs black with rot, a slathering pink tongue. It rears back, and my last thought is that everyone watching live TV is going to see the Chosen One get eaten, and somehow that seems just right. I am hoping it will be quick when I am shoved violently aside and hit the ground hard. The impact wakes me up. I shake my head. My God. I'm okay. *I'm here.* I can move.

I flex my palms and feel the white heat flowing through them and shoot to my feet. Pike Paskell is standing between me and the bat, and his right hand is palm-up and flickering with a healthy flame. As I scramble to my feet, he leans forward and blows on the flame like he is making a wish; only his breath is like gasoline and fuels a huge plume of fire that envelops the Mantharas' face. It gives a terrible screech and rears backward. The flame catches its wings. The bat tries to launch into the air but cannot. It crashes into the stands in a huge fireball.

"You okay?" Pike shouts, but I don't even have time to thank him because I'm sprinting into the middle of the Square, whispering to myself, "I am the Chosen One. I am the Chosen One.".

I've never fought more than one monster at a time, but I

need to believe that I can. I speed past screaming classmates and shrieking Mantharas; I need to get somewhere high, somewhere where I can see everything. All around me is chaos: the crowd is trampling each other as they run to the exits, which have been locked from the outside. I stop suddenly. THE EXITS. This I can do.

I stop running and focus on the main doors to the square, my palms held out in front of me. I feel the white heat coming down my arms, stretching my veins as it passes through and then I feel it: the tingling of power. I'm ready. I take a deep breath and pull with both hands, imagining my power pushing against the doors. Then I release it from my mind. The metal doors hum and then pull outwards, away from me. The crowd looks back at me with amazement before stepping backward. I let out an anguished scream and thrust my hands forward. The doors explode off their hinges, flying violently out, spinning as they go. With my palm outstretched, I catch one of the doors in midair and turn it into a weapon, flinging it like a javelin into a Mantharas hovering above the crowd. It cuts the beast in two.

The crowd surges through the exits. I hear Mr. Ferguson yelling at the crowd; he's doing his best to keep them from trampling each other, but he's also yelling Grier's name. Grier... where is she? I spin around and see her lying unconscious on the ground near Leo and Agnes and my heart leaps into my chest, but then she's sitting up, shaking her head. Did she faint? *Of course she did.*

A Mantharas launches itself toward the three of them, talons outstretched. Rage funnels through my hands and I push the bat away from them in one swift movement and send it wheeling into the stands before I curl a metal bleacher up and send it hurtling through its neck. When I spin around I see I'm not the only one fighting; Pike has set fire to another of them. A group of students has somehow snared one with a vendor's plastic tarp and is beating it to death with their backpacks. One more is circling above a family; the mother covers her son with her body as the father is attempting to shield them with a light rain, another useless Exceptional gift. The podium that Grier used in her showcase is to my right; I send it hurtling through the air towards the bat. It smashes through one of its black, leathery wings. The bat tumbles down to the stage, taking out the black curtains behind it. It leaps up, crazed and bloodthirsty but I hold out my palms and wrestle control of its narrow head. "Steady," I whisper to myself. "Steady..." *This is gonna be gross*, I think, but with my other hand I begin twisting, like I'm opening a bottle. The bat's head pops off in a gush of black, steaming blood. I dry-heave, but I don't stop moving.

Two bats are left in the arena now. One dive bombs the escaping crowd, plucking people up from the horde. I aim my palms its direction, wrestling control of its flight. It's harder than I expected, controlling the creature, and I almost lose it. That's when I feel arms wrap around mine from behind; it's Renata and she's holding my arms steady so I can use all my power. I let out a painful scream as I pull the Mantharas up and away from the crowd.

"Don't hold the whole thing, hold just a part of it," she commands. I focus in on the bat's chest, on something I can see....and there, just beneath its black skin and pale veins, I see a tiny movement: the thump of a heart. I focus on it and then suddenly pull my arms backward in a single, quick motion. The bat plunges to the ground, but its heart lands in the stands near a bunch of terrified girls, who let out a chorus of hysterical screams.

There is only one bat left, and it's climbing into the sky. I try to pull it back, but it's no use; my power is exhausted, and I slump against Renata. Then I hear a loud crack and the bat tumbles down to the ground just beyond the stadium. Standing behind me is a member of the Board of Proctor Moor, and in his hands is a hunting rifle. He lowers the rifle and takes a long drag from his pipe. He sees us looking at him and shrugs. "A weapon's a weapon, am I right?" Then he hops down and strolls across the green to take his trophy.

For the first time since I heard the first screech, I let myself rest, gulping in air with my hands on my knees. My palms are on fire. *What happened back there? Why did I freeze?*

I hear footsteps behind me, and I hear Pike's voice. "Hey, are you guys okay?"

"Maybe." I raise my head and look around the arena; on the ground in the stands. People are bleeding; maybe even a few are dead. The guilt hits me like a wave. *Why couldn't I move?* I'm about to thank Pike when I feel the ground rumble underneath me. *No.*

I step back and we watch in horror as the grass undulates beneath our feet. A long, winding shape takes form as the sod cracks in two. As this new monster moves up like a leviathan from the deep, I catch a glimpse of black scales marked with light purple under the rocky Connecticut soil.

Behind me Renata whispers, "It can't be." The ground parts in an explosion that showers dirt over us. I hear a loud hiss pass between protruding fangs, and I see the slithering of a heavy body as it pushes itself out of the ground.

Horror fills my chest as an Onyxcobra slowly slithers out, dirt pouring from the wide flaps on either side of its head. It coils its body until it stands more than twenty feet off the ground. The monstrosity's head is as big as a car; and when it rears up, the hoods on the side of its narrow face slide open, revealing two additional eyes. A four-eyed monster from the deepest caves in Southeast Asia - so rare that it has only been photographed a handful of times - is now staring straight at me. Its forked tongue tastes the air.

Behind the Onyxcobra, I see a group of students trying to sneak past its tail towards the rear exit. The snake whirls on the students, its four eyes focusing as it opens its mouth. I don't have enough strength to do anything and brace for their deaths, but instead the snake slowly, methodically turns back to me.

That's when I understand. *This snake is here for me.*

"Valora..." utters Renata, the fear in her voice far as terrifying as the reptile in front of me. "RUN!"

The Onyxcobra whips around and lunges toward me. I take off sprinting the other direction, away from the crowds that are still pushing out of the exit. I'm running across the green, heading toward the stage where a half hour ago I smiled proudly as I made a bicycle pedal through the air – stupid tricks that exhausted my power for when I needed it most. *Idiot.*

Behind me, I hear a hissing, too close. As I look back over my shoulder, the hood of the cobra rears back, ready to strike. I flinch, but without warning the snake's head is blown aside and crashes momentarily into the chairs at my right. I don't stop moving, but I see from the bleachers a woman in her forties with a baby on one hip and another small child hiding behind her. Her other hand is outstretched, commanding a strong wind in the snake's direction. This stranger, this mother, has just saved my life.

I make it to the stage stairs and turn around. The snake has recovered and is slithering toward me, so I throw my palms up and send a row of chairs hurtling towards it. They bounce harmlessly off its glittering scales as it rears back. I try to throw it sideways, but I'm too tired; I can't move something this big.

Quick as a flash, the Onyxcobra bursts through the line of chairs and is plunging towards me. I know I don't have time to make it to the exit , so I take my only option: I leap into the narrow trapdoor in the stage and fall about eight feet into a dark room littered with stage equipment. A pile of dusty tarps breaks my landing and envelop me in a cloud of white. I stumble to my feet, disoriented in the darkness. I look up just in time to see the snake's face hurtling down towards me, the side of its head slamming against the trapdoor. *What do I do? What do I do?*

A whimper escapes my lips. The cobra keeps slamming its head into the trapdoor, each time the hole widening. I look around. *Slam.* There's no exit down here, at least not one that I can see. *Slam.* I scramble away from the trapdoor, back into the darkness, searching for anything. I can't think. *Slam.* I pull back a tarp to find a soft couch and an old carousel horse. No hidden doors, no exits; just junk. The slamming stops. I slowly turn my head, knowing if I breathe it will be the last thing I do. In horror, I watch as the snake slowly coils its long body down through the entrance, searching for me with its four hooded eyes. My hands are shaking as I cover my mouth in an effort not to scream. Somewhere above me I hear the shouts of other people; they are trying to get to me, but they'll be too late. I back myself against a wall, trying to tuck myself away, but it finds me quickly in the small room.

Through the swirling particles of white dust, I see the snake's tongue first, slithering in and out, followed by its fanned head. It raises up until its head is perfectly level with mine as it stares at me. White dust seems to circle around us in slow motion as I raise my head to meet its eyes. I wish I felt brave, but instead I'm so scared and my heart is pounding so hard that I think I might die of that first. A tear runs down my face. Chosen One or not, I'm going to die afraid.

I want my Mom.

As the Onyxcobra rears back, exposing its white fangs, I suddenly glimpse a dozen extra arrows that Grier used for her demonstration lying in a small clutch a few feet away from me. My hands unclench, and I send any ounce of remaining energy out from my core, out through my palms. My desperation makes it strong as I send all the arrows veering straight for the monster's face.

They pierce its four eyes, its nostrils, its throat, tongue and cheeks. It thrashes back and forth with a heinous scream, its tail bringing the room around us down. If I don't die in its jaws, I may be buried, and so I look around the dark room for something...anything...and then with a scream, I throw my hands up in the air with desperation. The carousel horse goes soaring upward and its golden rod pierces through the bottom of the snake's mouth and then up through its brain, pinning the creature to the ceiling. The snake lets out a single screech and thrashes about for a few seconds before it gives a final hiss and goes limp. The pink ceramic roses that adorn the horse become covered with a steady flow of blood.

It's dead. I'm still alive.

The reality of what just happened washes over me and I curl into a ball, replaying it in my mind.

I almost died. I should have died.

I shudder and pull my knees to my chest and the words that I've kept at bay for so long come for me: *I'm not strong enough for this. I can't beat Erys. This fight will kill me.* The giant snake hangs over me, its body still twitching. I hear voices, people coming through the walls and the trapdoor to find me. The world spins as I grasp for consciousness, fading in and out. Strong arms wrap around me and I look up to see Leo, Grier's Leo, and he's yelling my name. I see my sister above him, looking terrified, and I remember their almost kiss, the way he looked at her, the way he *knew* her. My head is spinning and I'm not sure what is real, but I know this: *I want to be known that way; I want someone to know the truth: that I don't want to be the Chosen One. I'm not enough and I don't want this anymore.* Leo is there, and his eyes are so kind. I reach up and kiss him hard on the mouth, wanting to be known.

12

GRIER

"You girls need a snack? Something to drink?" Our mom twists around in her seat, gesturing to the square cooler parked between our feet on the floor of our dad's enormous SUV.

Valora, feet tucked up, arms wrapped around her legs and her chin on her knees, shakes her head imperceptibly as she stares out the window at the snow-dusted hills.

"Sweetie?" My mother's face is plain and kind, her wide brown eyes earnest under the same unruly brows I have. "I baked some of the oatmeal cookies you like. I think there might be some tea you like in there, too. Grier?"

"Hm?" I force a false cheer into my voice. "Oh! Sure, Mom. I'll have some tea. Thanks." I rummage around in the cooler until I find the thermos of a tea my mother had seen me drinking once and forever assumed was a favorite. Still, she gives a satisfied smile when I twist the cap and I know I've done my daughterly duty. All our lives, our mom has been the quintessential mother hen, clucking over us, making sure we aren't hungry, thirsty, too hot or cold, or otherwise uncomfortable...at least inside the narrow scope of what she could control. She might be the mom of the Chosen One, but she was my mom, too, and she never treated us differently. She loved us both fiercely, and I loved her for it. I can tell that she's barely hanging on to her own sanity since almost losing her daughter at Green Hills.

I glance over at my sister, who is wearing an uncharacteristically baggy pair of black drawstring sweats and a dark red hoodie, and notice she hasn't moved. Valora almost seems frozen in place, unable to move even if she wanted to. I examine her, willing myself to really look at her for the first time since the attack. I didn't see it live, but it's been playing nonstop over media ever since.

What made her freeze when she should have been fighting?

I feel the rage that's been consuming me since that day start boiling up again, my heart and stomach twisting. Valora couldn't fight, but she sure didn't have any trouble at all kissing Leo. I'm about to turn away when I see one corner of her upper lip raise in a faint snarl.

"What, Grier?" She doesn't look away from the window. I want to ask her what happened, I want to reach out across the void, but all I see is her *taking my first kiss*. This girl, who has literally everything, took the one thing that was mine, because that's what Valora does. She takes.

"Grier?" My dad's voice pulls me back out of my thoughts.

"Yeah?"

"I was saying to your mom that it's absolutely phenomenal, what you did at Green Hills! I sure wish we'd have been there to see it!"

"We were worried sick about you both, of course," my mom breaks in. "When I saw the news alerts of the attack, I just…"

"You knew Valora handled it," my dad interrupts, and my mom presses her lips together, but doesn't say any more. My dad continues. "And thank god she's okay. But Grier, we had no idea you could do all those things with your gift! It sure was great of that teacher to take such a keen interest in you."

Valora turns from her window and levels her gaze at me. "Sure was," she whispers. Anger boils in my belly, but I don't acknowledge her.

"Thanks, Dad. Yeah, I think he's taken it upon himself to encourage students who *are actually in school to learn something.*"

I can feel Valora's glare flitting off my skin. Our dad, oblivious, goes on. "The fantastic Rigmore sisters! Can't you just see it? You know, Marnie – you know her, Valora's press agent - saw your performance. I was thinking we should talk to her, see what she can do for you."

"Yeah, Grier! Wouldn't that be great? Imagine the accolades!" Valora's tone is cruel, but there's a strange heaviness to it.

"Valora," our mom gently admonishes.

"No, it's fine, Mom." I keep my voice artificially light, but aim right for my target. "I don't actually need the adoration of strangers to validate *my* existence."

Valora snorts. "Oh, right. Because your little sideshow tricks at the Green Hills were just for your own personal growth."

"Valora! That's enough," our mother snaps.

"I'm sorry, Valora." My tone is even, measured. "I didn't realize I'd be taking something so important from you. Besides, you still got to save the day." I whisper, "Like always."

And it almost killed her, a flutter of guilt reminds me, and I see the faintest tremble in my sister's chin, an almost imperceptible widening of her eyes.

"Girls! Please!"

"Sorry," Valora mumbles, and turns back to her window.

"Sorry, Mom. Really." But neither of us is.

The rest of the drive passes in silence, but I can't stop my mind from churning over the attack. It all comes rushing back at once: the Mantharas, my portals, swallowing the little girl. It was all still a blur, fragmented snippets of screams, of black snake scales and buckling grass. Of the fear that I would never see my sister again. And then, to top it all off, the sight under the stage: my bloody and broken sister reaching for Leo, her fingers entwined in his thick black hair, kissing him like she needed him to survive.

I squeeze my eyes shut, pressing my palms to my eyelids. The carnage was extensive: twenty-nine people, about half of them students, had been severely injured, requiring surgeries and blood transfusions. Two deaths. Canterbury Pavillion was effectively destroyed, as a gaping crevasse now tore through the grounds where the massive Onyxcobra had emerged. School closed early for winter break, just days after the attack. I have no idea when Leo left, or what Valora did in the day and a half it took our parents to make a hasty return from Greece to collect us. Agnes let me hide in her room, and aside from making sure I didn't starve, wisely left me alone. The damage done to Proctor Moor was more than physical. Something had been broken in our world; the new reality was monsters on a grand scale. And in return, my own mental monsters had come out to play.

"Gene," I hear my mom murmur as the SUV slows and turns onto the long road that leads into the woods, and then finally to our family home. "What is all this nonsense?" The gravel shoulders, normally empty, are lined with vans and SUVs.

"I'd say it looks like the girls are getting a proper welcome home!"

My mom sighs. "It's been a very rough few days. Didn't you call Marnie and tell her we'd set up interviews when we'd had some time to rest?"

"I did, but that doesn't mean they won't try." His voice is tense, and I'm not sure if he's annoyed by the presence of the press or my mother's response to it. From here I can make out a crowd of about sixty bundled reporters and photographers, all waiting with cameras and microphones. I'm suddenly nauseous and drenched in a cold sweat. *What do they want from us right now? Are they here to see me, too?* Valora curls into herself, pulling the hood of her sweatshirt over her head and tugging it over her face.

My mom turns to us, her worry lines etched deep. "We're not letting anyone in, girls. They can't follow us in the gate, even if they want to," she reassures us as flashbulbs begin to fire and the crowd rushes to our vehicle, clamoring and shouting questions.

"Valora! Rumor has it you almost failed to defeat the Onyx-cobra!" a sharp-featured blonde woman with a slash of purple lipstick across her mouth shouts, slapping her leather-gloved palm against my window. "What do you have to say about that?"

"They can't see in, girls," my mom raises her voice above the chaos. "You don't have to respond! Gene, the gate. Now."

"Grier! When were you going to share your gifts with the world? Did Valora make you stay silent all these years?" a ruddy-faced man with wire-rimmed glasses and a bushy mustache shouts in my mother's window.

I scrunch down in my seat, twisting away from the window as the heavy, twelve-foot-tall cedar and iron gates glide open wide enough for our SUV to pass through. My father puts his foot on the gas, and the handful of reporters at the front of the vehicle leap away as we roar through the gate opening, the heavy doors sliding closed behind us.

"Girls, are you alright?" Concern pinches our mother's face. I nod, and Valora grunts in response.

Our dad pulls the SUV to a stop under the wide, covered drive along one side of our family's sprawling grey Colonial home. When Valora and I were ten, we were moved from a modest little house in town to this six-bedroom, three-story beauty on twenty-four wooded acres. We didn't understand then what it meant that Valora was the Chosen One, or how important it was to make sure our family stayed safe. A high stone fence encircles our home and its outbuildings, discreetly topped with electrified razor wire invisible from the ground. An intricate system of cameras and sensors covers the remainder of the property, all monitored from a small stone cottage nestled in the trees some one hundred yards from the main house. This is all arbitrary as the main protection is unseen: the same chemical that coats the ground at Proctor Moor coats the grounds around our house, which makes it impossible for Erys to set foot on the property.

"We got the decorations up last week!" my mom chirps happily, helping my dad unload our luggage from the back of the vehicle. "It seems silly to put so many up when you can't see the place from the road, but I always think they look so nice..."

Our house will undoubtedly look like a Christmas card when darkness falls. My mom works hard to give us as much normal as possible at home. Warmly lit wreaths and lifelike flickering candles bedeck the windows, and I know inside, a towering tree will be dripping with golden lights and beloved ornaments, no stair railing left unadorned.

No star though. Not yet.

"It looks beautiful, mom," I assure her, and she smiles.

Inside the house, I tell my parents I'm tired, and just want to rest.

"What would you girls like me to make you for dinner?" Our mother is already rummaging in the sub-zero. "I could do pasta, or some chicken. Oh! Or I could thaw some soup..."

"I'm actually not that hungry, mom, so I'll just make myself something later," Valora mumbles, hugging her arms close to her body. She looks thinner than usual.

"I'm not hungry, either," I say, ignoring Valora's snort. "I'm going to go read for a while, I think."

"Oh! Oh, well, sure." Our mom nods, disappointed. "Well,

you just let me know if you want something later, okay? Gene, help the girls take their bags upstairs?"

"Sure thing." My dad grabs the handles of both of our rolling suitcases, and I notice that Valora doesn't protest and insist on carrying her own. At the top of the stairs, she wordlessly takes her suitcase from our dad, then disappears into her room, the heavy door closing with a decisive *thunk*. Dad turns to me, unsure of how to react to my sister's uncharacteristic silence. I force a smile onto my face and reach for my own suitcase handle.

"Thanks, Dad."

"Of course. Say, Grier, think about what I said earlier. We can give Val's agent a call. You saw the crowd outside; people are interested in you! Working with an agent and a publicist means we can handle the paparazzi, get ahead of things."

"Okay. I'll think about it." I mumble, not wanting to talk about it anymore.

He pats me on the shoulder, turning to head back down the stairs. I close the door behind me, then head straight to my oversized blue chaise and flop down on it. Valora's room may have a walk-in closet, but mine has a windowed reading nook.

From the windows, I can see out onto the grounds surrounding our house: the pool with its winter cover frosted in snow, my mom's gardens dormant for the season. I stretch one hand toward my laptop that's sitting on my desk. It's been unused in the months we've been at school, where laptops and smartphones aren't allowed. I haven't portaled anything since... well, since the little girl. I shake my head and take a deep breath, focusing on the laptop, feeling the familiar tingle as I easily portal it from my desk to my lap. Like it's nothing. Despite my mood, I smile with satisfaction. I lean back against the chaise as it powers up. *I should message Agnes*, I think, but I know she's going to want to talk about what happened. It had to have driven her crazy not to bring it up when I was hiding from the world in her room. She saw everything: saw me move the little girl, saw Leo lift my sister from the rubble. Saw Valora kiss him.

And I don't want to talk about that.

My laptop's chiming snaps me back to reality. I have dozens of message notifications—some from Agnes, one from Allen, but most from a sender I don't recognize at first. I click on the first one.

Grier,

Agnes gave me your email address. Please...I want to talk about Valora.

Your friend, Leo

My stomach lurches, and I feel anger bubbling up inside me again. I know exactly how the rest of that email is going to go. *Your friend.* I know exactly how this email is going to go: *"I didn't think I had feelings for your sister, but now..."* I unclench my fists, slap the laptop shut, and shove it to the floor.

"Mrrrrrrrrrw?"

I jump and look over to see our cat rising from her favorite napping spot on one of my pillows. She stretches as she yawns hugely before settling back down into a grey cat loaf. She stares at me, unimpressed, and slowly blinks her enormous green eyes.

"Come here, Mimi!" I pat the chaise, beckoning her. Another yawn. We are at an impasse, then inspiration strikes. I may not be able to hold onto Leo, but I can still impress Mr. Ferguson.

I reach my palm out toward her and concentrate, my wrist and palm tingling, a faint ache spreading up toward my elbow. Mimi blinks. Nothing. *What the hell?* Frowning, I glance across the room at a low, wooden stool sitting next to my turntable and shelves of records and flex my fingers, concentrating. I easily move the stool to the other side of the room, and back again.

Mimi bleats again, then turns her head away and closes her eyes, thoroughly unimpressed. "I can do it, Mimi," I tell her. "I swear." One ear turns slightly in my direction, but she doesn't move. Determined, I take a deep breath and focus again, this time holding out until the pain in my fingertips and wrist is so intense I feel tears pricking up in my eyes.

"Damn it!" I mutter, standing up and shaking out my arm. *Maybe she's too big?* I stare out the windows, and my gaze lands on a female cardinal perched on a branch of a maple tree. She's little. I rub my wrist before extending my hand again. Nothing. The bird stays on the branch, and my arm is throbbing. Baffled, I collapse into the chaise. Mimi pads across my bed and leaps gracefully onto me, head-butting me before settling in on my lap, purring.

"Sure, now you come sit with me," I groan, stroking her soft fur. Had I imagined moving the little girl? No, she was real, I know it. I felt her moving through me. Everything that happened that day was real, and I can't stop it from racing through my mind, over and over again.

13

VALORA

SOMETHING HAS CHANGED IN ME AND I CAN'T EVEN ESCAPE INTO my dreams. Even now, when I'm as comfortable as a person can be; wearing no pants and snuggled up in my own bed – I still can't sleep. Every time I close my eyes, the images of Green Hills flash through my mind like an old-fashioned projector: the Mantharas coming over the banners, the dripping fangs of the Onyxcobra, the way its scales felt as they slid over my body. The worst thing, though, is I can't stop remembering the surrender inside my mind when I knew I was going to die. Any relief from the sheer terror I felt in that moment was welcome, and the idea of it all being over was so tempting. I had felt glad to hurtle myself towards death in that moment, anything to escape the fear. If it wasn't for Grier's arrows, I would be decomposing in some snake's stomach right now. The Chosen One would be defeated, and Erys would have filled the world with monsters already.

And I would be free of it all.

I shake my head, shoving away these terrible thoughts, but they return, swift and relentless. I can still feel the moment I froze in place – a panic attack, Renata called it - before Pike shoved me aside. I let myself smile. No one has ever shoved me aside. I let myself think about him for a few greedy minutes; his brown skin and his curly black mohawk; those chestnut eyes. Pike is a welcome distraction, but as I struggle to focus on his face, the same nightmarish images creep up from deep inside my brain.

I was so alone down there, under the stage. The memory is too much, and I lose control as a sob rips out of my throat. *I am so alone.*

Which is why I kissed Leo. There was shouting and the snake's head thrashing back and forth and walls folding in around me. A shower of dust, the smell of blood. And then there he is, Leo, a halo of light around his head. I remember reaching for him, and Grier's face behind him; how scared she was for me. I remember wanting to be known. The rest is a blur.

It wasn't because I want him. *Ugh.* No, he's much more Grier's speed, but now I can't even look at her. And when I do, the hatred in her eyes just lights my own fury, and I'm lashing out when I should be saying sorry, but doesn't she understand? I was half-conscious. Half-dead. My feet were planted in my grave. I know this, because in this haunted stillness I'm finally able to decipher the dread that has nestled in my heart for the past year. The whisper.

It's the truth that *I am not strong enough.* That I can't defeat Erys. That I am going to die. I roll over onto my side, curling myself around a pillow before I stuff it into my mouth so that no one hears my sobs.

Hours later, I stand and face my computer. Now that I have nothing left to lose, I might as well see my fate, in all its hideous glory. I pull it onto my lap and grit my teeth as I pull up the video of the death of Everett Proctor. It's all over the internet, no matter how much his estate tries to snuff it out. It's the most watched video in the world after that kitten stuck in a hamster ball. I find it easily enough and after a second thought, pull Mimi into my lap. She purrs as I push play and take a deep breath.

It's a shaky clip; the neighbor who filmed it was obviously scared out of his mind. He's in a house overlooking the Proctor's woodland compound in the Litchfield Hills, where the last day of Everett Proctor's life played out. I know the backstory by heart: Everett had been hunting Erys for years before he had finally found her – and her monsters, in the deep swamplands outside the Everglades. He had gathered a few powerful friends to plan an attack against her. But she had shown up first, just outside his enormous farmhouse. Until now, no one had actually seen her; she was a ghost, a rumor, but then she was there, and monsters crept out of every corner of the surrounding forest, all of them targeting Everett Proctor and his family.

His children had been sent away the day before, thank god, but his wife Sophie wasn't so lucky. I watch on the screen as she runs out of the house mid-attack, the monsters pushing her out from the inside. A Willowmouth chases after her – a tree-like creature with clawed hands and poisonous bark, deceptively fast. It catches her and rakes bloody fissures down on her arms and face. I watch as Sophie's face swells and turns grey with the poison. She can't breathe as her throat swells up; there's nothing anyone can do. Everett blasts the first wave of monsters away in a rush of stunning telekinetic power and kneels before his wife, cradling her in his arms, frantically screaming her name as the life goes out of her. In the background, a young Renata watches in terror, then just a new member of Proctor's resistance. I see the helpless devastation on her face. I wipe away the hot tears on my own.

Everett gently puts his wife's body on the ground, crossing her arms over her chest. I watch him realize he can't kiss her one last time because of the poison. Then he slowly stands to face Erys as his palms glow white. His power – telekinesis, just like mine but so much stronger – is unleashed. He pulls trees from their roots and sends benches and lampposts hurtling her way. He kills monsters with a power that my own can't rival. He has so much more control than I do; such a bigger reserve of energy. My palms burn watching him.

He dispatches monster after monster as he makes her way to where she calmly stands, the bodies of innocents piled at her feet. The shaking camera zooms in and we see a quick glimpse of her. Erys pulls back her hood and Everett stares at her in shock. Her hair is black, short and styled straight back from her head in a pompadour. Her reptilian green eyes, sunken in deep shadows, glitter. A vicious scar traces across her forehead, but it's hard to notice due to what is floating just a few inches above her head: The Baleful.

Baleful are rare creatures full of mysterious power that live in the deepest, darkest, and most dangerous places on earth. Like a perfectly spherical octopus with a metallic pearl sheen, it floats above her head, its many tentacles floating in an invisible current. It gives her power. It is at her command. Some say it's the first monster she ever commanded.

Erys stares at Everett for a long moment before a sneer coils on her lips and she points a blackened finger at him. Suddenly, a multi-headed creature that I've never seen before shoots out of the arm of her cloak. The half-snake, half-squid with its multiple tentacles pins down Everett's arms. I sit back and clench my hands. *This is where it ends.*

Without his palms freed, he can't do anything.

My heart rate accelerates as Erys lifts her hands and Everett's feet rise off the ground. This was the moment of terror felt around the world; the moment when we all learned that Erys, in addition to being able to control monsters with her mind, was *also a telekinetic.* A nightmare come true. Everett screams as his neck begins to turn slowly around, a wicked smile breaking over Erys's face. As Everett's head twists, a knife buries itself deep in Erys's side. She screams and looks up to see Renata standing before her. God, she was so fierce. Is so fierce.

As Erys knees hit the ground, she points at Renata and a horde of monsters heads her way. Everett is screaming for Renata to run as his head begins twisting again. Instead of running, Renata reaches for the monster that is squeezing him, and struggles to pull him free. A few others join her, inspired by her bravery. Erys is climbing back to her feet now with blood pouring from her wound, and she raises her hands to finish the job. The Baleful twitches, it's arms curling around her shoulders. I press Mimi's fur against my face. Renata pulls hard at the monster binding Everett and in that one second he gets one hand free. He and Erys scream as they raise their palms to each other. There is a huge crack as their powers hit each other.

She breaks his neck at the exact same time that he sends a wave of telekinetic force at her, so potent that I can SEE it on the screen. The blast lifts her off her feet and sends her flying off camera. He slumps to the ground, his head turned backwards, the creature still wrapped around him as he dies. His eyes are on his wife's corpse as his body stops moving. Sweat is pouring from my brow as I slam my computer shut. I need to throw up, maybe.

We all know what happens next: Erys disappears with her monsters for the next twenty years. The monster incidents seem to slowly taper off, at least until Thackeray Chadwick publishes his prophecy about the birth of the Chosen One and then promptly dies.

I set the computer and Mimi on the floor of my bedroom, my head pounding. I haven't watched this video since I was much younger, and this time it was worse. I cover my eyes with my palms, seeing his wife on the ground, Everett's head turned backwards. Only in my mind, it's my head on the ground, and in front of me are Grier and my dead parents. I climb back under my covers, my body involuntarily shivering. I can't control my thoughts and instead of fighting them, I helplessly let them drag me under.

A couple of hours later there's a sharp rap on the door. My voice is hard. "WHAT?" The door slams open and I see Grier's figure.

"Mom says to come down for dinner." She pauses. "She says it's mandatory." My sister raises her nose. "It stinks in here."

"Thanks." I launch out of bed and push past her rudely.

My family is waiting at the table, which looks lovely with my mom's Christmas linens and a red poinsettia as the centerpiece. I plop down in the seat next to my dad.

"Oh, I think Grier was sitting here," he mumbles awkwardly and points to a half-consumed glass of sparkling cider. I see a lipstick mark on the edge. *Grier is wearing lipstick now?*

I give my dad a withering look and slink over to the chair beside my mom, who pats my hand gently. I love her. I lay my head against her palm and let her run her fingers through my dirty hair. Grier comes down the stairs, her head held high. She gamely takes my chair next to my father and smirks at me. *Really, Grier?* I'm so exhausted by her. My mom pretends not to notice the iciness between us and gestures to the food.

"Dig in, girls! Teriyaki beef and garlic noodles." My heart twists a little in my chest. This is my favorite meal. I try to smile as I reach for my plate.

"Thanks, Mom." Wearily, I scoop a huge serving onto my plate and begin eating in silence. The rest of my family helps themselves, and my mom leans in.

"So, what do you girls want for Christmas? I'll make sure Santa knows." My dad winks at her and they grin at each other.

Grier leans against her palm for a second. "I was thinking some new records, maybe?"

"Of course." My dad grins at her. "What about some new clothes? We should get you an outfit like Valora's, one that makes it easy to best display your powers...maybe something with shorter sleeves, so people can see your wrists moving when you create the portal?"

Grier swallows a bite of food. "Um, maybe. That sounds good, I guess. I would love some new books, or maybe a gift card for some makeup or something." My dad leans back in his chair, his mind somewhere else, crafting how best to capitalize on Grier's new fame. I know he used to be a normal dad, protective and caring, back when we were really little. I don't remember the last time he was more of a father and less of a manager, though.

"So, Valora, what would you like for Christmas?" he manages, awkwardly.

I take a long drink of my cider, wiping my mouth with relish. "I don't know...what kind of makeup repels an Onyxcobra?"

"Valora," intones my father with his warning voice. "I don't like this attitude."

"No, I'm serious. Are there any books on defeating a monster-controlling witch? Maybe some sort of vinyl that I can throw at a Mantharas?" My anger is boiling over and it feels great as it pours over our table. *That video has made me feel reckless. Why care when I am going to die, anyway?*

"Why don't you calm down and just eat dinner?" hisses Grier across the table. "Mom made it just for you."

"Calm down?" I tip my head back and laugh. "Calm down. Yes, that's what I need to do. Be calm while the world prepares eagerly for the spectacle of my death."

"Valora!" My mom sounds shocked, but I'm just getting started.

"Don't worry, Grier, Dad will make sure you'll have the spot-light soon enough – he's good at that. It's about the only thing he's good at." The words flow out of me like a poison river. "Good luck fighting Erys with a confetti cannon."

"Well, I might do better than you did. At least I would *move*," Grier mumbles, taking a drink. I close my eyes, flex my palm and her glass gives a shudder, then explodes. When I open my eyes, Grier is sitting still in shock, her hand holding just the stem of her goblet. There is glass in her hair and she's dripping with cider.

"VALORA!" My dad's voice is louder than I've ever heard it.

"WHAT THE HELL?" Grier screams, throwing the stem onto the table. I sit back, shocked at my own actions. My sister's face is bleeding from a small cut. *What have I done?*

"Oh my God, I'm sorry, Grier. I didn't mean to..." I leap to my feet.

"What is wrong with you?" my sister fumes. "Why do you have to destroy everything I have?"

"What is she talking about, Valora?" My mother is standing now, her arms out, trying to protect us from each other.

"Nothing!" I don't want my mom to know about this.

"Nothing to you, maybe," fumes Grier. "Because my life is small and insignificant to you." She lowers her tone and there are angry tears in her eyes. "But that wasn't. My first kiss, with Leo, the boy I like. She took it."

"Valora?" My mother is concerned. "Is this true?"

"I...I didn't really know what was going on. It was after the fight. I just wanted..."

"To take him for yourself! Because you have nothing." She leans back, blood dripping over her lip. "You know, I used to want to be you, but now you're the last person I want to be."

Grier's words land hard. I'm stumbling to answer her, my anger and guilt creating a potent mix inside me. *How can I make her understand?* I hate the way my mother is looking at me.

"Look, I didn't want to kiss Leo. I honestly don't know what happened. I was half-conscious, Grier. You would think you would cut me a little slack because I had just almost died, but no. *It was a MISTAKE.*"

"You know what was a mistake? Ever thinking we could be friends." Grier wipes her lip and throws her napkin on the floor. "I'm done trying."

"Trying?" I shriek, throwing my arms out. "You've never ONCE tried to understand me, or help me. You don't even watch my fights, because that's how little you care if your sister lives or dies."

"That's not true..." Grier starts, but I interrupt her.

"In fact, I'm not sure any of you really care. Except Mom, maybe." I spin to my father, rage coming off me in waves. "Look, you can turn Grier into the new Chosen Rigmore if you want, but the fact of the matter is that Erys is coming for me, for us, and we're all going to die."

A gloomy silence settles over the table. "I'm publicly done being the Chosen One. I'm not doing another interview, I'm not taking another picture. I quit being the face of this family and I don't want to be the Chosen One anymore."

Then I say it out loud, the words that have always been there, the cold mist slowly making its way through my brain for years: "I'm not enough."

"No. Valora, you are! You can't quit," breathes my mother quietly. "It's your birth legacy. The Chosen One is who you are, Valora." Grier is watching me with red-rimmed eyes.

"Screw this legacy." I turn to head up the stairs before spinning back around. My family is sitting in shock at the table, but I breeze past them and scoop up my plate. "I'm taking this to go." Then I leave them and my legacy downstairs.

14

GRIER

THERE'S A STUNNED SILENCE AFTER VALORA STORMS UPSTAIRS. My parents both stare after her, then turn to me. My mother's eyes are wide, her face drained of color, but my father clears his throat and picks up his fork. "She'll get used to sharing the spotlight. Imagine it. Two Rigmore sisters!"

Shut up, Dad, I think.

"Gene." My mother's voice is barely audible.

"There have always been two." I hiss at him through clenched teeth, my cut lip beginning to throb.

He glances up at me, chewing. "Hmm?"

"There have always been two of us!" I snap.

"Grier, I know that. I meant..."

I can't listen to him for another second. I hear my mother call after me as I rush out of the dining room, through the kitchen, and out into the dark, frigid night. I stumble out over the snow-encrusted ground, not caring that I'm dripping with cider, bleeding, and wearing a pair of slippers. My entire body thrums with anger, my blood pounding in my ears. The night is still, the temperature just below freezing. The air feels heavy with silent anticipation, as it often does right before snow begins to fall. It's lovely and inside I am breaking.

No one has come after me. Our dad is probably still sitting there, eating his dinner and wondering what the big deal is. Our mom has probably gone upstairs to try to make peace. I glare at the warm light glowing from Valora's bedroom windows.

Somehow the fact that kissing Leo was nothing to her makes things worse, not better. He was nothing to her. *I'm nothing to her.* But *I'm* the terrible sister because I don't show up with the masses to cheer her on? *Like she even needs me there.* Guilt and anger scorch through my chest in equal measure, and I turn to the trees, throw my head back, and scream. I scream until I run out of air, my throat aching as the sound carries out into the night. My nose is running, and tears are streaming down my face, mingling with the blood from my cut lip and the now-sticky cider. I choke back a furious sob and turn back toward the house. From the still trees behind me, I hear a rustling, and I whirl around with my heart pounding.

My eyes adjust to the darkness, and I'm relieved that instead of some hideous creature Erys managed to get past our security, it's just a fat black squirrel. It scurries around the trunk of a nearby tree, eyeing me suspiciously. Without thinking, I throw one hand out toward it. A surge of energy burns through my arm, and the squirrel disappears into my shimmering blue portal.

Holy crap. I blink, momentarily stunned, and stagger backwards a few steps. I can feel its little claws click-clacking across my mind.

Panting to catch my breath, I extend my hand and focus on the wide, paved area halfway between the tree line and the house. A small portal appears, and the squirrel drops to the ground. I stare open-mouthed as it sits there for a moment. The squirrel streaks toward the trees, a black, furry blur, and then proceeds to sit on a branch and chitter angrily at me. I burst out laughing, half at this little creature giving me a piece of its mind, and half in total disbelief.

I can do it. I can portal living things. My mind races. What was different about this time than when I tried to move Mimi? How was this similar to when I moved the little girl in the arena? I close my eyes, letting out a frozen breath. I was afraid at Green Hills, terrified but also elated at my performance. Now, I'm consumed by anger. The portals are connected to my emotions. It's the only explanation that makes sense.

My heart is pounding, but what I'm feeling is deeper and warmer than adrenaline. It's the feeling of coming home. This is my gift. It is mine, and it is connected to me in a deeper way than I thought. I let a soft smile pass over my face as I wrap my arms around myself and head toward the house.

I slip into the kitchen and close the door silently behind me, creep past my parents and pad quietly up the stairs. Valora's door is closed. I type Allen a quick email about what happened before pulling off my cider-soaked shirt and tossing it into my laundry basket. I retreat to my bathroom, where I stand in a steaming shower, letting the near-scalding water beat down on me until the water runs cool. Afterwards, I wrap a towel around my hair, and step over to the mirror above the sink, wiping the steam away with the sleeve of my robe. The cut on my lip is smaller than I thought, more of a nick than anything. I touch it gently with my fingertips, right where my bottom lip begins to curve upward on the left side. Even in the joy of discovering more about my powers, one sentence of our fight keeps coming back around: "That's how little you care if your sister lives or dies!" I stare at myself through in the foggy mirror. That isn't true. She knows that isn't true.

Doesn't she?

In my pajamas a few hours later, I settle into my reading nook and pull up my email, scrolling through my unread messages. Emails from "Marnie the Publicist" fill my inbox, along with requests from agents who represent Exceptionals, all cc'd to my dad. Scattered among them, I see emails from Leo, one each day since I've been at home. My heart lurches, and I feel tears spring up in my eyes. I don't want to read them. *Not yet. Do I?* I press my fingers to my eyes and take a deep breath, unsure of what I want. As I exhale, my new message notification chimes. It's Allen. I feel an unfamiliar thrill run through me as I click to open the message.

Hi, Grier,

I'm so glad to hear from you! My apologies for not checking in sooner. As you might imagine, things at Proctor Moor are in a bit of upheaval at the moment. It goes without saying that you saving that little girl's life was nothing short of incredible, Grier. Your performance at the Showcase was great to be sure, but your true ability showed through in the horrific aftermath. You saved a life. There is nothing more admirable.

This brings me to my next point: I'm not surprised to hear that the caliber of strength of the portals are related to your emotions. There hasn't been a lot of documented research on emotional resonance affecting Exceptional gifts, but I can assure you it is indeed likely that this is the case with you. I am sorry, though, to hear that you had a falling out with your sister. Family relationships can be difficult, and I don't doubt that your sister's situation makes this especially true. Prophecies can cause all sorts of confusion. Hold your head up, and know that your place is not in the shadows.

Merry Christmas, Grier.

Allen

I can feel my cheeks burning, and I realize I'm grinning. My entire body is buzzing, and it takes me a minute to recognize the feeling: the glow of my potential. The world hasn't even begun to see what Grier Rigmore can do. I shut my laptop and stand, stretching my arms above my head. My stomach growls to remind me I never really ate dinner. I shove my feet into my slippers and step into the hallway. The television is on and I hear my mom talking to someone on the phone about our upcoming Rigmore Christmas party. *Ugh, that's right, that's coming.* I inwardly groan.

I'm about to head down when an enormous, framed print hung at the top of the stairs catches my eye. *The prophecy.* There it is, the original Thackeray Chadwick prophecy written in his own hand right after he jotted my parent's name down on a napkin, the famed words that have driven my family's existence. I tilt my head, for the first time really reading every word written in elaborate script.

"As the seas rise, all will be crushed under a great revenge. Yea, even the Suffering Servant, with good heart, will not be able to stand against the Cursed One. Family will crumble, as dust divides blood and the betrayer unknowingly pulls the light to power. If the Chosen One does not stand, lands will be devoured by monsters gnashing their teeth. The fate of all will hinge on the bonds of one severed."

The Suffering Servant, that's Valora is there ever was one. The pissy thought stops me cold, and from somewhere deep inside of me a question I've never dared to think whispers. *What if Valora is just the Suffering Servant? What if...oh my God... what if she wasn't supposed to be the Chosen One?* I shake my head. *No. That can't be right.* It's always been Valora. All our lives. She's powerful, a weapon. But the train in my brain is running off the track now, smashing through decades of assumptions. *What if she's not the Chosen One?* We're twins. Thackery Chadwick wrote down our parents' names right before he wrote the prophecy. That's how the press knew it was for us, but...what if Valora isn't the Chosen One? *What if it was supposed to be me? What would that mean?* The cat meows at my feet, breaking me out of my fog. I scoop her up in arms and shake my head.

"Okay, kitty, let's go." I cautiously laugh at my absurdity all the way down the stairs, but the idea has taken root in my brain, and it's digging deep.

15

VALORA

I T ' S BEEN TWO DAYS SINCE THE FIGHT AT THE TABLE, AND MY family might as well be a million miles away. I've taken to running in the woods in the afternoons, when the sun is high in the sky and the weather is just above freezing. The ground crunches under my feet now with short satisfying cracks as I race through the trees. Ahead of me on the trail, downed branches block my way, long surrendered to the weight of the snow. I flex both of my hands out in front of me and they slide gently off the trailhead. I whirl my fingers and the snow curls and leaps ahead of me. I try not to sing "Let It Go" in my head as I run through the flurry. Something fun to distract me, to distract my mind, because I can't stop thinking about the video. Not the violence of it, even though that plays constantly in my mind; it's the *look* that Everett gave Erys.

It's been interpreted a thousand different ways: that he knew she would kill him, that he knew it was their destiny to fight, and so on. But here's what I see: recognition. He knew she existed, but when he saw her face, it was like *he knew her*. I know how it feels to be in the middle of a telekinetic fight. Everything whirls around you and you must silence the noise or else. In that moment Everett Proctor couldn't shake what he knew. That's why he lost, because he lost focus. *Because he knew her.* I'm sure of it.

I hear a footstep behind me and whirl around with my hands out, but it's only one of the twenty anonymous men in black coats that wander around our property while we are home. Being the Rigmore security detail must be the most boring job in the world. I honestly feel bad for him, out here chasing after me as I tear my way through the woods. The figure in black attempts to blend in with a tree and I shake my head. "I can see you!" I yell, and the man gives a half-shrug in apology. I sigh as I begin running back to the house, blasting myself a wet path of grass just because I can. I send all the snow back his direction.

I check my phone; it's almost three o'clock, which means I need to start getting ready for the Rigmore Chosen Christmas Party. Yes, that's what it's actually called. I always loved it, but now the party seems cruel and unnecessary, important people coming to see the Chosen One lift the star onto the tree while they toast their champagne and eat petit fours. I promised my mother that I would go, but that's all I'm doing. I'll make an appearance, show that I am alive and well and then I'll go back to my room with Cicely and the girls. We'll sneak champagne and eat too much and watch *Home Alone*. It might be fun – for the first time in weeks I'm looking forward to something.

Up ahead, I can see the house transformed, a Christmas dollhouse, lovely to look at and frozen in time. When I step inside, I am blasted with the smells of Christmas baking: gingerbread and sugar cookies, hams, and apple cider. My mouth waters and I head to the kitchen. I hear my Nan's voice through the swinging kitchen doors and I smile; I'm glad she's here. I am about to head up to my room when my father appears at the foot of the stairs. We haven't spoken since my outburst at the table the other day. He lowers his glasses and looks at me, his face stripped of all emotion.

"Valora, your mother may have told you that we need you to make an appearance tonight." I nod, stung by the lack of affection in his tone. "You will not make a scene, is that understood?" His words are so cold that my eyes prick with tears.

"Seriously? Dad?" My voice croaks on the last word.

He straightens his back. "I've also decided that Grier will put the star on the tree tonight, so you don't have to worry about that. One less thing to stress about." He smiles like he is being kind. I nod numbly, aware that even my family is pulling away from me. My palms warm, aware of what I am itching to do: tear down the decorations, burst the Christmas tree into needles, but instead I trudge up the stairs to my room, slamming the door with a quick flick of my wrist. On my bed sits my party dress, picked out for me by my mother, who really does have good taste: the high-waisted skirt is made of pale gold sequins that reflect the light. The top is pure black and tightly fitted. Next to it sit black tights and black heels. It's beautiful, tasteful and just a little sexy. I let my hands drift over the fabric and try to fake a smile. I may be a broken vessel, but maybe I can still look good.

An hour and a half later, I smile at myself in the mirror. I look great, minus the dark circles under my eyes; my hair falls straight across my chin, the gold shimmers on the dress pick up on its subtle highlights. I turn slightly, watching my face in the dimming light. The golden girl, the Chosen One. This is who they see, but it isn't what I see: beyond the sparkle the mirror reflects someone scared, someone tired; a girl who sees monsters every time she closes her eyes.

I walk into the hallway at the exact same time Grier does.

She won't meet my eyes, but I look her up and down. She looks beautiful. Her long-sleeved dress is a deep green with black lace detailing on the bodice. The flared skirt hits her at the knee, marked with a layer of lace that looks like black stars. Her curled hair falls on the side of her face, honey brown spirals dusting her pale cheeks. Dark red lipstick marks her lips...and her cheek. Without thinking, I lick my finger and reach to wipe it off, and she rears back from me like my touch is poison.

"You have lipstick on your cheek." I say softly, hurt by her reaction.

"Oh," she says, shyly raising a hand to her face. "Thanks, Valora." It's the most she's spoken to me since the fight and I'll take it. I head downstairs and as soon as I turn the corner, I see the flash of cameras. I try smiling like I always do, but something is preventing my face from doing so; it's like I'm frozen again. I don't smile, but I make my way down, trying my best to ignore the people reaching out for me, saying my name like we're friends when we aren't.

"Valora, have you met my daughter? She's about your age..."

"Valora, hi! I'm friends with your dad. Do you think you could read my book?"

"Valora, I watched the video of Green Hills yesterday –that snake got your tongue? Right?" Ugh, PJ Hammerton is here; the closest neighbor we have and also a creepy chauvinist pig who fancies himself hilarious when he is anything but. When we were little, Grier and I called him the mole because that's what he looks like: a hairless mole who peeps out of his den once a year with squinty eyes and sour breath. He leers at me as I pass, and I stealthily duck under his outstretched arm and make my way around through the main room and into the kitchen to avoid the throng of people in the hallway.

I grab a warm apple croissant and am reaching for a glass of champagne when I hear my mother's voice. I keep the croissant, but quickly put back the champagne. My mother bursts into the kitchen, rushing about and making sure everything is perfect.

"Have you seen Grier?" she asks me breathlessly.

"She's up in her room still, I think," I answer, my voice flat.

She squeezes my arm. "If you could just try to make things better with her..."

"Mom." How can I explain to her that it's not like deciding to cross a bridge? There is no bridge; there never was. There is only the chasm. But my mother's face is so hopeful that I lie. "I'll talk to her, promise." She nods and kisses my cheek, and I lean against her for a moment. Then I dart out the back of the kitchen and enter into my father's office. I pull out my phone as I take a bite of croissant, closing my eyes for a minute at its buttery goodness.

Are you almost here? I text Cicely. *When you get here, I'll sneak us a bottle.*

I have almost finished the croissant when a text pops up.

Not coming. Sorry.

My breath catches in my throat and my heart gives an unfamiliar tug. I read the words again, the shortness of it saying much more than the words. *Not coming. Sorry.* I frown and flip onto Cicely's social media. There's nothing there, just a picture of her skiing with her parents, but I see that something new has popped up on Gillian's page and I open the photo. It's from tonight. Gillian and Anna are smiling together in a cheesy selfie. They both look beautiful, but that's not what I focus on because in the background of the photo, surrounded by the warm glow of Christmas lights, are Cicely...and Julian North. He has one arm wrapped lazily around her waist, their body language is so casual that I know this has been going on awhile. She is looking at him with such adoration that my hands clench unconsciously and a few of my father's books shoot off the shelves and fall to the ground.

My heart feels like it has been punched through. I know I

shouldn't care about Julian and Cicely, and I don't really – after all, I broke up with him – but this feels horrible, like ice in my stomach, accompanied by a feeling of falling. Below the photograph people have commented: *Love you guys! Congrats to Julian and Cicely! Enjoy the party!* I know I shouldn't be surprised by this; Cicely has always wanted Julian and he has always wanted someone he can flaunt on his arm.

Well, there you go, Julian, I think meanly, *enjoy your useless rainbow unicorn.* I realize, in that moment, that I have lost my friends. I am now the outsider. Angry tears roll down my face as I stare at the picture and I don't have time enough to wipe them away when the office door bangs open. I spin away, trying to hide my face, but I'm unsuccessful. I hear the kindness in my Nan's voice and it makes everything worse. She steps toward me, looking fierce in a sharp green pantsuit.

"Valora? Honey, what's wrong?"

I can't hold it in anymore and I explode in a mess of tears. She reaches me just as I sink to the floor and wraps her arms around me. She smells like my childhood, like lemon candy and winter coats, and I want to lose myself in that time when I was just a child, when being the Chosen One had no downside to it, when I believed in myself as much as everyone else does.

"Tell me everything." It's not a request, and so I do: I tell her about Julian and Cicely, about the hallway and the carnations, about the Onyxcobra and my panic attack, about my fears. About the Erys video, about Grier and her showcase, about kissing Leo. It takes almost an hour before it's all out and when I'm done talking, I feel like the weight of grief that pulled me to the floor has lessened; I'm lighter. She cradles me in her arms, skin like fine paper.

"Listen to me," she whispers. "No one in this world has been asked to do what you have. You have more pressure on you than Everett Proctor ever did, not only because you have to be the Chosen One, but you have to do it while being a teenager, which by itself is enough to make anyone crazy." She lets out a long sigh. "When you were born, I remember that I took you and Grier – just hours old – in my arms and looked at your tiny faces. You weighed almost exactly the same, you know, and as I held you, it was as if I could feel the weight of expectations that would be put on you, Valora. You were heavier on my arm. I begged your mother to forget the prophecy, to change your last name, because it publicly tied you to the prophecy. Your mother was exhausted and drifting in and out of sleep, but she agreed. She has only ever wanted the best for both of her daughters. But then your father came in and..." I can just imagine how that went.

"He wanted me to be the Chosen One," I whisper.

"Yes. It gives him a purpose that he never had in his own life. His own gifts that weren't strong enough. But I think...I think there's something more there," she answers.

"I just don't know if I can do this. I'm spiraling." She nods for a moment, thinking.

"Have you ever considered that this may need to happen? Valora, for as long as you've been alive, a long shadow has clouded your future, the shadow of Erys and the shadow of expectation. But...maybe you're also stuck in place by some of your own bad choices." I raise my eyes to her and flinch at her steely gaze.

"What do you mean?" I ask, though I'm pretty sure what is coming next.

"Your friends sound terrible. They affirm everything that is shallow about your life: your status and the things that come with it." She brushes a strand of golden hair past my ear. "I often wonder who you and Grier would be without all this. What would your relationship be like?"

I sit up and look at her face. "Tell me what to do," I plead.

She touches my cheek. "I can't. But I can tell you that we are all some combination of our yesterdays. To move forward on the right path, we have to honestly see what has led us to this place, before we walk straight into darkness." She kisses my cheek and I know she's left a rose-pink smear. "Don't walk into the darkness, Valora. Pivot to the light." Her face becomes fierce. "And don't let *anyone* tell you that you can't be afraid. You have more reason to be afraid than anyone who breathes. You need help – *real* help, not from those idiotic friends of yours. May I suggest your sister?"

I can't help the snarl that curls my lip.

"Grier won't even talk to me. She's never really cared about what happens in my life."

I can feel Nan's sharp retort from a mile away. "Can you say the same about yourself? Have you ever cared about what's going on in Grier's life?"

I pause for a moment and think...*no*. "I'm fighting monsters...she's..."

"Fighting monsters, too," my grandmother snaps. "Everyone is fighting monsters. You're just the only one fighting *actual* monsters." I nod, and there are flashes of cruelty in my memory: when I've ignored Grier, when I've teased her, but worst of all – when I have let others do it. Shame rises in my chest.

Nan pats my legs.. "Now, you best get up before some degenerate takes a picture of you lying on the floor and sells it to the tabloids for a million dollars." I nod and climb to my feet. She lifts my face to the light and with the corner of her silk scarf wipes under my eyes. "I would not be a teenager again for all the money in the world," she sighs, and I can't help but laugh.

"It's not all bad," I say. "There is a boy."

"Ooohh." Nan steps back, impressed. "Darling, tell me everything."

I spend the night talking with Nan, and head straight to my room when she leaves the party. After I throw on my favorite flannels, I pick up my phone and text Cicely back one single message, as terse as hers was:

Enjoy him. I didn't.

I lean back and breathe deeply, feeling for the first time in a long time that maybe everything will be okay. I hear a male voice outside the window and lean over to look outside. Grier and Leo are out there. I quietly open the screen and feel the warmth of power flowing in my palms. I circle my wrist slowly, gently. When the magic happens, I get to see it, and it melts the last shard of anger in my heart.

16

GRIER

IT'S ALMOST TIME FOR THE PARTY. I SHOULDN'T HAVE PICKED such a dark shade, I tell myself, standing with my face inches from the mirror as I carefully check for stray lipstick. It was kind of Valora to point out the smudge on my cheek. I wouldn't have noticed, and then it would've been in photos. I take a deep breath to calm my nerves, then reach for some tissues and blot off as much of the dark red lipstick as I can. My lips stay stained a plum red, but it's more my speed, and I breathe a little sigh of relief as I swipe on some clear gloss. Much better. I smooth down the front of my dress, checking myself from every angle I can see in the mirror. I look good, and for the first time in a while, I don't try to talk myself out of the compliment. *Here we go.*

"Honey, are you coming?" I hear my mom's voice outside my door.

"Yep, just checking my makeup." I open the door and step back so she can see the dress she's chosen for me. She bustles in, her silver silk wrap jacket rustling softly, heels clicking on the hardwood. "You look beautiful, Mom!"

She smiles and reaches for my hand. "You, too, honey. Ready?"

I squeeze her hand and nod, and we head downstairs. We're met with a dazzling burst of flashbulbs, and for a moment, I'm disoriented by it all.

"Smile, Grier! You'll look prettier if you smile!" a man's voice calls out. The Mole. Ugh, gross. *Don't tell me to smile, asshole.* But I do, and when I reach the bottom of the stairs I am immediately surrounded by reporters.

"Grier, how are you recovering from the attack at Green Hills? Do you think you'll be training to use your gifts to fight?" A petite brunette woman in a red velvet cocktail dress holds a digital recorder toward me.

"Um," I swallow. "I don't..."

"I know you're all dying to ask Grier questions, but I think we're just going to let everyone enjoy the party tonight. Thank you, and please help yourselves to hors d'oeuvres and a drink at the open bar," my mom steps in, politely but firmly.

Disappointed, the small crowd disperses, and my mom turns to me. "Go talk to whoever you want to, and politely say 'No, thank you,' to anyone you'd rather not chat with. Say 'No comment' if the question involves your sister. Enjoy yourself, honey. Nan's here somewhere; and I assume Agnes is coming?" I nod. "Great. Have fun. Next year, let's just go on a cruise." With that, she gives me an exhausted kiss on one cheek and bustles off into the crowd.

I swipe an apple croissant from a passing server and make my way into the formal living room.

"Champagne, Miss Rigmore?" another server offers. I pause. I've never been offered anything but sparkling juice at my parents' annual holiday bash, but... I glance around.

"Yes, thank you." I pluck a crystal flute from the silver tray, taking a tiny sip like it's something I do all the time. The bubbles dance pleasantly across my tongue.

"There's my girl!" My face immediately flushes at the sound of my father's voice behind me, and I briefly wonder if I can ditch the champagne before he sees it, but it's too late.

"Hi, Dad." I force a cheerful smile across my face and turn to greet him. His eyes flicker briefly over the champagne flute in my hand, but he makes no mention of it.

"I think we have enough of our guests gathered to have you place the star on the tree here in a few minutes. Why don't you find a good place to stand, and I'll get the star."

"Are you sure Valora doesn't want to do it? She always..."

"This will be an exciting moment for you!" he cuts me off and squeezes my shoulder before striding away. I consider another sip of champagne, but instead furtively slide the flute onto a table and make my way towards the towering Christmas tree, covered in glittering ornaments. The only thing the tree is missing is its star. I feel a sudden pang of uneasiness in my belly, but push it aside when the pianist in the corner stops playing and across the room my father raises a glass and clears his throat.

"Friends and family, may I have your attention, please?" his voice carries out over the chattering guests, and they fall silent. "Welcome to our home, to our annual Chosen Christmas Party!"

A polite smattering of applause ripples through the crowd.

"Thank you. We are so pleased to have you here, celebrating with us. As many of you know, the placement of the star on our Christmas tree is a beloved tradition. I'm thrilled to share that this year, our daughter Grier will be doing the honors." There are murmurs of surprise, and I feel all eyes turn to me. My dad reveals the heavily ornate star. *God, that thing looks heavy.* I know I can portal it; I'm just afraid I'll drop it down the side of the tree, sending broken shards of glass and crystal into the crowd. I take a deep breath to steady myself, closing my eyes for a moment.

"Grier, we are ready!" My dad's voice is overly cheerful. *Chill out, Dad*, I think, then open my eyes and smile. The crowd around me backs away respectfully as I stretch one hand out toward the star and focus my energy on it, fingers flexed. The shimmering whorl appears, expands, and the gilded star disappears. The house full of guests cheers and claps delightedly, and I can't help but grin. *I get why Valora loved doing this so much.*

I take another deep breath to steady myself for the placement and turn toward the tree. The portal appears inches from the top of the tree, widening, and with a soft rustle, the star drops directly onto my target. It tilts precariously to the left, then the right, and the crowd gasps before it settles securely where it belongs. My father hits a switch and the tree and star burst into light, sending a dazzling glow into the entire room. I beam, and the crowd breaks into applause.

After that, the night is filled with people clamoring to talk to me, asking questions about my gift, how I discovered it and what my future plans are. It's overwhelming, and I'm grateful when, through the crowd, I see Agnes removing her coat. *Thank goodness.*

"Would you please excuse me?" I say as politely as I can, then slip away and make a beeline for my friend.

"Oh my god, I'm so glad to see you!" I exclaim, hugging her before stepping back to admire her pretty midnight blue dress with a narrow black belt. "You look gorgeous!"

"Hi! Um, Grier..."

"I just got to put the star on top of the tree!" I rush on. "It barely stayed on, but it worked. Also, I have some surprisingly strange feelings about Valora not putting it on, but..."

"Grier," she interrupts me, grabbing my shoulders.

"What?"

She blinks nervously, then turns to her left. My eyes follow, and my heart leaps into my throat. Leo.

"Hi, Grier," he offers softly. He's standing there holding flowers, all six-foot-three of him, in a slim-cut charcoal grey suit that fits like it was made for him, his dark brown eyes imploring.

Stunned, I glance back at Agnes. "He flew in from L.A. yesterday to stay with me." She twists her hands nervously. "Don't be mad. He begged to come." I blink, but before I can say anything, my mom rushes over.

"Agnes, hi! Welcome!" She hugs my friend, and turns to Leo, smiling. "And who is this *handsome* young man?"

Leo clears his throat and offers a hand to my mother.

"Mrs. Rigmore, I'm Leo Irsan. It's a pleasure to meet you."

My mother's eyes widen with recognition, but she recovers and smiles warmly. "Leo. So wonderful to meet you. I have - *or haven't* - heard about you from my daughter." She gives me a panicked shrug. *Oh God.* "I'm glad you could join us this evening! Please, make yourselves at home."

"I see some old neighbors of mine, so I'm gonna..." Agnes glances past me. She's a terrible liar. "I'll find you guys later!" she calls over her shoulder, practically running from us. Leo and I stand awkwardly, staring at each other.

"Leo, I..." I start, but he interrupts me.

"Grier. Please. Let me say something. I never...I didn't..." He trails off, black brows furrowed. "Um, could we go talk somewhere? I know it's your party, and it's probably a bad time, but...."

"You don't want to have this conversation right here, among a hundred or so relative strangers?" I cock my head and glance up at him, a slight smile on my lips. He laughs, his face breaking into that heart-stopping grin, and I feel whatever remaining resolve I had to stay angry with him begin to thaw.

"Not ideally, no."

"I know a spot." I reach for his hand and lead him through the crowd, past the dazzling tree and the bartenders pouring champagne into flutes lined up like glittering soldiers. I lead him out through a set of French doors onto a small patio off the side of my father's home office. It's far enough from the beaten path of the party that a server shouldn't interrupt us.

"Grier," Leo steps toward me, his voice nervous. "I brought flowers. I don't know if you're into flowers, but I figured you'd think red roses were cliché, so I got these. I asked the florist what they mean – she's kind of a hippie, so be warned – but she said that anemones have two meanings: one, anticipation for the future and two, protection against ill omens. That's when I knew I'd get these ones. Because I hope there is a future here and also I really don't want you to get eaten by a monster." His words are rushed, but he pauses for a second. "At Green Hills, all I could think about in everything that was happening was you. I've never been so afraid."

"They're beautiful," I murmur, taking the anemones from him. "Roses are definitely overrated." My heart is thudding in my chest as I set them down in the snow. He reaches for my hands and I slide them into his.

"Grier. I'm so sorry about the kiss. I don't know what happened that day to Valora. I don't know why she kissed me. I wish she hadn't. I didn't know that was going to happen, and I—"

"Leo." I stop him right there. "I know. I'm sorry, too. I was so angry: at you, at Valora, at the world. I thought..." I take a deep breath, hardly believing I'm about to admit this aloud, "I thought I'd been right all along, that you'd only ever wanted to get closer to my sister. You have to understand: that's been my whole life. From the time I was old enough to understand it, people have used me to get close to her. It's not an excuse, but it's something about me that will always be hard to shake. But I'm working on it. I'm...working on a lot of things."

Leo leans in, his long fingers closing tightly around mine.

He's so close, he has to be able to hear my heart pounding, and the blood rushing in my ears. *God, he smells incredible.*

"Grier, I don't care who your sister is. I've only ever wanted to get closer to you." He reaches up and gently grazes my cheek with his fingertips, his hand coming to rest at my neck, thumb ever so slightly brushing my jawline. "Don't you know that? Couldn't you see it?" His black hair, normally swept up and back, falls over his forehead. His breath is minty, warm against my cold cheek. The air around us is charged and silent with anticipation. I inch closer, closing what little space there is between us and tilting my face up toward his. In my low heels, he's still several inches taller than I am.

"I wasn't ready for you. You came into my careful life like... some sort of meteor."

"And now?" His other hand slides to the small of my back, and pulls me closer still, and he leans down so that the tip of his nose is just ever so slightly touching mine. I smile, and reach up to pull his face closer. He kisses me softly at first, his lips brushing against mine, full and soft.

My entire body is buzzing with electricity, and I feel a rush of warmth spread through me, my knees suddenly like jelly. I pull him toward me again, this time not letting go. I want him and he wants me. His lips find mine again, urgently. I run my hands over his broad shoulders and down his back, marveling at how finely muscled he is. His one hand tangles in my hair, and I feel the other splayed across the curve at the small of my back, pulling me in, pressing my body against his. I've never been kissed like this. I've never been kissed, period, but I'm melting into Leo, and it's as though the entire world has stopped, and the only thing that matters is us, this kiss, right now. Good God, I'm on fire.

"Are you chilly?" he murmurs after the kiss, and I smile softly, shaking my head.

"Not at all. You?"

He shakes his head and gently plants a kiss on the tip of my nose. "It's snowing."

I glance up, and sure enough, fluffy snowflakes are drifting lazily around us, swirling in a circle as though we're in our own little snow globe. But it's not snowing anywhere else. It's like magic, like our own little miracle. That's when I see Valora's hand out of her upstairs window, swirling gently. In that moment I think, *thank you*. But that's the only thought I have before Leo wraps his arms around me tightly, and I let myself fall into him completely.

PART II

17

GRIER – ONE MONTH LATER

WE'RE IN MY ROOM, STRETCHED OUT ON MY BED, TANGLED UP AND swollen-lipped. We've been back at Proctor Moor for just over two weeks now post-Christmas break, navigating our way in this new normal. School life has become infinitely better; the giddiness and passion spreading through my body and mind is akin to what I imagine being intoxicated feels like, and I feel it all the time.

For Valora, however, the new normal isn't better. Something has shifted perceptibly, and what was once a student body that revolved around my sister's very existence now seems scattered. No one really knows what to do with Valora, and so she seems curled in on herself, not really caring one way or the other. Her ridiculous friends, all of whom I noticed were conspicuously absent from our Christmas party, aren't constantly in our suite anymore. It's nice not having them around, because it also means Leo and I can be alone together more often than not.

Like now, where we've been holed up for the last hour, records spinning on my turntable and this boy wrapped around me. We're interrupted from our little universe when we hear Valora slipping in through the entrance to our suite. We both sit up, smoothing down our hair and straightening our clothes in a useless attempt to look innocent.

"Hey," she nods, acknowledging us before collapsing onto an overstuffed chair.

"Hello, Valora," Leo greets her, shifting uncomfortably next to me. He's so formal with her, it's almost amusing. We have all made a fragile peace.

"Hey. We're, um...we were just going to head out," I tell her as I stand and take Leo by the hand. I pause. "How was your day?"

Valora doesn't pry her eyes from the ceiling. "Uneventful. I'll see you guys later." One corner of her mouth twitches slightly upward. "Make good choices."

I glance over my shoulder before the door closes and see her still staring up at the ceiling. My heart pulls a little for her. The feelings and resentment that had been building up between us this year were released in, leaving behind a strange hollowness. It's an uneasy armistice, and now that I have Leo, I'm not sure what step is next to reach my sister, but I know one thing: I'm going to try.

"Where are we headed?" Leo slips his hand into mine as we head toward the atrium.

"I have to meet up with Allen in his office in a little bit. Walk me there?"

"Of course." He squeezes my hand. My heart tilts sideways and I feel my cheeks flushing. Maybe someday this'll wear off, but I hope not.

"Grier!" My name echoes across the atrium, stopping me in my tracks. "Hey, Grier! Over here!"

Cicely. She's perched atop one of the study pod tables, her legs draped over Julian North's lap. *Wow, really?* They are gross together, and I hate that they betrayed my sister. Sensing my hesitancy, she hops down and strides across the atrium, students parting ahead of her as she tosses her hair over one shoulder. It changes from a pale, minty green to a deep cherry red.

"Hey!" Her voice drops to a whisper. "So, Grier, look. I know we've had our differences." Another hair toss, this time turning it a rosy copper.

"Differences?" I snort. "Yeah, that's totally how I'd describe it."

"Sorry," she pouts. "But look, let's let bygones be bygones. We're having a low-key room party tomorrow night, and you and Leo should come by."

I blink. "A what?"

She's momentarily stunned, but recovers. "A room party? You've been to a room party before, right?"

"I...uh, no. No, Cicely. I haven't."

She laughs, like I've just said the funniest thing. "Right. Well, it's in Gillian's room, nine o'clock. I raided my parents' liquor cabinet over break." Her eyes flit to Leo's face, and she lets one hand rest gently on his forearm. "You should come."

"I have a thing," he deadpans, and I have to bite my lip to keep from cracking up.

There's a quick flash of the real Cicely, a brief vicious flicker in her eyes, but she turns to me and smiles brightly. "Well, Grier, you should totally come even if your cute import can't."

I refrain from punching her and deserve a medal for it. "I have the same thing he has," I shrug. "Thanks, though. Enjoy.." Sliding my arm around Leo's waist, we keep walking. We wait until we're almost up one curving flight of stairs before laughing.

"What was that about?!"

"That," I sigh sadly, "was about Valora."

We reach Allen's office, and Leo pulls me in close. "See you at dinner?"

"You got it," I promise. He leans in for a kiss before heading back toward the staircase.

Allen's door is cracked open, but I still knock, peeking in when I hear him call, "Yes?" His face breaks into a smile when I step into the office. "Grier! I was wondering when I might see you. Come in! You said in your email that we have a lot to discuss."

I'm surprised by the sudden flutter of nervousness in my belly as my mind races back to the night where I stood on the landing at home, staring at the words of the prophecy everyone had long assumed was about my sister. This might sound completely insane once I share my thoughts out loud, but I can't get it out of my head. "Um, can I close the door?"

There's a pause. "Sure." He gestures to one of his chairs and leans forward. "What's going on?"

Another deep breath, settling into what I'm about to say. "So, my family has this huge print of the Chosen One prophecy hanging in our house because, of course we do. I've never really paid attention to the prophecy itself, just accepted it for what it was. But then when I was home on break, I was staring at this print, *really looking* at the words. The family divided stuff, but especially the suffering servant thing and seeing what my sister has gone through, I just wonder...."

"If she's the Suffering Servant and not the Chosen One?"

"Yes," I breathe, relieved to hear someone else say it. "I mean, it's probably just overly poetic."

Allen taps his lips. "Thackeray Chadwick was a strutting peacock with an enormous ego, but that doesn't mean he was wrong. That was his gift, prophecy."

I nod. "Right, but I just keep having this thought..."

"What if it isn't Valora? What if it's you?" His voice is calm, quiet. We sit in silence for a moment, then I nod.

"Grier," he begins slowly, lightly drumming his fingertips on his immaculately clean desktop. "It may surprise you to find out that I have suspected this myself for quite some time." I blink, stunned, and he continues. "For longer than you've been alive, the prophecy has been interpreted this one way. Unquestioningly, the Chosen One has been Valora. I've always felt that the prophecy, as with all great works of literature or sacred texts, should be open to interpretation. After all, if we are talking about such gravely high stakes, should we not consider all options? We owe it to ourselves, to others, to not get caught up in this blind faith in one singular interpretation of the prophecy."

He leans back in his chair, and I let his words slowly sink in. Allen sighs, shaking me from my thoughts. "Of course, this isn't exactly something one can just bring up. Exceptionals cling fiercely to what we believe we know. We don't like to be wrong, and we don't like change, particularly when it challenges our very way of thinking. Willful ignorance is powerful, Grier; dangerously powerful at times. Erys knows this, mark my words. She is counting on it."

"What does this mean? What do I do?" I feel panic rising in my throat. Though the radical idea that I could be the Chosen One has been drifting around my mind for the past two weeks, I hadn't truly considered the weight of that possibility. *The Chosen One.* God, those words are so heavy.

Allen stands, then comes out from behind his desk and sits next to me in the other orange chair, placing one hand on my shoulder. He squeezes gently and I sit forward uncomfortably. "Don't be afraid, Grier. Take a deep breath." I comply. "This means we have work to do. But look at what you've done in just the last few months. Think of that awkward, anxious young woman who walked into my classroom this past fall, and then consider the young woman sitting here in front of me today. You are understandably overwhelmed and afraid. The world will see soon enough; let's not let that get in the way now."

"What do you mean?"

"I mean, I think for the time being, making public any speculation about the legitimacy of Valora as the Chosen One will only be an unnecessary distraction, and it will wreak havoc on your family life." I almost laugh. *You think?* "Let's focus on your training, particularly your ability to portal living things, large things, and at which distances. We need to focus on honing your skills and researching how we can best apply them in weaponized scenarios. Do you understand? Grier, your progress is wonderful, but at some point, we have to acknowledge the *why*. *Why* are we doing this? *Why* is it of the utmost importance that you realize your full potential? Because it's about what it means to be Chosen One."

I'm silent, absorbing the weight of his words, trying to find my own. "It means I have to kill Erys." The words sound strange coming from my lips and I'm suddenly overwhelmed by the reality of my situation. *God, how has Valora carried this her entire life?* My stomach churns, and a numbness spreads through my hands. At my distress the tiniest wisps of blue portals begin appearing at my fingertips.

"Grier." Allen's voice is gentle as he leans in toward me. "Look at me. You're only getting stronger, Grier, and look at the upper hand you have. Your sister, she has to fight these monsters as they come. She has to struggle, and it's damn near cost her her life. You may not watch her fights, but I do, and she's not able to get it done. She's amazing, don't get me wrong, but fighting a telekinetic with another telekinetic will never work. What are they going to do, throw things at each other until they both die? No. It's primal. Unable to tip the scales." He closes his eyes and shakes his head, as if the memory of Valora, broken and bloodied after the Onyxcobra, is almost too much for him to bear. "You have the upper hand in that you don't have to *battle* these creatures to win. Your weapon is your ability to simply send them away."

He lets that sink in for a moment, then stands and paces around the room.

"We know what must be done, Grier. We've acknowledged

it here, and now we plan. Now we plot." His voice is intense, hushed, and he kneels in front of me, his eyes blazing. "The next beast Erys sends, we will be ready. You will be ready. Rest assured, I will be here to guide you every step of the way. You have my word." Then he pats my shoulder and stands up.

"Thank you. This is a lot to process, but thank you." Though so much lies ahead, I feel lighter somehow. I needed to tell someone.

"Of course. Now, the afternoon is growing short, but there is some time left. We have a lot of work to do. Are you ready to jump in with both feet?"

I nod firmly, more certain of this than I've ever been of anything in my life. Somehow the fact that I'm maybe the Chosen One *feels* right, like it's something that has been waiting in the shadows of my heart all this time. My life makes sense: the unrest I've felt growing up, the inability to watch Valora's fights...maybe this is why. Perhaps a balance has been righted within me. Perhaps it's destiny, or perhaps I'm just floating on Allen's belief in me, but either way, I'm ready. Let's see what I can do.

I turn toward him and open a portal.

18

VALORA

I USED TO LOVE PROCTOR MOOR. WHEN I WALKED THROUGH THE halls, I felt like this school was built for me, and in a way it was. People support the school because the Chosen One goes here; they get huge grants from the Department of Defense to keep me safe, and to continue to implement Everett Proctor's chemical protections on the grounds around the school. When I used to walk down the hallway, my fellow students would either part in front of me or casually try to have a strained conversation with me in hopes that I would find them down to earth and want to be their friend. That never happened, not once, by the way. Although, in hindsight maybe it should have, since now I find myself pretty friendless.

Oh sure, I could probably grab some friends from the middle tier of the Proctor Moor social structure, the lacrosse players and the shiny choir girls. But even if I wanted to, I wouldn't know how to start. How does one make friends when everyone knows everything about your life already? How do you build relationships when you know they will want something from you the minute a bond is made? I've never had to think about things like this before; friends were always part of the package when you are the Chosen One. But now, that package has turned on me.

I see Cicely at the end of the hallway. She's leaning against the lockers and Julian is leaning over her, one hand of his stroking her hair, which changes colors each time he touches it. Twinkling aqua, candy-apple green, a soft periwinkle with pink accents.. When they see me, they lean their heads together and snicker. I spin away from them and take the long way to class, my heart in my stomach. When I sit down next to Anna, she stands up and moves, but not before silently mouthing "I'm sorry" to me. I'm not even mad; I understand. If she is kind to me it's a betrayal to Cicely, and her own social status will be in jeopardy. *I am starting to see why Grier hates Proctor Moor.*

Speaking of Grier, she saunters in with Leo as class is starting. They are holding hands and hesitantly let them part when they sit down. As cynical as their new love makes me, I am still happy for Grier. Also, when I see them together, I realize that I never felt this way about Julian. Not even once. My eyes glaze over as Mr. Ferguson - Allen, as Grier calls him, which is really weird, but then again I call Renata by her first name – goes on and on about Holographic Theory in Earth's early age and *oh my god why is he so boring.* Grier is sitting alert in her front row seat, her eyes glued to him. I tilt my head and watch the way she responds to him; scribbling down his every word, the way her body is alert to each change in his movement. He looks at her for most of class, smiling at her, winking one time when he makes a point.

I narrow my eyes, a rogue thought coming to the surface. *Is there more going on here than I think?* I look to Mr. Ferguson and then back to Grier. *No, there can't be.* She's falling in love with Leo. I know because I see it all day long and it's gross.

Mr. Ferguson finally wraps up class with a long homework

assignment that I won't do. I go to close my notebook, but instead stare at it, shivers running up my spine. I've been doodling on my notebook the entire class without thinking about it, and now I really look at what I was drawing: a huge Onyxcobra circles the outside of the page, its hood flared wide at the top. Mantharas cover the midsection, their wings punctured and torn. On the upper right corner, a Mistspawn's tentacles reach out, curling around the notebook spiral. In the center is a smeared black blur in the shape of a person with a hood. Erys. I look with surprise at the underside of my hand, now covered in black ink. I push back from my desk and leave the notebook behind me as I grab my backpack and run out into the hall. My head is swirling. Lunch can wait; I'm not hungry in the least and I need some quiet.

I turn the corner of the Rigmore wing just in time to see Grier and Leo slip through our door. I clench my fists together and spin on my heel, and almost take out Renata, who is standing right behind me. "Valora! Slow down!"

"Sorry," I growl before remembering my basic manners. "Are you okay?"

"Yes, but you won't be if we don't start your training up again. You need to come see me."

I drop my head, unable to meet her eyes. "I'm not coming back, Renata."

She puts her hands on her hips as her black eyes bore through me. She's terrifying. "And why is that exactly?" I want to keep looking at the floor, but instead I use all my willpower to meet her eyes and hold her gaze. I want her to see me. "Because no matter what I do, I'm doomed. Because no matter how much I train, Erys is going to kill me one way or another. I'm not strong enough, Renata. That cobra almost killed me. Would have killed me if I hadn't gotten lucky."

"Not if we keep training, Valora! At least give yourself a

fighting chance!" Her accent grows thicker the more upset she becomes.

"No. No! All my life I've been told what I'm going to do. All my life I've been put on this pedestal and then forced to scale it time and time again. It's impossible. I'm exhausted, Renata, and I'm going to spend what little time I have left on this earth without a spotlight on me."

Renata leans forward, grabbing my collar a little roughly. I step back with surprise as she spits out, "Erys isn't waiting. Erys isn't resting. And you are right, she is coming for you, she and her monsters. I'm trying to save your life, you ignorant child! I have seen what she can do! You don't know her power, I do. I know what she can take from you." Tears fill her eyes as I push her hand away. "You are breaking my heart, *mi cielo*. I always thought it would be Erys. Not you, never you."

Her words are too much for me and I turn and walk swiftly down the hall, my hand clutching over my heart as I walk, plumes of power spreading over my fingers. The edges of the floor curl as I pass over them, her words playing in my head.

"You can't hide from your fate, Valora!" she yells behind me, but I am going, and I am gone.

I can't go to the room, because I know that Grier and Leo will be there, making out to some terrible acoustic album. I try not to replay the argument with Renata as I walk, but it's almost impossible. I forget sometimes that she has seen Erys, has fought her. It's much more real for her than I could ever imagine, but I can't take on her fury. The scene of Everett Proctor's death tugs at the corner of my mind; one scene in particular – when Everett looked at Erys. He knew her, I feel deep in my chest. Was she a teacher? A friend?

At the end of the hallway I take a sharp right, heading where I've only been down once or twice in my entire time at Proctor Moor: the library. The Proctor Library is the pride of the school for good reason: the arching walls of books are grand, and the white wooden ceiling, carved like the inside of a whale, makes you feel as if you were inside a dream.

I never come here.

I approach the reference desk and clear my throat. "Um, hello?"

The librarian turns around and I almost snicker: she is exactly the person you hope a librarian would be: soft and kind, with horn-rimmed glasses and a mustard-yellow cardigan. "Oh, hello! It's you." She giggles awkwardly and I smile and do a half-nod.

"Yes. Hi. I am needing some help and I'm not sure where to start."

She claps her hands "I would love to help you, dear! Anything for the Chosen One!" I cringe.

Behind me, I hear a few students snicker and my face flares red. The librarian shoots them a nasty look and then reaches out and takes my hand. I'm surprised, but I keep smiling, even as I feel her somewhat sweaty hand squeezing my own.

"I need every piece of information on Everett Proctor." Her eyes widen and I can see the gears turning in her head. *The Chosen One just asked me for information on the dead Chosen One, OMG, OMG.*

She nervously waves her hands at the rest of the students dismissively. "Sorry! Can't help you. We're closed for the afternoon." They groan and she ignores them as she slaps a closed sign on the desk.

"Now, Miss Rigmore, if you'll follow me..." We disappear into the book stacks and she begins grabbing from the shelves. "This one is a good choice – a bit dry for my taste, but very accurate. This is a collection of all the news clippings about his death here, and his fight with Erys. Here is his collection of essays on telekinesis and the inner workings of genetic chemistry, though I'm sure you have studied these in class." She hands me the piles of books and heads back up the aisles, pointing excitedly. "You know, I think we just got in a new book about him. A sort of unofficial thing. It's not coded yet for our system, but I'm sure they wouldn't mind if it was for you, so I'm going to run to the back and sneak it out." She giggles. "It's a bit like being a sidekick, isn't it! I'm the Robin to your Batman!"

Then she's gone and I'm left standing somewhat bewildered in this woman's wake when I hear quiet laughter from a book stack behind me. And from somewhere inside of me, a coiled rage strikes out. I drop the pile of books with a thud and throw my hand out. The books on the shelf across from me fly forward into the aisle where I heard the laughter. I hear them hit something, followed by a mumbled "OW!"

Two dark brown eyes peek through the shelf at me. "Oy! Did you just throw books at my head?"

"I don't know, did you just laugh at me?"

Pike Paskell's eyes light up. "No so much at you as at that woman losing her marbles over being able to help you."

I look around, making sure she's gone before heading around the shelves.. "Yeah, she's a bit overeager."

"Overeager, is that what you call it?" He bends down and picks up the books, putting them back on the shelf. Using just the power in my hands, I pick up the last one, fold it shut and quietly put it back on the shelf without ever physically touching it. Pike shakes his head. "You know, I've seen you use your powers to fight many a gross creature, but seeing you use it to do ordinary things is somehow more astounding." It's a compliment, and it's a good one. My cheeks flush.

"Thanks, though I'm not sure it's going to make any difference." The words are out of my mouth before I can stop them. I visibly flinch and step back, embarrassed at my sudden vulnerability. He stares at me.

"What do you mean?" he asks softly, and there is something

about the tone of his voice that unleashes a torrent of emotion. I sit hard on the ground, books falling all around me like rain.

Without a word, Pike sits next to me and reaches for my hand. It's bold; most people never touch me. It feels...friendly. I search for the words to try and explain, but it's too much and all I can manage is the raw truth:

"I'm going to die." I say it plainly, and watch for the shock on his face, but it doesn't come. Instead, he nods.

"Okay."

We sit in the silence left behind by my bombshell. After a minute, he lets out a long breath, his mohawk pressed back against a shelf full of Greek history. I admire the pattern of flames shaved into the sides of his buzzed head. "If you're going to die soon, then what are you doing here? Why aren't you skydiving or traveling the world? Why are you checking out every book ever written on Everett Proctor?" He picks up a book. Everett is on the cover, hands on his hips, looking out from a cheesy backdrop. "My mom worships him, but I always thought there was something weird about him."

"I used to think that, but now, I don't know. The pressure, the media, family, all of it. It can make a person..." I clear my throat, trying to ignore the lump there and the fact that Pike Paskell's shoulder is touching mine, and that the brown skin of his hand feels like fire against my own. "It can make someone go a little mad."

He squeezes my hand reassuringly and then lets it go and it's like being plunged into icy water. I try to ignore it as I pluck the book out of his hands. "If I'm going to die, I want to understand my enemy." I turn the book over. "I guess I'm hoping that there is something in one of these that helps me. I feel like I'm missing something."

He nods. "Well, that sounds much more interesting than my Trig homework. Can I help you? We can go to the quad and study, or maybe..."

"Could we go to your room?" His head jerks up, and I quickly course-correct. "To study. It's just that Grier is in my room with her new boyfriend – "

"Oh, yeah, that Leo kid. He's cool."

"And I don't want to be..." I gesture out to the main body of the library. "Out there with all the people, wondering what I'm looking at."

"Wondering why you are with me." He shrugs. "I get it, Valora. I have a mohawk. I'm black. I'm British. I'm not exactly Julian North."

Thank god, I think. "Honestly, it's not that." It's the truth, and as painful as it is to say, I'm on a high from having a simple, honest conversation. "It's that I'm not the most popular right now. And I'm avoiding a certain ex-friend. I'm one step away from eating lunch in a bathroom stall."

He grins. "I doubt that. You're still Valora Rigmore. But, my room it is. Though I have to warn you, I'm not, let's say, 'great' at doing laundry."

Before I can laugh, the librarian explodes back around the corner. "There you are, right where I left you! You'll never guess what I found!" She shakes a brightly bound book in her hand. "*The Letters of Everett Proctor*, not even released to the public yet!" I stand and reach for all the books on the floor.

"We'll take it!" Pike reaches out for the book and she reluctantly hands it to him.

"Keep it safe and don't share it."

"We won't, promise," grins Pike.

She reaches out and takes both of my shoulders, her eyes blazing with intensity. "I truly hope you find whatever it is you are looking for. We're all counting on you, you know, and when that bitch comes, I hope you give her hell."

As soon as we clear the library, Pike and I nearly collapse from the laughter that follows. The rest of the afternoon is grand, and for just a few hours I forget, as I laugh at Pike's ridiculous room, all about the Chosen One stuff. It's a miracle, even though we find nothing of worth in the books. When I get back to my room a few hours later and beaming pretty brightly, Renata is waiting for me. The minute I see her pale face I know something is wrong.

19

GRIER

SQUEEZING MY EYES CLOSED, I CONCENTRATE ON THE TINGLING IN my fingers. Then, in a matter of seconds, I open them, visualize the target, and send out my portal. It's so easy for me now to move inanimate objects that I barely have to think about it. I hear Leo gasp, and I spin around, eyes open. There it is: a large, potted fiddle-leaf fig, balanced just so on top of an end table, which is resting on an armchair, which sits on a sleek wooden desk, which is nestled on top of the cushions of a wide sofa tucked away in a cozy corner of an out-of-the-way common area in Proctor Moor.

"The new world record in magical furniture stacking is five!"he announces grandly.

I laugh."Magical, huh?"

He crosses the room and takes my face in his hands, kissing the tip of my nose gently. "Magical, *sayang*," he murmurs, and warmth courses through my veins. I slide my arms around his waist and nestle my head under his chin, where it fits just so, where I can hear his heart beating. He wraps his arms around me and rests one hand on the back of my head, his long fingers intertwining in my hair. I try to focus on what I'm doing, reminding myself that this stacking is for a purpose, and that purpose comes with fangs, claws, and poison.

I shudder, then feel the temperature in the air around us rise slightly, Leo's warmth spreading outward. "I'll never need a blanket when I'm with you," I sigh, relaxing into him and trying to push the nagging fears from my mind.

"Could maybe use a watch, though."

We both jump at the sound of Agnes's sharp voice.

Agnes. Crap. We were supposed to meet up with her after she finished tutoring.

"Oh my god, Agnes," I begin, but she holds up a hand and interrupts me.

"Look. Just let me say this, okay?" She sounds tired. "I'm so happy for the two of you. SO happy. Grier, you've been my friend all my life, and Leo, it kind of feels like you've been my friend for a really long time, too." One corner of her mouth lifts in a slight smile. "I get that you want to have time together, and I don't begrudge you that. I don't want to interrupt...*alone* time, or be a third wheel. With that being said, I don't want to be forgotten about. Like today."

The hurt in her voice is far worse than any amount of anger ever could be, and I feel a wave of remorse crash over me. I don't have an excuse; I've been a crappy friend. She was right.

"We..." I begin, then correct myself. The royal we is beyond obnoxious. "I...Agnes, I'm sorry. It's my fault."

"I'm sorry, too," Leo offers. Agnes tilts her head and pushes her glasses up her nose, a gesture of hers as familiar to me as any of my own. "It's Grier's fault," Leo adds in a stage-whisper, elbowing me, and Agnes cracks a grin.

"Grier's the worst," she agrees, and I groan.

"I am. I am the worst."

"You really are." Agnes smiles as relief blossoms in my chest. I'll have to work harder at this boyfriend and best friend thing. "Though, I thought I'd find you guys making out, but it looks like you were practicing...some sort of weird feng shui?" She gestures to the tower of furniture and crosses the room to peer up at the plant perched at the top. "I mean if this is what you guys are into, then who am I to judge."

"She portaled them." The pride in Leo's voice is unmistakable.

"Whoa!" Agnes's eyes are enormous. Even when she is angry with me, she is proud. I don't deserve her.

"Allen has been helping me hone my skills." I feel myself blushing, though I'm not quite sure why. "I have to go meet him before dinner, actually, so I should probably put this all back." I start toward the pile of furniture, but Agnes stops me.

"No way, you have to do it the cool way. Portal it. You owe me for this afternoon!"

"Fair enough." I close my eyes and stretch out my palms. If my power can save people like these two, then every minute, every second is worth it.

I'm about to say as much aloud, when we're all startled by Renata Flores rushing toward us, black eyes blazing. I turn around with a smile on my face, but it dies when I see Valora standing behind her. Valora, who on any other day would be the first person anyone would notice in a room, has shrunk behind Renata, fragile and shaken. Our eyes meet, and immediately I know something is wrong. Something is incredibly wrong.

"Grier, come with me, please." Renata's voice snaps me back to attention.

"Is everything alright, Miss Flores?" Agnes steps up beside me, her arm protectively locking with mine, but Valora steps forward.

"Grier." Her voice is hoarse, raw, and I notice that her eyes are swollen and red-rimmed. "I need to talk with you." She gestures for me to follow her. She's shaking, and I reach for her hand, but she pulls it back before I can, raising it to her cheeks, where tears fall without ceasing. Her voice cracks and she leans forward, clutching her chest. "Nan is dead." Her voice breaks and tears spill down her cheeks as I stand there, dumbfounded.

No. "No, it can't be. I just got a letter from her two days ago," I whimper, the room spinning around me as I struggle to stay upright.

Valora nods. "She's dead. And no one will tell me what happened." I sway, and suddenly the floor is rushing up from below. Valora steadies me. Renata pushes us gently toward the door.

"Grier, go with Valora. Stay close to her." If only she knew the impossibility of what she is asking. The rest of the afternoon is a blur of tears and travel and an aching, open wound where my heart used to be.

I'm standing at her funeral and even though it's been a week, I can't believe Nan is gone. I keep telling myself that this isn't real; this is some sort of movie playing out in my mind and any minute I can stand up and turn off this overflowing font of grief. My hands twitch and I cling to the skin on my upper arm, and I pretend for just a minute that this is Nan's arm, that I can touch her papery skin, see the smile that crinkles the corner of her mouth.

But I can't, because she is in a box at my feet. A rush of nausea passes through me and I taste bile. *I don't understand. I just saw her.* Nan was the healthiest 78-year-old I know; she walked every morning, lifted weights, and had plans with her friends almost every night. She swore that she would live to a hundred, and I believed her.

The pastor is speaking ancient words of comfort, but it's like he's in another dimension; his voice is nothing more than background noise. I feel myself reaching for the holy words, hoping to find that source of peace. "And may the God of all comfort, strengthen and preserve you..."

Beside me, Valora stands stoically while I sob loudly, and for once the coldness of her emotions doesn't annoy me; her silent grief makes me feel better about my messy cries. She loved our Nan so much. When I saw Valora's pale face, I knew something bad had happened and I knew that from this second there would be a *before*, then an *after*. Now we are in the *after*, and it's as horrible as I had imagined.

My parents stand together at the edge of the grave, my mother softly crying. Nothing I have learned has prepared me to see my parents' devastation; it's almost harder to take than my own. I watch my mother sag against my father, watch him wrap his arms around her as he struggles to stand himself. Then he straightens up and cradles her head with one hand, gently wiping her tears away with a tissue. His face is pale and drawn. A dark reality has soaked into his starry-eyed dream. Nan's death has shaken him.

In that moment, seeing him at the graveside holding up my mother, I decide to forgive him for all that he has done. For his blindness and his selfish words to his daughters, for the way he has used Valora and then me, for his inability to differentiate between fatherly pride and his own ambition. I forgive him because I cannot have anything else heavy in my heart. I am full up.

I have a strange thought, observing them: we cannot die. My mother cannot stand over our graves and weep. I cannot let that happen. They said that Nan died of natural causes. That she was old. She was found at home, in her favorite chair, a book at her feet. Quietly. Quickly – that's what the report from the coroner said. But I know my Nan, and I know that she would never go quietly into that good night. Also, my grandmother *hates* reading. Trashy TV shows? She's all about that. But reading? No. That's not her thing – I know because I was always trying to change her mind. I bite my lip and taste blood. *Something is wrong. Someone is lying.* My parents are a bit too stricken, and the panicked look upon the pastor's face speaks of something else.

But that's for later. For now I'm pretending that my feet are roots, digging deep into the earth, rooting me to her forever. The pastor finishes talking and makes the sign of the cross over her coffin. My mother steps forward, my father holding tight to her shoulders. With a cry, she throws a handful of dirt down onto the coffin of her mother, and the other people around us follow. My father nods at me, but I'm frozen. I can't move, can't do this one last thing for Nan, a woman who raised me as much as my own parents did. But I am not strong right now. I am broken.

"Grier." I look up in surprise and see Valora standing next to me. She reaches out her hand and takes my own, gently opening my fingers. Then she puts a handful of dirt in it.

I curl my fingers around it, feeling the cool texture, and I walk to the edge of the grave.

"I hate this. I hate this," I sob.

"I know," she whimpers. I open my hand, but my dirt does not fall. Instead, the dirt begins spiraling in the air, controlled by the power in Valora's hands, a power that Nan always loved. She would have loved mine, too. The dirt falls piece by piece onto the coffin like snow. Valora lets out a sob beside me and without thinking I reach out and pull her into my arms. Together we sink to the ground, in our own little circle of devastation. Whatever barriers there are between us fall away and we blindly fumble toward each other in our shared grief, even if just for a moment. I hold my sister until everything else falls away.

20

VALORA

THE RECEPTION IS AT THE COUNTRY CLUB NEAR NAN'S HOUSE, IN A pretentious room full of chandeliers and palm tree wallpaper, the smell of coconut air freshener and money drifting through. It's tacky, yet fabulous; Nan would have loved it. I'm standing in the corner trying not to look like Wednesday Addams in my black dress, hoping to disappear into the gaudy wallpaper. Everyone is milling around giving their condolences, but then they glance at me. I can see their mouths moving: *Is she still the Chosen One? Is she okay?*

Grier is doing a great job of representing the Rigmore sisters as she makes her way around the room, thanking guests for coming. I'm about to go bully the bartender into giving me another drink when I spot a familiar figure crossing the room. My posture straightens as the mortician shakes my father's hand. Then he turns and makes his way toward the door, walking more swiftly than he needs to. He's tall, with curly black hair and dark eyes, and he looks very uncomfortable in his black three-piece suit.

I know this man; well, barely a man. His name is Mateo, and he is Renata's cousin. He was always hanging around her when I was in middle school, a pouty teenager who would sulk about during our lessons, always finding a reason to come to the door and watch. He's always been a strange one, which makes sense, seeing how he ended up becoming a mortician. I set down my drink and make a beeline for him, weaving my way through the ballroom. He is heading toward the elevators, down a long hallway decorated with pictures of palm trees. Mateo turns back and sees me before breaking into a sprint down the hallway, his coat flapping around him. Hell no, he is not getting away from me. I dart after him, pushing past hordes of well-wishers and curious onlookers who are wondering why Valora Rigmore is chasing a man down a hallway. The crowd falls away as I turn another corner.

"Mateo! Wait!" He makes a hard right, veering away from the elevators and towards the stairwell, but that's a mistake. If I can kill a Mistspawn, I can certainly catch an out-of-shape coroner. I throw out my hand, and the rush of power sweeps his feet out from under him. His face hits the thick carpet and he groans, rolling onto his back. Immediately, I curl my hand and his body comes sliding toward me as he kicks his legs helplessly. He looks ridiculous, like a beetle flipped on its back. I bring his body to a stop at my feet and look down at him. "Going somewhere, Mateo?" I snap.

He groans and climbs to his feet, brushing his hands down his sleeves. "This is a new coat, Valora. And I'm going to have a hell of a carpet burn from that."

"I could be wrong, Mateo, but you look like a man with something to hide."

He sighs and adjusts his round glasses. "The universe has quite the sense of humor today. How is it that I am now in a presence of the person that I most needed to avoid?"

I smile at him. "Why is that? Afraid of my charming personality?"

He looks skeptical. "You were never near as charming as you thought you were."

I pull my hand up toward my face and his body raises upright, his toes barely touching the ground. I feel no shame; Nan is dead and my patience is worn thin. My voice is jagged in my throat. "Why. Are. You. Running. From. Me. Mateo?"

"Because I was told that I couldn't talk to you," he rasps. "Let me down. Please. I'm not one of your monsters." He's right. I look around us; the ballroom hallway is empty, save Grier, who is making her way toward me with a concerned look on her face.

"Get in the elevator," I snarl at him, putting his feet back on the ground. We both push into one at the end of the hall and I frantically push the buttons, but it's too late. Grier is upon us. Her hand shoots into the gap and holds open the door.

"Where are you going?" she hisses when the doors open. "Valora! You can't leave Nan's reception!"

"I'll be back," I reply. "Don't worry about it." Grier eyes Mateo and then looks back at me with a confused look on her face that says *him?* I sigh and yank her inside the elevator. "It's not that. Also, gross. I have standards. I'm asking him about Nan." Grier watches as I turn and twitch my fingers. Mateo's tie lifts off his chest and I point the end of it right at his face. "And Mateo is going to tell us everything." I think Grier will protest, will tell us to get back to the reception, but instead she reaches out and pulls the emergency stop switch. The old-fashioned elevator jerks to a stop. She gestures to him, her eyes burning. *Whoa.* She's kind of scary at this level of intensity.

"Speak," she orders.

Mateo is still watching his tie, which I'm making sway back and forth in front of his face like a snake. Finally, his shoulders shrug forward in defeat. "Fine, but you guys can't tell anyone I told you. I swore to your parents that I wouldn't. Swore to

Renata that I wouldn't. She'll kill me." I stare coldly at him. He takes a deep breath.

"Your grandmother was found about a mile from her house, on the south side of the lake, you know that patch near the rear of the property, where the golf carts can't go?" I nod. "She..." He shifts nervously. "This won't be easy to hear."

Grier steps forward, her teeth gritted together. "Keep. Talking."

His mouth twists. "Okay. Just don't say I didn't warn you. Her body...it was found in the top of a tree." A whimper escapes Grier's lips, but Mateo keeps talking. "A white pine, very tall, like... couldn't get to it from a ladder tall. We had to call in a crane to get her body down. It was pretty clear by the location and shape of the branches that were...interacting with her body that she didn't climb the tree. Something dropped her there, after she was already dead." Grier and I exchange pained looks. I put my hand on her back. Tiny blue portals are flickering at the edges of her fingertips. I focus again on Mateo's voice.

"Your grandmother, I'm very sorry to say, was electrocuted. That was the cause of her death. Her burns were deep and extensive. The pathway must have gone straight through her heart; probably passed through from arm to arm. It was so strong that even her internal organs were burned. Her brain suffered a lot of damage; the voltage could only have been above 11,000 volts to cause that kind of muscle and tissue damage."

The elevator seems to sway and blur around me; it feels like the floor is falling away.

"But, how..."

Mateo puts his hand carefully on my arm. "I don't know. The burn seemed to originate from her fingertips. But I need you to know," he pauses for a deep breath, and we both look up at him in teary disbelief, "I saw no signs of prolonged pain. This shock, it stopped her heart almost immediately. The rest of her wounds, those came after her heart stopped beating. In my professional opinion, your grandmother did not suffer. She might not have even known. Whatever monster did this, it was quick and brutal." *Whatever monster did this. He has no idea how right he is.*

I watch as Mateo releases the emergency lock. The doors open and he steps out, then pauses. "Your parents didn't want you to know." He gives us a half bow. "I am truly sorry for your loss, girls." Then he is gone, blended into the folds of the country club and its finery. The doors close again, and I lean back against the walls. Grier looks at me, and I see how hard she is trying to hold it together.

"Erys," I whisper, my lips trembling.

"Are you sure?" she asks, her eyes wide, trying to hide her shock.

"She's come for us. *She was always coming for us.* She ordered one of her monsters to electrocute Nan and then she raised her up on a tree for all to see. How else to get a body that high other than to lift it yourself? Only a telekinetic can do that."

Grier bites her lip. "Or a monster who can fly. And what monster can do that? Electrocute someone?" she asks.

I shake my head. "Does it matter? It's one of the hundreds at her disposal."

Grier kicks out a leg next to me and we sit rigidly together, wanting to comfort each other but not exactly knowing how to navigate it. She clears her throat. "Why would Mom and Dad hide this from us?"

"They want to protect us. It's the only thing they can protect us from." I give an ironic laugh. "Nan's house didn't have the protections around it like the school did. Or like our house has. Erys is coming, and there is nothing I can do to stop her." I press my palms against my eyes. "I couldn't protect her!" The words explode out of my mouth in a half-wail. "I should have protected her, but I can't. I protect anyone, not you or Dad or Mom!"

Grier stares at me for a long moment and I see that she is weighing saying something, but then she retreats back into her typical Grier silence. Finally, she says, "Do you want to go back to the reception?"

I shake my head. "No."

"Me either," she says. "Is it okay if I stay here with you?"

"Sure, I mean, if you want."

She nods and sits. "Want to tell our favorite Nan stories? Remember when we found all those raunchy letters from her lover in Paris in her attic, tucked behind the dollhouse?"

"Remember how they were dated from only five years ago?"

"I know, that's what made it so great." She lets out a delicate laugh, as breakable as a bubble. Sitting in the elevator, we cobble together a pot of good memories and somehow it brings Nan back, if only for a second. I feel her there with us in that moment, her love silently stitching shut the wounds we have inflicted upon each other.

21

GRIER

Dear Allen,

Thank you for the beautiful flowers you sent for my grandmother's funeral. It still doesn't feel real. This week has been such an overwhelming blur, but I know one thing is for certain: I can't ease my way into this. It doesn't feel right to keep this a secret from Valora and I'm not sure it can wait much longer. If I'm the Chosen One, it's time to be prepared. I don't want you to go easy on me anymore. I'm ready. Bring on the monsters.

Grier

One week later, I am running to keep up with Allen's long strides, the bitterly cold air burning my lungs. The Proctor Moor grounds are silent, save for the crunching of our boots on the thin crust of ice glazing the snowy path. The winter sun is shrouded by gray cloud cover. I'm keenly aware of the presence of security guards near the main building, though the black-clad men are remarkably discreet. As we leave Proctor Moor behind us, I don't see anyone else. I know they're further out in the woods and patrolling the moat, tucked away in places unseen.

Allen's voice is muffled but firm from behind his scarf.

"Careful, now. Watch your step." I can't believe it's been only been six days since the funeral. "You're absolutely certain you're ready for this, Grier? Fully preparing you, this level of training, means I can't keep you entirely safe any longer. It can be quite dangerous. You do realize that." I envision my Nan's body perched on a tree branch and shake away the thought; the same one that currently is haunting my dreams. Determined, I nod. *I'm not safe anyway,* I think. *No one is.*

"I realize that. No more warnings, Allen." He nods slowly and then reaches one leather-gloved hand out and grasps my shoulder through my puffy winter parka.

"Alright. Follow me. We don't have a lot of daylight left, so we'll need to move quickly."

When we reach abandoned Canterbury Pavilion, I stop dead in my tracks to take it all in: the wrecked stadium, seats cracked and thrown, the great rifts raked where the Onyxcobra surfaced and coiled its way toward my sister. The wintry ruins are eerily beautiful, almost as if everything has been left untouched since the attack, save for the blanket of thin snow covering everything.

"Grier?" Allen's voice jars me back to attention.

"I'm coming." Carefully, I make my way around overturned seats, taking Allen's offered arm as I navigate the rubble leading up to the front of the stage. I see the yellow caution tape over the trapdoor, the place where my sister almost died.

Allen turns and pauses, then takes a small, locked metal box from his pocket. "You've proven you can move large objects, and you can confuse the hell out of a squirrel. That's impressive, Grier, but if we are being completely honest, it isn't terribly helpful in the face of great evil."

The thought of fighting great evil with a fat squirrel strikes me as particularly funny, and I'm unable to keep myself from smiling. Allen looks at me sharply.

"Sorry," I check myself.

He strides across the stage and carefully places the metal box on the floor and produces a small key from his pocket. Gingerly, he reaches down and unlocks the box before sprinting back to me. I watch, mesmerized, as the lid of the box rattles, then shoots up three feet in the air before clattering to the ground.

"What—" I begin, but Allen holds a finger to his lips.

"Wait," he whispers.

I hold my breath, my heart hammering, and watch as two long, curved antennae appear over the edge of the box. They quiver slightly, then out hops...a grasshopper. A vivid blue-green, average sized grasshopper.

I turn to Allen, confusion mingling with irritation. "Are you serious? What, do you want me to go step on it? I meant it when I told you I was ready. I-"

He holds up his hand and stops me mid-sentence, a smile beginning to play across his lips. "Do you really think I'd bring you all the way out here to fight with a regular grasshopper?"

My cheeks burn. "I...no..."

"Orthopetra. Genus, Monster." He gestures at the insect, which hasn't moved. "This rare but deadly little creature came to me on the black market. He spits, you see, as any grasshopper does, but instead of merely unpleasant tobacco-like liquid, he spits a toxin that absorbs through the skin almost instantaneously. By the time you've noticed, it's likely too late. Within two or three days from initial contact, blood clots begin forming in the brain, and the victim will suffer an almost always fatal stroke." He chuckles to himself. "Frankly, the fact that Erys hasn't used these as a weapon thus far is sheer luck on our part. The destruction and death these benign-looking little monsters could cause..." he stops when he sees the expression on my face. "But they're incredibly rare. Perhaps a dozen in captivity. Including this little fellow."

I take a deep breath and try to steady myself. "So...do I just, um, do I just portal it? That seems simple enough. I can do that." *I can, can't I?* I feel an icy pit form in my stomach, and my mouth is suddenly dry. If I screw this up, Allen and I could die. *Oh my god.* "Where do I put it?" My voice is raspy, tremulous. "How do I know I got rid of it, and didn't just send it to some poor family's backyard or something?" I fight to keep the panic from rising in my throat.

"Grier, part of this is figuring it out. If you are successful, it will be rather anticlimactic, I'm afraid. It won't be a long, drawn-out battle like you're used to seeing Valora fight."

I never watch her fight, if I can help it, I think, a pang of guilt making me wince. The Orthopetra is rubbing its legs together, its antennae twitching as a long rubbery nozzle extends from its mouth. Suddenly, it looks more like a monster than an insect.

Allen lowers his voice to a whisper as he stands behind me. "Focus on it, Grier. Concentrate. Wait until it attacks. You must be able to portal a moving target when *you* are its target. Steady now."

I take a deep breath and stare at the insect. It looks harmless to the casual observer, but I know what it is. It's a monster. I know who is responsible for its deadly venom. The same evil that stopped my grandmother's heart, the same evil that left her body hanging in a tree. A coil of fury tightens in my stomach, and shimmering blue simmers at my fingertips. I grit my teeth as the Orthopetra lets out a high-pitched chirp, its antennae pointing directly toward me. I stretch one hand in its direction. *Come at me, twerp.*

It leaps, and a whorl appears in the air between us as I dive to one side, but I miss. It's moving so fast. Allen lands behind me with a shout. The Orthopetra lands, just a few feet shy of where we'd been standing, and the portal dissipates. It chirps at us, like it's playing a game.

"Anticipate, Grier! Think ahead!" Allen hisses, as it shakes its head in an eerily human-like manner, as if gaining its bearings before zeroing in on me again. This time I'm more prepared when it jumps, but I stumble over a pile of rubble on the stage floor, and tumble to the ground before I can even open a portal. I dodge it, but barely. It spins around again, angry now.

"Be aware of your surroundings!" Allen yells as he tries to help me get to my feet. I push him away.

"Don't help me!" Now I'm worried about him and me and it's making my head spin. The Orthopetra chirps again, loudly, and launches itself at me before I've even steadied myself. Panicked, I shove Allen backwards and throw one hand out in front of my face, feeling a surge of energy flow through me. Allen and I both go sprawling across the stage floor, and I squeeze my eyes closed tightly. *This is it.*

But the monster dodges the portal, soaring up into the air above our heads and then plummets downward, its face level with mine. I hear its jaws click together as a stream of venom hisses right toward me. I have no time, and so I throw up both my hands at once: one portal swallows the venom. In a second, I project it to come to rest on the grass across the field, and then I'm back, opening up a second portal to swallow the insect. It disappears in a flash of bluish light and I blink in surprise. *Two* portals. Opened and deposited within milliseconds of each other.

"Grier!" I hear Allen's voice cheering and dare to open my eyes. It's gone. I did it. I scramble to my feet.

"It's gone." I breathe, in shock. Something skitters across my unconscious.

Allen shakes his head. "Almost."

"Right." Panting, I stretch my fingers out in the direction of the moat surrounding Proctor Moor, closing my eyes and concentrating on it. Once the telltale surge of warmth flows through my palms and out my fingertips, I exhale. I watch as the monster drops into the moat. "Can they swim?"

He shakes his head *no* before dusting himself off, collecting the little metal box and putting it in his pocket.

"You've defeated your first monster, Grier. How are you feeling?"

I'm sweating, with stray hairs sticking to my forehead and neck, and I'm still trying to catch my breath. My knees feel like jelly, and I don't know how I'll manage to make it back to the school building, but a newfound power courses through me, deep and intense. It was exhilarating.

"More." I say, as he reaches into his bag.

That night, I make my way down the spiral staircase towards the boys' dorm as though I'm in a dream. I nod dazedly at the cheerful greetings of fellow students I pass in the halls, and it isn't until I'm knocking at a cedar door that I even truly realize where I am.

"Hey!" Leo grins in surprise when he opens the door and pulls me inside his room. "What's the matter? Are you okay?" He settles me on the old loveseat shoved under his lofted bed, and drops down next to me, my hands in his. I shove my coat off, throwing my hat and gloves to the side.

"I have to tell you something." The words tumble from me, and I couldn't stop them even if I tried. I realized this tonight, that I can't keep this huge part of my life from him. "You have to promise not to freak out."

He smiles confusedly for a moment. "Okay. Now I'm nervous. What are you talking about?"

"I think I'm the Chosen One." I'd never said the words

aloud to anyone other than Allen, and they hang in the air between us, leaving Leo stunned. "It's not Valora. It's me," I rush on, giving him an abbreviated version of what happened with the little girl, the prophecy hanging in my family home, my revelation with Allen. The Orthopetra.

"An Orthopetra?!" Leo sputters, turning angry. "That was ridiculously stupid! You could've been killed, Grier. Are you sure it didn't spit on you? Are you absolutely sure it's not on your clothes anywhere?" He's panicked and checking my coat, my jeans.

"Leo." I lean in and kiss him, hard. "I promise. It didn't touch me. It's gone. I portaled it into the moat. It's dead." His fingers are in my hair, and he presses his forehead to mine.

"If it had...Grier, God. I'm not sure what to think about this, but I do know this: risking your life to practice portaling isn't the answer." I look on his face and see that he's so worried about me that I'm probably not going to get anywhere with him today.

"Look, Leo, I'm okay. I am." I take his face in my hands. "Please, you can't tell anyone, not even Agnes. I just needed someone to know. I needed you to know. I know it's strange and new and scary, but I need you to be in my corner. I didn't want to keep it from you for another second."

"Grier." His voice is low, intense. "I am always in your corner. No matter what, I promise. But don't ask me to be okay with you risking your life."

"That's fair. But I want you to know it all." I'm hoarse, my heart thundering in my ears. *I can't even handle how much I want him.* I'm high on him, high on the monsters. "This is a lot to take in, I know. A lot to reckon with."

He kisses me, sweetly and softly. "We will reckon with it. I'm here. What do you need?" he murmurs, pulling me closer.

"Right now? Just this. Just you." Leo's lips meet mine again, fierce and possessive.

22

VALORA

I HAVE FOUND THE MOST PERFECT SPOT AT PROCTOR MOOR, A secret spot. You go past the teachers lounge and hang a sharp right. If you go past the empty classrooms and turn left down a small unassuming hallway, you'll find it: a wide window seat that overlooks the orchard and the hills beyond it. You can sit, you can lay, and not a soul on earth will find you. You can be here for hours, crying about your grandmother being electrocuted to death and no one will see. I'm here now, skipping class and reading the Everett Proctor books from the library. I turn over to lay on my stomach, the sun on my skin, one leg dangling off the bench.

God, I've fallen so far. This is the kind of introvert crap Grier does.

I've found nothing of use in these books. They cover the same subjects again and again: his silver-spoon upbringing in Savannah; his father's business dealings on beach-front real estate and their eventual move to Connecticut. The books then move to his adolescence, filled with cheeky shenanigans and tales of glory; then his eventual graduation and the realization that he could combine Exceptional talents and his own genetic chemistry. He meets his wife Sophie, has children. In the meantime, Erys rises out of the swamp, along with her monsters. He fights her. She kills him brutally. End of story. I lean my head down on the book and sigh. Nothing here can help me. I lift my head and bring it down again on the hardcover, banging my forehead against the spine.

"That looks like it hurts." I stop and jerk my head up. It's a male voice, but not the one I want to hear. Julian North is standing next to the bench, looking like a supermodel, smelling like an entire bottle of body spray. I immediately feel embarrassed and sit up, curling my legs underneath me and pushing the books back. He tilts his head.

"Whatcha reading?"

"Does it matter to you?" I reply sharply.

He gives a half-hearted shrug. Still the same Julian, I see. "I guess not." He shoves my books to the floor and aggressively sits down on the window seat.

I scoot away from him. "What do you want, Julian? Also, how did you find me here?"

He laughs. "You think you are the only one who knows about this little slice of patheticness? The nerds always come up here to hang out, find themselves. Anyways, I, uh, I wanted to say I'm sorry about your grandmother. I know you were close." He reaches out and touches my cheek and I flinch backwards.

"Nice transition, Julian. God."

He looks hurt. "Hey, calm down. It's just me. You know me, Valora." For a moment I let him run his fingers through my hair, because in that second it feels nice to be touched, to not be so alone. He was always good at this, the touching part. I flash back to nights on the beach at his house, of sand on my back and his body above mine. Those times are like pretty pieces of paper in my memory: lovely, but thin. Easy to punch through.

His peach lips part. "Cicely doesn't have to know. She's not like you, Valora. She gives me everything I want. But sometimes I like begging."

I push him backwards with a groan. "Thank you for reminding me, Julian."

He pushes his hair back from his face and leans in for another kiss. I stop him with my hand. "Reminding of you of what?"

"Of why I broke up with you. You're disgusting! You've been with Cicely for what, like five minutes and you are already cheating on her?" He shrugs and I struggle to pull away from him. "Do you even like me, Julian? What is it you like about me? Tell me."

He looks puzzled. "What do you mean?"

I pull free of his grasp and stand up. "I mean, what do you actually like about me? Because now when I look back on us, I'm not sure we ever had an actual, real connection. I was with you because I didn't want to be alone. You came with built-in friends. You're...not unattractive." This is a giant understatement but I keep going. "And you, you got to be with the Chosen One, so that sent your own popularity skyrocketing. It was a relationship of convenience, nothing more. Don't you see that?"

Julian stands, and I see a blush rising up his pale cheeks. "We felt things for each other, real things."

"Shallow things, forever ago." I reply. He grabs my arm angrily, and there is the real Julian I know; the insecure boy whose shortcomings make him possessive. I slowly look down at his hand and back at his face. *He forgot who he was touching.* His fingers begin pulling back, one by one, not by his own decision. My hands flare with heat as I move his fingers off my upper arm. I could break them if I wanted to, but I won't. He doesn't deserve the effort. Instead I slap his arm hard against his side and hold it there as he struggles. "You are going to walk away and never talk to me again; otherwise, you will find yourself on the front lawn of the school, and it won't be through the door."

He sneers. "You're a freak, Valora. Just like your sister, just like...him." He nods to the books on the floor before looking at me with cruelty etched across his face. "And you're going to die, just like him. At least that's what I put my money on."

I watch him walk away before I let my defenses collapse. My eyes blur with tears as I kneel to gather the books. *The Letters of Everett Proctor* has fallen facedown, and I pick it up, letting my fingers rifle through the index at the back of the book. I turn to the Vs, wondering if my own name is mentioned in here; yes, there it is: Valora Rigmore, my birth a footnote in this book, but instead of turning to the page that mentions me, my eyes fall onto another word.

Valenseas.

I blink. I know that word. *I know that place.* I flip to it and read the introduction to a section of poetry:

"In 1985, Everett's father rented a summer cottage at 50 Merchant Avenue in Valenseas, a tiny island just off the coast of California. Two years later, his father purchased the house, which had been erected in 1944 and was enlarged and remodeled to suit his family's needs. In and around this house, Everett Proctor spent part of his childhood summers, acquiring a keen interest in sailing and practicing his Exceptional gifts on the waterfront. He would often return there alone as an adult to meditate. His poetry here reflects his time admiring the waters of the island and the slow life he enjoyed there."

I sit back. Valenseas is not a big town. It is tiny, in fact; a seaside hovel with only a handful of houses and a huge swath of coastline. I know this because I have also spent a few summers there...visiting Renata and her family. Not once did she mention that the great Everett Proctor lived just a few doors down. I close my eyes and bring my fingers to my temples.

Why would Renata hide this from me?

I knew she was part of the group that fought against Erys, I knew that she knew Everett, but – were they more than that? Were they childhood friends? My mind flashes back to the video of that final battle: the part where Erys brutally killed Everett's wife. He had bent over her, wailing loudly and in the background, Renata looking devastated at the violence of it all...or was it something else? A wave of power pushes out through my hands when the realization comes, blowing the books across the narrow hallway, peeling the carpet up. I can't believe I've never put it together before, but we trust the ones we love. There is a reason that she knows so much about him. There is a reason that she is so passionate about my training, for me to defeat Erys at all costs. Because Renata was more than his friend.

Because Renata was the lover of Everett Proctor.

She's in her office when I push the door open, and the relief I see on her face is palpable. Wearily, she stands up, her long red skirt swaying ever so slightly in the breeze from her open windows. Renata always has the windows open, whether it's freezing or sweltering outside. She says fresh air is the stuff of life. She walks over to me, shaking her finger.

"Valora, thank God! I know that much has happened to you since we last met, but I believe that we can turn that righteous anger into power-" I stop her cold by holding up the biography. "What is that?" she asks, uninterested.

"Valenseas," I reply. "A quaint beach town off the coast of California, where Everett Proctor spent his youth. A place that I know well, because my mentor and teacher lived there all her life, though she never thought it worth mentioning to me that the Exceptional who our school is named after was her neighbor growing up."

Renata raises her chin. "You knew that I knew Everett. We fought Erys together."

"Yes, I knew that, but you spoke of him as if you were mere acquaintances. How could that be if you spent every summer with him from childhood into his early youth?" I narrow my eyes at her as I throw the book to the ground. "You cannot ask me to bear the weight of the world and not share the truth with me, Renata."

She stares at me for a long moment before quietly shutting her office door. I take a seat. Before she begins, she reaches inside a small plastic bag and tosses a peach into the air. I smile and raise my hand, holding it in the air. This is what we do. "Good. Counter-clockwise rotations, please, Valora. Swiftly as you go."

I look her dead in the face. "If I spin this peach, you will tell me the truth."

She nods and begins. "I first met Everett Proctor when I was just a girl of ten. We had only lived in this country for maybe a year so far. We lived in that same small house that you've visited; my mother cleaned summer homes for a living, working herself to the bone so that I could go to a fancy private school. Everett and his family arrived when he was eight years old. He first became my summer friend; and then he became so many other things: my first kiss, my first intimate encounter." I know I'm supposed to be enthralled with her story, but that sentence kind of makes me kind of barfy. I make a face, but she doesn't see.

She continues, "We fell in love as all young people do: passionately. Over the school year, we would write letters back and forth and pine away for each other until summer. I would sit on my porch with my mama and wait for their car, always a new model, to pull up at the beach house in Valenseas. The tires of his car spinning on the gravel was my favorite sound in the whole world."

Here she closed her eyes and swayed on her feet a little. "We couldn't tell his parents about our relationship; he swore they would keep us apart. For all their charity, the Proctors still carried bitter values in their hearts. They didn't care about my race, but they cared about class. Their son, such a gifted Exceptional, could never marry a poor immigrant girl." She shook her head. "Eventually we both went to the same university, and that's when he met Sophie Provence."

I can hear the hurt in Renata's voice, even now. She sees the pity in my eyes and sharpens her tone "Faster, Valora! Less bouncing! Anyway, Sophie Provence was everything the Proctors wanted in a match for Everett. She came from money. She was marginally gifted, so that she could truly let Everett shine. Everett didn't know what to do; he loved me, but he didn't want to disappoint his father, and so we walked away from each other. It was the hardest thing I have ever done, and it left my heart utterly shattered. I thought I saw agony in him too." She paused, lost in the past. "After he was married, we continued to see each other a few times a year in foreign cities, in hotels, shadiness and the stench of infidelity all around. It had been years when Everett showed up at my door, disgustingly drunk and holding a letter in his hands. A private investigator who had been digging around his father had found something: Everett's father – a man who he had worshipped his whole life – had another family in Florida, in a small house near the Everglades, that he barely kept out of abject poverty."

My brain is whirling. *Florida. A small house near the Everglades. A swamp.* The peach drops and splats onto the floor. Neither of us even look down.

"Erys," I whisper.

She leans over me "What I share with you can never leave this room: Erys is Everett's half-sister. She was born to a mother who rejected her from a very young age, who hated her Exceptional gifts and gave her little more than a bed to sleep in.

During the day, her mother would send Erys out to fend for herself in the swamp."

My voice shakes when I find it. "And her telekinesis..."

"Came from Everett's father, just like it had for Everett."

"*His sister.*"

I remember the look on his face in the video when she took off her hood, a look of recognition and sadness, just seconds after Erys had killed his wife.

"Erys was forced to raised herself in the swamp. Imagine being a child, so poor and alone, and surrounded by the terror of living in the Everglades, filled with terrible creatures. In the meantime, in your father's 'real' family, your brother is being hailed as a man amongst men, a Chosen One. He has the best of everything. He has fame and money and acclaim. He's on the cover of magazines, on television, being interviewed." I think for a second of Grier, and what life must be like in the heavy shadow of Valora Rigmore. Renata continues.

"Eventually, Erys blamed Everett for everything she lacked in her life. It was surely easier than blaming her mother for her parental failure, or the father she worshipped, even though he only visited once a year and was undeserving of her adoration. While her rage at Everett grew, so did her ability to control other creatures. Everett's father stopped visiting once Erys became unnerving, and it vaulted her over the edge. When she was fifteen, the Baleful found her, and her powers grew exponentially. In one of her rages, she sent a Sea Whelp to kill her own mother; her body was later found in its belly." My stomach turns. "Erys started seeking out monsters in the depths of the swamp, on high mountain tops, in desert caves and other nightmarish places on the earth. Slowly, she amassed an army that she could summon at will. Distance doesn't matter; once she wrangled control of them, they are always at her beck and call. As she was gathering these demons from the four corners of the earth, the more famous Everett became, totally unaware of this growing threat, of the sister who was more monster than human. The rest you know: that random monsters began attacking people. Hundreds of people near rural areas went missing; monsters were to blame. Kids snatched from their parents. Farmers, eaten by giant worms. And finally, after she had made her own world, she came for Everett, and for his family. She desired his fame. His happiness. Such trivial things that had come to mean so much to her."

I step back and take Renata's trembling hand. "That day, that terrible day when we stood against her and her monsters, I watched her kill Sophie, his wife. I watched her die in Everett's arms, and I watched the truth pass over his face: he loved her. His wife was always the one he would have chosen. I had lied to myself for so many years; I never realized that I was truly the mistress until that moment. And as I felt hate for him race through me, Erys began to twist his head around." She shudders. "I will never forgive myself for not acting faster." She releases my shoulders as my heart aches for her loneliness.

"I'm sorry I didn't tell you. I tried to give you as much information as I could. If I ever told the truth about Erys, the Proctor legacy would fall. They'd find out about our affair and I'd lose my position here. Most importantly, I wouldn't be able to train you. I couldn't save him, but maybe I can save you - and in keeping this secret, it's all that I can do to give the man I loved one small last thing: his dignity."

I stand up. "You should have told me Erys was his sister."

"It wouldn't have changed anything. Everything you know is still the same."

I turn and pace around the room. "It changes everything! You have a personal vendetta against Erys, because she killed the man you loved. That's why you train me so hard that my hands blister. That's why you are so convinced I can beat her when you know that I don't have a prayer!"

Renata whirls on me. "No, no! Valora, I would never let you

confront a danger you cannot defeat. You are like a daughter to me. But you have no choice but to fight her. You're the Chosen One. Someone has to, otherwise she can destroy this world between her powers and her monsters. They grow stronger every day."

"She already hates me, Renata. Don't you see that? I'm just like Everett, with all the attention and the gifts..." I let out a cry. "She killed my Nan! She was electrocuted and put onto a tree. But you already knew that. One more secret you tried to keep from me."

She touches my cheek softly. "I cared for your Nan. She was the only person who knew about Everett. She kept my secret for 20 years, even though she didn't like it. I'm sorry, Valora. Sometimes I am a sad old woman, holding onto a past that she cannot fix."

Everett. Renata. Nan. It's all too much. I step over the remains of the peach and walk out the door, leaving my mentor crying behind me. My steps hasten, and I once again find myself running through the school, as though I can leave it all behind me. As I run past the cafeteria, I come to a hard stop when I notice a small monster wiggling its way through a crack in the brick, no larger than a baseball. It's a Black Qually, an inky river creature, like a crab but meaner, with a bite that contains a multitude of poisons. I curl my hand and watch as the creature is slowly crushed to death.

Then I turn and continue my sprint, hoping to outrun a destiny that has claws and teeth.

23

GRIER

"I CAN'T BELIEVE YOU MADE THIS FOR ME. *GRIER.*" HE LAUGHS, and my heart thuds wildly. "This is incredible." Leo grins, and shovels another forkful of nasi goreng, Indonesian fried rice, into his mouth. He's always groaning about how bland the school cafeteria fried rice is before dousing it with something from his own personal stash of hot sauces.

I knew he'd missed out on weeks of home-cooked Indonesian food when he spent most of Christmas break in Connecticut, hoping to make things right with me. Before we came back – and before my Nan died - I'd done some recipe hunting and gathered whatever ingredients I knew I wouldn't be able to pilfer from the school pantries. "Did I get it right?"

"You nailed it," he moans, probably lying. "Oh, this is so awesome." He scoops more of the spicy rice, flecked with tiny, tongue-searing bits of bright red chili peppers, onto his plate. "What do you think? Do YOU like it?"

I nod, gulping ice water like I'm drowning. "Uh, yeah! It's just a little spicier than I thought it would be." That's an understatement; my sinuses are cleared and my eyes are beginning to water.

Leo, meanwhile, doesn't seem to even notice the heat. *"Pedas itu baiiiik, sayang,"* he laughs. "Spicy's good! How'd you manage to make this, anyway?"

"Oh, you know, it was nothing. I bribed a few of the student cafeteria workers to let me raid the kitchen and use it after hours," I tell him nonchalantly, enjoying how the cool, crisp bite of cucumber and the thick, sweet soy sauce mingled to tone down the heat.

"Bribed?" He wiggles his eyebrows. "Tell me more."

I shrug. "Couple of underclassmen. It wasn't my proudest moment, but I maybe I offered them some of Valora's used clothes. Just ones she won't miss."

Leo snorts, chuckling as he leans over the dishes to kiss me. "Not underwear, I hope."

I almost snort out my milk. "God, no. Just shirts. I'm not that terrible of a sister."

He takes another huge bite. "Well, you'd make my mother proud. This tastes just like home. I can't believe you did this for me." He gazes at me with such adoration, it takes my breath away.

"It was fun, and I like cooking." I slip my hand under his, intertwining our fingers. "Besides, I needed a break from training. Allen will get over it."

Leo stands and pulls me to my feet, leading me away from the makeshift picnic I'd set up in my room, toward my bed. He stretches his lanky frame next to me on my bed, and I wind my arms around his neck, pulling him in. The way he kisses me makes me dizzy, filling my brain with such a delicious fog, I'm not sure I can even remember my own name. My palms are tingling, and I know if I opened my eyes, I'd see tiny sparks of blue flickering at my fingertips.

The next afternoon, after classes are over for the day, Agnes and Leo head to the library to work on a history project, and I head toward my room. I'm about to duck through the doorway to the Rigmore Wing when I'm stopped by Renata Flores, her black hair even wilder than usual.

"Grier, I need to speak to your sister." She sounds frazzled. "She hasn't been in class the last few days and has ignored my requests to see her in my office."

"Do you want me to see if she's in our room?" *Why is my sister ignoring Renata, of all people?*

"She needs to come to my office. Please, can you just convey my message if you see her?"

I nod. "I'm only going to be here for a little while, but I'll leave her a note if she isn't here."

Renata looks at me sharply, examining me as though she wants to say something more, but she doesn't. Instead, she thanks me before striding briskly away.

"Okaaayyy," I mumble, letting myself into the wide hallway outside our rooms. Valora is there, sprawled on her bed, schoolwork scattered around her. "Renata's looking for you," I tell her when she glances up at me. A stormy look crosses her face, and she sniffs dismissively, shrugging before turning back to her books.

"She wants you to go to her office, said she needs to talk to you." When she doesn't respond, I press on. "She seemed sort of panicky. Are you trying to avoid her or something?"

"I don't need Renata all up in my face right now, and I'm not interested in anything she has to say to me." Valora's tone is measured and bitter, her words clipped. She still doesn't look up. I let my bag slide off my shoulder and onto the floor, weighing my options. "Was there anything else, Grier?" She raises one eyebrow at the sound of my bag hitting the floor, the irritation in her voice making it clear there had better not be.

She flips a page angrily and I think, *Are we really back here again?*

"No," I mumble and turn toward my corner of the room. Behind me, Valora sighs the exasperated sigh of the endlessly put-upon. I turn to face her again. "You know what, yeah. You don't need to shoot the messenger, Valora. Renata wants to see you, and I'm just letting you know. That's all. Feel free to keep hiding from her though. That'll help."

Valora stares at me for a long time, expressionless, then slowly sits up and closes the books in front of her, setting them aside. "Grier," she begins calmly, letting just the faintest tinge of venom into her voice, "I don't expect you can begin to understand, and I don't need you to tell me I'm hiding from anything. This has nothing to do with you."

You have no idea, I think, anger rising in my throat. "That's right, everything's always only about you," I spit. "Glad to know we're back to that status quo just when things were getting better here."

"What the hell is that supposed to mean?" Valora hisses.

"Oh, please. It's the same thing it always is with you. Nobody can possibly understand how hard it is to be you, and if anybody tries," I try to match my tone to her condescending detachment, "you don't let us in."

She cuts me off. "Yeah, Grier. Nobody CAN imagine. Would you like to carry this weight on your shoulders? Would you like to know that Erys is out there, thinking of ways to murder you and a few of your loved ones for good measure, because it's your damn job?"

"Yes." I blurt it out without thinking.

Valora's lip curls. "What?"

"Nothing." I turn to go, but I know that it's out there and it can't be put back.

"Wait, Grier - what? Are you serious right now?"

I take a deep breath to steady myself. I cross the room and perch gingerly on the edge of her bed.

"Yes. Valora, calm down. Please, just hear me out. Do you ever wonder about the prophecy? With all the bad things happening, with some of the things people are saying, with you struggling." My words are rushed, and I'm trying to stay ahead of myself, make sense of what I'm trying to say. Valora's expression is unreadable. "Do you ever wonder if it's me and not you? The Chosen One?"

There's a long pause, and I swear my heart is pounding so loud she can hear it. My sister stares at me for a long time, then throws her head back and laughs. "Oh, my god, Grier. That's amazing." Her face falls when she sees that I'm not laughing. "Oh shit, you're serious."

"Yes."

She shakes her head. "No, Grier. I don't ever wonder that. Ever. Because it's ridiculous. How would you even..."

"Why is it so ridiculous?" I cut her off, and I feel my face growing hot. "Why is it so ridiculous, Valora?"

She's on her feet now, her own cheeks flushed bright red, eyes blazing. "Are you kidding me? Grier, I don't know what sort of fame and glory you think you're angling for here, but trust me. You do NOT want this." She turns her back on me.

"How do you know what I want? Being the Chosen One isn't something anybody wants. It's a duty. It's a burden. It's something you feel like you can't handle right now, and that's understandable. You've had the pressure your whole life, and maybe, maybe it was for nothing. So no, of course I don't *want* this but what if I HAVE to take this? What if it's up to me and I look the other way because I don't want to step on your toes? You are like a wall. No one can get in, no one can even talk to you about this. If we could just talk...Valora, please! People could die if I don't speak up."

Valora wheels around and leans forward so her face is only

a few inches from mine. "Don't you dare insinuate that I'm a coward who can't handle this and that you are some savior coming in from left field to rescue us all," she hisses through clenched teeth. "You don't deserve the title. You haven't done the work, amongst a million other, better reasons!" I don't react, don't flinch or crumble like she's used to me doing, and this seems to only make her angrier. She leans back, crosses her arms over her chest, and tries another approach. "Who's filling your head with this nonsense, anyway?"

"What's that supposed to mean?"

"I'm saying someone is stroking this new ego of yours just the right way. Let me guess: about five foot ten, graying hipster who everybody thinks is just the coolest teacher ever?" She's pacing around the room, her voice dripping with condescension. "Is this some little fantasy your special friend Mr. Ferg... oh, sorry, no, *Allen*, has concocted for the two of you?"

"What are you even talking about?" She's completely unhinged now, lobbing any insults she can think of at me. "I'm sorry; am I not allowed to have a mentor? Is that just your thing? Because last I checked, you're not even speaking to yours."

"Mentor," she snorts. "Right. You keep telling yourself that's the sort of relationship you have with him."

"What other kind of relationship would I even have?!" I sputter, aghast. Of course she would ruin this, *of course.* She climbs up on her bed, and I hop up with her, inches from her face. Things are rising off the floor in her anger, and my portals are flashing at my fingers.

"You've got to be kidding me!" she screeches. "You honestly think he's just a good teacher who sees something in the nerdy girl in the shadows? *He's grooming you, Grier.* He fawns over you, tells you how special you are, tells you how you aren't like all those other students. He sees something in you that nobody else does, doesn't he?"

My stomach lurches and twist at the implication of her words. She's jealous. She has no idea what she's talking about.

"Tell me one thing. Why do you think you can be the Chosen One? Give me a real answer, not one that Allen has fed to you."

Damn her, she's so much better at fighting than me because she's so hollow inside, but I have honesty on my side, and I wield it unflinchingly.

"Because you don't want to do it anymore. And I do."

"That's not enough, Grier. This is my destiny."

"It doesn't have to be!"

She stares at me long and hard. "If I could give this to you, I would. If I didn't think it would kill you in a second, I would. But you are my sister, and I will not sign your death warrant."

"You have no idea what I can do. Because you aren't willing to see me as anything but your lower-tier sister."

But she's done listening to me as she leaps down from the bed and grabs her backpack. "This is the most insane conversation I've had in a long time, and I've had a few lately. I don't know what you are trying to prove here, but this is a low blow, Grier." She pauses. "I knew you struggled with the comparisons growing up. I can see now that I should have tried harder not to separate us. You're becoming unhinged."

She's right. I am unhinged. I feel like I'm going to kill her. "You know what? I tried to give you a little grace. You've been through some shit lately, and I get that. But now you're just desperate and mean. Now you're just jealous." The words are cruel, but I don't care.

"Jealous!" she shrieks. "Why the hell would I be jealous of you, Grier? You think I'm jealous that you have some creeper teacher trying to brainwash you into god knows what?"

I stare at her, willing myself to keep steady. "No. You're jealous because I have real things in my life. I have a boyfriend who doesn't care if I'm famous. I have a best friend who doesn't care, either. I have a mentor who sees my potential, who believes in me because of what I can do and not just because of some stupid prophecy written by a dude who died seconds later." My voice is calm, quiet. "You're jealous because I have all of those things, and for once, you have nothing."

Valora's eyes go dark and the color drains from her face. She flings one arm out, and one of the books on her bed flies into the air toward me. Without thinking, I throw my hand out toward it and it disappears into a portal next to my head, reappearing across the room and thuds heavily onto the floor at her feet.

"Now what?" I say coldly. "You want to break another glass on my face? Will that make you feel powerful, Valora? Make you feel strong?"

She stares at me, hard, and for a second I think she might just fling something else at me. "You don't have any idea what you've gotten yourself into, Grier." Her voice is eerily calm. She turns and storms out of the room, slamming the door so hard everything on the walls shudders. Outside, I hear the breaking of glass and wood as Valora shatters the posters of herself. I'm left alone, shaking and trying to catch my breath, my entire body charged. *She's wrong. She's wrong about everything.* I keep repeating it to myself. She has to be wrong. She has to be.

24

VALORA

GRIER THINKS SHE'S THE CHOSEN ONE. I SNORT AT THE INSANITY of it as I stalk down the hallway towards Mr. Ferguson's office. *Grier.* Grier the Chosen One. Grier, who burns her toast eighty percent of the time. Grier, who once broke her ankle walking on flat ground. Grier, who can't even stand up to *Cicely.* I try to imagine my sister fighting the Gallsoul that I faced in Mystic. If I remember correctly, she threw up immediately following our battle.

Not only is trying to imagine Grier as the Chosen One impossible, it's impractical. I repeat the facts as my sneakers hit the floor loudly. Fact: Grier's gift is not weaponized. Sure, she can move things from place to place, but how is that useful in dispatching a charging monster? At most, she could discombobulate, or portal herself a knife, which would be helpful, but how would she wound? How would she kill? I shake my head. She was talking utter nonsense.

The remnants of a deeply buried memory shakes free inside of me. *There is a knock at the door...my father is yelling... someone whispers something to me.*

I shake my head to rid myself of whatever it is. The fact is, if

Grier was the Chosen One-.I stop walking for just a second, swaying on my feet. *She would die. So quickly.* I calm myself and let out a long breath as I make my way down the wooden stairs. This is a dangerous idea, one that could spread like a cancer. I have to stop it at any cost. And I know exactly who gave her this disease. Students scatter as I pass; they can tell I'm on a mission and that anyone who gets in my way will have hell to pay.

I can't even consider the possibility. I can't. *I cannot watch my sister die.* I come to a hard stop in the hallway right in front of the floor-to-ceiling windows, where outside the trees are bursting with the new life of Spring. *I cannot watch my sister die. My God.* That's why Grier never watches my fights.

The understanding makes me pause, makes me reconsider. *Maybe I should go back and talk to her.* I want so much to talk to her – not fight, just talk - but I don't know how. I pause, weighing my choices, but Cicely appears at the end of the hallway surrounded by her new gang of female groupies.

"Hey!" she shouts at me. *Shit.* I turn away. This isn't going to be good. I spin around and continue on my path to Mr. Ferguson's office, ignoring her voice calling down the hallway.

He's in the south wing of the school, where all the hard sciences are. The lights are off in the hallway when I make my way down it; classes are over for the day and most of the students are soaking up the sunlight in the atrium. His office door is open and I glance inside. It's empty. I step back; at the end of the hallway, a single light flickers in the physics classroom. I stalk down there, anger streaming from every pore. Grier's words continue to play in my mind as I dramatically fling open the door with my powers. When I step inside, Mr. Ferguson is sitting at a long lab table, writing some notes in a spiral notebook. He's immaculately dressed as always: signature bowtie, cool blue sweater, yellow gingham shirt, jeans that are too tight for any teacher to be wearing.

He looks up with a start when the door almost flies off its

hinges. "Hello, Valora. That was quite an entrance. What can I do for you?" He turns back to his notes, apathetic to me as always. This should have been my first clue that something was off: teachers are always interested in me. The fact that he focused in on Grier so intensely speaks of something else. I slam the door shut behind me, this time using my actual hand.

"I need to talk to you," I say forcefully.

"Sure. Have a seat." He is still nonplussed. This is part of his act, I'm sure.

"No, I'll stand."

"Alright. What can I help you with? Are you wanting to catch up in my class? We've missed you as of late. But you know...'training.'" He puts it in air quotes. I want to strangle him. I think I might.

"I'm here to talk about Grier."

With a sigh, he slowly puts down his pencil. When his eyes meet mine, I see a slight hint of panic. He tilts his head. "And what about Grier?"

"I know." I narrow my eyes and step toward the table. "I know what you want from her."

"And what is that, you think?"

"Don't make me say it."

He stands up too quickly and the stool falls to the floor behind him. "No, I'm interested in what you have to say."

I raise my chin. "Fine." I close my eyes for a second, putting together all the information I have. It's so clear now; how did I not see it earlier? I open them and stare right as his deceptively handsome face. He's a trap; a human trap for girls like my sister. I clear my throat. "I know that you're *grooming* Grier. You ask her to stay after class, spend time with her after school hours, often at night. Tell her that no one sees her potential, and then you exploit that."

"Is that right?"

I don't move. "You probably had been looking for someone like Grier – an insecure student that needed a positive male role model in her life, thanks to my failure of a father – and secured her trust, slowly over time. You have built her a private castle with secrets and compliments and lent books - a place where no one can find her but you. But I'm here to stop you. I'm here to tear your castle down."

He watches me with careful eyes as I come around the lab table. "Perhaps Grier is grateful because she feels like someone finally sees her for the person she is."

A person that I've never been able to see, I silently chide myself. I should have tried harder, but this isn't my fault.

He lifts an eyebrow. "And do you think that Grier is unworthy of this extra attention? Do you yourself, the great Valora Rigmore, believe that she is someone special? Or do you believe that she is exactly who she appears to be on the outside: frumpy, shy, unworthy Grier? By the way I've seen you treat her, I would say no. You couldn't even let your sister have a chair at the front of the room. Not. One. Little. Thing."

I feel like this is a distraction, but I look inside myself anyway, and face the shame waiting there. "No," I say finally. "I don't always see her as I should. Grier and I have always had trouble connecting with each other and I'm not sure why. And yes, living in the Valora bubble doesn't let me see others as much as I should." Tears gather in my eyes. "And I have to live with that guilt. I know that she is much more than she seems on the outside, but *you're not the one to bring her out of her shell.* You're her teacher, not her boyfriend. And for you to convince her that she's the Chosen One is not just cruelty. You've manipulated her greatest insecurities into a dangerous fantasy. It's unforgivable." From the curl of his lip at the word "boyfriend," I know that I'm spot on.

I step menacingly toward him.. He can feel the power

curling out through my palms and I see him swallow nervously. "I don't know where you thought this was going to go, and I'm willing to give you the benefit of the doubt that it hasn't happened yet, but I'm telling you now: stay away from my sister." I step closer to him and with a sudden curl of my finger, I wind the bowtie around his neck into a tight knot. His smug veneer vanishes as he clutches at it with a panicked look. I watch as his panic escalates. He's scared, but he can still breathe. "Don't worry. I'm not a monster," I whisper as I step towards him.

"What are you going to do?" he gasps, his face turning red with fear, working to get his finger under the bowtie.

"I'm not going to kill you, if that's what you are wondering," I say calmly, releasing the bowtie. "But I am going to tell you to stay the hell away from my sister. See her in class and that's it. Let her have her goofy happiness with Leo. And if you don't...."

I step back from him as he collapses to his knees, pulling his tie off with a panicked breath. "I'm going to go to the board of Proctor Moor and tell them that you've been pursuing me the entire year, trying to convince me to have a relationship with you. It will be my word against yours." I lean over him, my voice dropping. "And guess who they are going to believe? The teacher with the too-tight jeans, or the girl who makes sure their salaries get paid? It will be the scandal of the decade. I can weather it...but will you?"

I turn away from him and begin to walk out of the classroom when he stands up behind me. "You're wrong, you know."

I turn back, exasperated. "About what?"

"About Grier, and about me." He smooths out his shirt and adjusts his collar. "I've never liked you, Valora. You're insufferably vain without reason. I always thought you were weak and vapid, until that day in the hallway with Julian, when I saw you use actual power and restraint. And now, this whole thing, defending your sister's honor...I'm impressed. Color me wrong."

"Defending her from perverts is my job," I finish, and his face goes rigid.

"I'm not a pervert any more than you're a hero," he snaps.

Something here feels dangerous, and I step toward the door. "Stay away from her."

"I don't think so."

I hear his voice over my shoulder, closer than it was before. Forget my offer: I'm going straight to Renata and then right to the Board.

I grab the door handle to leave and it feels like I have grabbed onto the sun. White bolts of electricity shoot from the doorknob up through my palm and I fall to the floor as my body seems to be cooked from the inside out. I see the crackling lines of electricity lace over my body from every angle and I feel like I am on fire and then, even worse, like *I am the fire.* The last thing I see before I lose consciousness is Allen Ferguson leaning over me. His eyes have gone black, and inside of them I see what looks like bolts of lightning. "I'm a monster." He hisses. "Just not the kind you think."

When I wake up, I'm in a place that I don't recognize; overhead are damp stone walls, slick with condensation. The floor is dirt. My head is pounding, a violent headache that bounces from the back of my skull to between my eyes, crippling and raw. There is a gag in my mouth and duct tape around my feet. My hands are behind me in handcuffs that cut into my wrists. I try to flex them but my fingers are stuck together with duct tape. I can't move my fingers, or my palms. He must have known that I couldn't call forth my power without having my hands in front of me. *Just like Everett.* I struggle back and forth, moaning against the gag.

"It's not going to help." Mr. Ferguson is standing in front of me. He walks swiftly back and forth, packing things into bags, organizing papers. My heart beats fast as I fully wake up. I try to scream.

"Okay, here are the rules. If you scream, the gag goes back. If you talk too much, the gag goes back." He leans over me, and I see black markings, almost like soot, curling down from his eyelids. "And if you call me a pervert again, I will burn your lips off."

Slowly, he reaches down and pulls the gag out of my mouth. Then, as a warning, he lets his fingers spark on the side of my face, singeing my hair. I watch with wide eyes as currents of electricity travel back and forth between them. The dim lighting over our heads flickers. Understanding dawns on me as I try to find enough moisture in my mouth to speak.

"The outages," I rasp. "That was you."

He nods. "Obviously. How you and your sister never put it together is beyond me, but then again you were both so worried about your own two lives that you never looked around, never saw the big picture." He stands up and touches his finger to a small desk lamp. It glows bright. I watch him with fascination. Besides Renata, I've never seen another energy gift like this, and nothing half as powerful. He drums his fingers on an old desk in the corner and little sparks shoot out.

"Who are you? What are you?" I whisper.

"I'm an Exceptional, just like you. Unlike you, I have two gifts. Memory, and this." He snaps his finger and I watch currents of electricity dance over his fingertips. Exceptionals with two gifts were rare, but not unheard of, but in every documented case, the second gifts had been even more useless than the first. Nothing like this. "I was born and raised all over the place. My father was in the Army. I've lived in France, in Africa, and finally here in Connecticut." He pauses. "The foliage is really something in Fall, isn't it?" He lets out a long breath. "Stunning, really. "

"What do you want? Why are you doing this?"

"Hmmm...such simple questions with such complex answers. *What do you want?* Well, I want what Erys wants. I was languishing here, teaching physics, never forgetting a word I read, and able to cause minor static electricity if I rubbed my hands together." He tips his head back and lets out an evil laugh. Then he looks back at me with a wry smile. "Sorry, I always wanted to do that. Can you imagine, though? What an utterly useless gift, if you can even call it that. I was wasting my life here, droning on about equations in front of students who cared as little as I did. I wanted something bigger. Needed something bigger.

"Two years ago, she came to me while I was vacationing in the Florida Keys. Beautiful and ruthless, Erys came to me in the night like a dream, offering me everything I'd been longing for. The thing I had been missing in my life: a targeted run of glorious purpose. A chance to be a part of something bigger than myself. To be part of the revolution."

He strides across the room, sending crackles of electricity shooting from his fingertips. "Of course, she took great risk. It could've backfired spectacularly. I could have run, gone to the authorities. But I didn't, and she has made good on her promises to me. Incredible how all it takes sometimes is just one person to believe in you. How transformative that can be, how much stronger and more powerful your gifts can become. Your sister knows," he sneers.

"What does she want?!" I cry.

" Actually, what Erys wants is simple: the revenge that she was denied. Imagine that you spent your whole life dreaming of revenge against your privileged, famous brother and then you finally kill him. But just when the spotlight is finally on you, it shifts to someone else: a baby, born under a prophecy, that you can't get to, no matter how hard you try." He shakes his head. "Sheep, all of them, worshipping you, a girl they don't know. A girl who, as far as I can see, has just gotten lucky again and again. See, once Erys has killed TWO Chosen Ones – you and Everett - the world will finally learn: There are no Chosen Ones. Only monsters. That's who should be revered. That's who should have the power, the fame."

I choke back a laugh. "So Erys wants some paparazzi? Her picture in magazines? That's it? She can have it."

He looks at me, the dim light glinting off his high forehead. "People have killed for much sillier things. People assume that if you have fame, then somehow you are deserving of power. Do something that gets people to notice you and then you can take them in, one lying word at a time. Being famous is the same as being qualified in this world – look at some of our leaders. Besides, who's going to stand against an army of monsters? Who will rebel against a leader who can send a poisonous snake into your child's nursery? Who can command a Tsunami Wraith to tear naval fleets apart? The world will bow to her, and quickly. But she needed a public display of power to cement that fear. She wants a good show, and so she had to wait until you were ready to fully demon-strate her strength. Killing a child is easy. She needed you to be strong."

I shake my head, straining to get my fingers free. He clicks his tongue at me. "It's not going to work. I know you can't use your gift if your hands are behind you. What a revelation! Grier and I have talked about your gifts many times."

Dammit, Grier.

He kneels beside me and leans toward my ear before brushing my cheek with his finger. I flinch. "Lovely Valora, you're just as stunning up close as you are on the television. You're much more my taste than Grier." Then he pulls back his hand and slaps me hard. The slap has a spark of electricity in it and my legs thrash beneath me. "But inside, you're as dead as Erys is." He stands back up and stretches.

"I'm very annoyed at the timing of your interruption. Honestly, I figured I still had weeks to plan, but I'm the kind of person who considers every outcome, including the one that I would have to put my plan in motion early due to some unforeseen circumstance. And that has come to fruition by your utter nosiness." He rubs his hands together. "But while I'm waiting, I think I may grade some papers. This school may not be standing for much longer, but that doesn't mean I can't fulfill my educator duties." He sits at a desk and pulls out a file.

I watch him incredulously. "Why do you think Grier is the Chosen One? Why would that matter?" I blurt out.

He sighs and leans forward on the chair. "Well, one because you aren't strong enough, but don't worry. Erys is going to skin you alive. When I talk about Grier as the Chosen One, I'm not talking about the same Chosen One you are. *You* believe you are Chosen to defeat Erys, but really it just means you are scheduled to die in spectacular, public fashion. *I* believe that Grier is Chosen to help bring Erys to power. That's what makes her the Chosen One. *It makes her the most important person in the world.*"

"You're delusional," I snap and he stands quickly, shutting his binder.

"I can see that working down here isn't going to happen, so I might as well get what else I need. I'll be back in a bit. Don't move...not that you can." He reaches out and touches a black metal pillar attached to the ground. I didn't notice them before, but now it's impossible to not see them: they are everywhere, dark pillars at different points around the room that blend in with the dark walls. "You'll stay here, or you'll die." Electricity shoots out from his fingertips as a purple blue light cracking with power lights up one of the pillars and then another. Soon, it's a web of live electricity, and I'm trapped in its center. If I stand, my head will be in the middle of pulsing currents. "If you touch one of these, you'll get a good strong kick of voltage, similar to a police taser. If you try to go through them, the currents will run through your body, burning your organs."

When I hear his words, I see my Nan, lying on a morgue table, her body cold. It is as if the floor has fallen away from me.

"My Nan." I raise my eyes to meet his. "You killed her."

"Oh, absolutely. Shattered you, didn't it? She went fast, poor old heart. She was calling your name, by the way. Yours and your sister's." He cackles. "How delightfully macabre it was, watching her crawl through the house you played in as a child, passing pictures of the Chosen One as her body shriveled under my power."

Bile rises in my throat. "You won't..."

He turns to me, exasperated. "Please don't say I won't get away with it, because I'm going to. This isn't a movie. I have thought over every outcome and there is no way that you and your sister don't die here. The game is over, Valora, and you never even got a chance to play. Now, I'm going to need you to be quiet." He flexes his fingers and a shot of electricity crackles out and stops about an inch from my face. "Don't move." He picks up a landline telephone and pushes a few buttons. His voice changes the second someone else picks up.

"Hey! Leo, it's Mr. Ferguson. I'm good, sir, how about you? Mmm-hmm. Hey, I don't mean to cut you off, but I'm kind of worried about Grier. Yeah. Grier. Have you seen her? You haven't. Okay, shoot. Well, um, I know she's not in her room; I just talked to Valora." He winks at me and my hands burn with rage at the frustration of being trapped and unable to rip this man in two. "I'm working on something in the lower level, near the Mat – could you meet me and we can figure out what's going on? I have some concerns about her. Okay, see you in three minutes." He hangs up the phone. "Well, that was disappointingly easy."

I look up at him through the sparking lines of electricity that separate us. "I'm going to kill you.," I spit.

He salutes me. "Your bravery is noted. I'll be back. Remember, don't move, unless you want to end up barbecued like dear old Gran."

"Nan," I hiss, holding back tears. "Her name was Nan."

He pauses for a second. "Nan. Okay. Semantics matter." He walks through the shifting lines of electricity as if they weren't there and shoves the gag back into my mouth. Then he slams the metal door shut behind him.

I let out a cry, pulling my knees up to my chest. All around me, lines of electricity are cracking and jumping from pillar to pillar as the electrons flow through the circuits. It's palpably hot, and I feel sweat drip down my chest. I can't move, can't flex my hands in any direction. I wish for the zillionth time that I could just use my mind to move things, but it doesn't work; it never does. I turn carefully on my side and lay my head on the floor. What do I do? *What do I do?*

A few minutes later the door slams open and Ferguson comes in, dragging a barely conscious Leo behind him. He waves his hand and the sparking lines of currents cease momentarily as he tosses Leo in beside me. Then he pulls both hands downwards and it leaps back to life.

He lets out a long sigh. "I really thought that today would be relaxing. It is what it is, I guess." I narrow my eyes. He takes out a pocket watch, glances at it and tucks it back into his pocket, and then walks over to a small wooden cage in the corner. My skin crawls as two glowing blue eyes appear in the darkness. "Tell Erys to get ready, at the place where the two waters meet," he whispers to the creature before opening the cage. I watch as the small monster flutters out; it's a cross between a tarantula and a wasp, with long legs that drift lazily beneath fluttering wings.

"Baulays," groans Leo next to me, one arm crossed protectively over his head. His hand is still trembling. "From the darkest parts of Louisiana." The creature gazes at us for a second and then flutters up and out of a crack in the stone wall. Leo and I both freeze as Mr. Ferguson turns towards us.

"Well, what do you think?" he asks, staring down at us with calculating eyes. "Shall we have your sister join us?"

25

GRIER

VALORA HAS NO IDEA WHAT SHE'S TALKING ABOUT. NONE. I'M fuming as I shove my way through the atrium. The hall is crowded with students making plans, studying, chatting about whatever trivial things normal students get to worry about. *Not monsters. Not prophecies and portals.* I ignore the curious glances as I push past blindly. Does Valora really think I want to be the Chosen One just for the adoring fans?It's not about that. It's about defeating Erys and who can do it. If anything, she should be grateful I'm offering her an out.

Anger curls my lips as I make my way to the study pods in the atrium, half at ground level, half suspended from the ceiling, swaying gently several yards above the floor. The furthest suspended pod is empty, tucked in a corner where curving wall of windows meets the balconies above. I yank on the heavy rope pulley, lowering the clear, teardrop-shaped pod to ground level so I can climb in.

I fall back against the nest of cushions in the pod and stare out the wall of windows. Outside, the sky is iron-gray. The Connecticut countryside is bleak, the hills covered in bare-limbed trees reaching their black branches toward the sky. I press my palms against my eyes and fight back the tears beginning to prick at the corners. For a minute there, I was actually starting to believe that Valora and I might be getting along. I thought our grandmother's death, awful as it was, may have actually brought us together. Like real sisters. Like Nan always wanted us to be. Nan. I choke back a sob, overwhelmed by sadness. Nan never made me feel like the lesser twin, like an afterthought. She never treated Valora and me differently, Chosen One or not.

My anger begins to bubble to the surface again, suffocating the grief. I knew Valora would be angry about the prophecy. But to blame Allen...to act like the only reason a teacher would see anything in me is if he were interested in...something else. Of course she'd think he was a jerk; he didn't blindly worship her like everyone else.

I take a deep breath and exhale shakily, and work to convince myself that this is all okay. Besides, if Allen were some sort of creep, why would he go to all this work to train me? Why would he go to all the trouble to teach me how to use my gift, if he just wanted to... I shudder. *No*. Allen is my mentor. My confidant. He's the one who knows who I am, who'd suspected what the prophecy really meant all along. He's the one who helped me see there was more to my gift than fun party tricks.

My gift. My powerful, useful, but ultimately non-weaponized. I can't destroy anything.

My face is burning, hands tingling, and I'm furious. *If Valora was right...* My stomach churns and I fight back a wave of nausea. If it was true, then I had walked right into one of the biggest clichés around: creepy midlife-crisis of a teacher preys on young student, and I let it happen because I was desperate to believe there was actually something special about me.

A deep, aggressive wave of shame rolls over me. *I should*

have known better. I gently flex my fingers out in front of my face and watch as tiny, shimmering blue whorls spark at my fingertips.

It wasn't all for nothing, at least, I think, willing the whorls to grow and shrink. Even if Allen's motives were predatory, I couldn't deny that the things I'd worked toward, or the way my gift had grown and changed. I couldn't deny that there was still a compelling argument for me being the Chosen One. Did Allen know this all along? What else could he have wanted?

"Proximity to power...everybody wants a little of that cast-off glow." I speak the words that Valora had once snapped at me when an underclassman tried to be her friend.

I need to talk to Valora. We will make it work because we have to. I'm not willing to give up on us just yet. I reach for the rope pulley to lower the pod to the floor. Just as I'm swinging my legs out, and my feet hit the ground, I hear his voice. "Grier, there you are!"

Allen. A shockwave goes through my body. *You can do this. Just make an excuse.* I turn to face him, glancing around the atrium and noticing it's completely empty, aside from the two of us, and try to keep my tone light.

"Oh, hey! Um, you startled me a little," I offer as an excuse for my shaky voice.

He smiles and says nothing, but I can see that he's examining me closely. "Grier, I was wondering if we might have a little chat?"

"I have to go meet Agnes. I told her I'd meet her, and she's waiting for me." My words are rushed.

"Ah. Sure, sure, but this will just take a few minutes." He reaches toward me to put a hand on my shoulder, and I flinch involuntarily, jumping back. He looks at me curiously, but his face betrays nothing. I realize I find him imposing. He isn't remarkably tall or bulky, but he's intimidating. "Well, I'd better say this quick then. You see, Grier, I've been thinking about our training sessions, and I honestly have been thinking it would be a good idea to have another teacher sit in with us." He lets this hang in the air between us for a moment, watching my face closely. My mind whirls.

"I know it might sound silly," he laughs gently, running his fingers through his hair, "and I hope I don't embarrass you by bringing this up, because of course it's completely ridiculous in our case, but you know how salacious gossip mills can be. There are, how do I put this...well, there are some real creeps out there. I believe we have a fantastic teacher-student relationship, and you and I both know that's what it is." He places his hand on my shoulder again, briefly, and I look up at him. "But I do think, just to make sure small-minded gossips don't get the wrong idea, particularly because what we're doing is of such importance, that we should include another teacher in our training sessions. Do you agree?"

I stare at the floor and nod almost imperceptibly. Has he been reading my mind? Or, worse, was there already gossip about this? Maybe Valora was spreading rumors...*no*, she wouldn't.

"I've spoken to Renata Flores, and she's agreed to sit in with us. I think that's a discussion the three of us can have together. I know you need to meet Agnes, but perhaps we could stop by Renata's office first?"

I'm silent, considering. Agnes isn't actually waiting for me, but he doesn't know that. I don't know what to believe at this point. What does he really want? Are these doubts just because, after all this, my own self-doubt is still drowning me?

"Grier?" He's waiting for me to say something.

"Why are we doing this?" I begin slowly.

"What do you mean?" He seems genuinely confused.

"Why me? I can't destroy Erys. Not really. I can move her, but I can't..." I take a deep breath.

"Grier," he smiles kindly. "We've been over this. You need to believe..."

I cut him off. "What do you really want from me? Valora said..." I shake my head, unable to get the words out. "I just need to know. What do you really want from me, Allen?"

He's not smiling now. His mouth is set in a hard line, and his eyes bore into me, and I notice with alarm that they've gone black. He steps closer, closing the gap between us, and grips me by the upper arm with a strength that makes me yelp in pain.

"Alright, Grier. I've tried to do this nicely, but clearly that isn't going to work out." His voice is a low hiss. "Dammit, now be the pliant girl I know and come with me." I pull back in an attempt to free myself, but his grip is too strong. The atrium is still empty, no students or staff passing by to come to my aid if I were to struggle.

"If you scream, I will kill you. Do you understand?" he explains matter-of-factly. When I look up, his eyes are flashing with lightning. I stare at him in disbelief, then nod. He yanks me out of the atrium and pulls me into a darkened hallway.

"You're absolutely right. Your gift is essentially useless," he spits. "But you noticed too late." He jerks me close and pulls a small cellphone-sized device from his pocket and the screen flickers to life. He hands it to me, and my heart drops. There, on a video monitor, are my sister and Leo, hands bound. They're surrounded by a sharp, glowing net of white currents.

"Electricity," Allen tells me, pride in his voice. "They aren't going anywhere, and neither are you. Now. I'm going to need you to comply with everything I'm about to ask of you, or here's what will happen: I will kill your sister. Then I will kill your boyfriend. I will even kill Agnes, just for good measure. Then I will kill you. I could kill you instantly, should I have the inclination, so don't think I'm not serious. In a second, just like I killed your grandmother. Do I make myself clear?" His voice is still bright, cheerful, but his eyes are black and soulless.

Trembling, I nod. *Oh, god. Nan. Valora. Leo. Agnes. I'm so sorry.*

"Good. Follow me. And save your energy. You're going to need it."

26

VALORA

It figures that Mr. Ferguson would forget to gag Leo. "What does he want with Grier? Where is she? Is he going to hurt her?" His frantic questions are making it hard for me to think as well as increasing my panic level.

Above our heads the electricity net sparks and fizzles a bright white as a shower of sparks passes overhead. The hairs on my arm are still standing up. I shrug at him.. I have no power here, and the way he is expecting me to save us is making my heart break. *I can't do it.* The only thing I know is that we may die here.

"Where did Allen take her?" Leo is next to me now, his brown eyes looking into mine with desperation.

"Mmmmm," I mumble through my gag.

Leo's hands are shackled behind him as well, his feet duct taped together like mine. He motions to me with his eyes and then scoots closer, getting to his knees in front of me. He leans forward so that his cheek is close to mine and I jerk back in a panic.

"It's okay," he breathed "Trust me." Then his eyelashes brush my cheek and his lips are on the side of my face, and I violently shake my head back and forth. *No, no!* This already destroyed my relationship with Grier once; I won't let it happen again. I jerk away from him a second time and Leo rolls his eyes as he sits back. "Sit still!" he snaps.

I stare at him for a long moment and then lean forward, pressing my face against his. I feel his lips on my cheek, and then, using his teeth, he rips the gag down and out of my mouth. I let out a sigh of relief. "I'm sorry, I thought you were...."

Leo shakes his head. "I know what you thought and I in return have two thoughts about that: One, I'm not attracted to you in the least."

"Same," I mutter, relishing not having a disgusting piece of fabric shoved in mouth. I stretch my jaw, working out the soreness.

"And two: WHAT IN THE ACTUAL HELL IS HAPPEN-ING?" Leo explodes. "Mr. Ferguson told me that he was worried about Grier and wanted me to look for her with him. The next thing I knew my skin was on fire and then he was dragging me down a dark hallway. I think I passed out."

I look above us at the currents leaping back and forth. "Probably. I did." I ponder my next words, because saying them aloud makes them true.

"Mr. Ferguson works for Erys," I finally utter.

Leo's eyes widen. "What?"

I nod my head, trying in vain to pull my hands out of my restraints. My hands are too big; they don't budge. "He's been trying to convince Grier that she is the Chosen One, but not in the way she assumes. He's also apparently a doubly-gifted Exceptional who can also control electric currents – that's what happened to you: he electrocuted you."

Leo's face goes pale. "He's been working with Grier all semester to build her powers," he says slowly.

"But why? That's what I can't understand. I thought he was

using her to get to me, but then he had me and didn't seem to care. Grier's going to bring Erys to power, but how?" I shake my head. "What would he want with Grier? Does he need her to move weapons?" Leo's eyes glint in the sparking light and I see it; he's hiding something. "What is it? Tell me."

"I know what he wants." Leo says slowly, his brow wrinkling in understanding.

I sit forward. "Tell me now."

"Grier can move living things," he says carefully.

I give him a withering look. "Your comic timing is terrible."

"I'm not joking, Valora."

"When? I've never seen her do that, and I live with her. The biggest thing I've ever seen her move is that desk at the showcase. What, can she move like a bug or something?"

Leo's face is incensed when he turns back to me. "I think it's safe to say you know less about your sister than any person in this school. She moved a person at the Green Hills Showcase during the attack!"

I laugh a little; it escapes from my throat like a shard of glass. "What?"

"Yeah. A little girl, right before a Mantharas grabbed her. It took so much out of her that she fainted afterward. Since then, she has moved chickens and squirrels...and your cat."

"Mimi?" I squeak. *How could I not know this about my own sister?* But if it's true that she can portal living things, people... The realization punches through me. I sink to the ground and curl around my knees,. Oh God. Oh no. "If she can move people...." I close my eyes. "Then she can portal Erys directly into the school."

With Grier's help, Erys could avoid the outer grounds, moving right past Everett's defenses. She's coming for me...and everyone else." I hear the roar of blood in my ears. *It's all going to end tonight. This is it.*

"Arggghh!" As I react in shock, Leo has become unhinged

trying desperately to wrestle his hands out of his handcuffs to no avail. "What can we do? Maybe I could try just sprinting through the current. Maybe it won't be any worse than before."

I shake my head. "That was barely anything, a low current. At this level, we'll die if we do that. Just like my Nan."

"He killed your Nan." It's a statement. Leo sighs. "Yeah, of course he did. That makes sense; Grier told me about the autopsy. I never wanted to upset Grier so I never said anything, but I did think it was weird they were spending so much time together."

I lean forward, pulling at the handcuffs. "I thought he was trying to have an inappropriate relationship with Grier."

He grits his teeth. "I'm going to kill him."

"You and me both." *I might actually kill him,* I think silently. "How can we get out of here?" I ask Allen is smart; the room is completely bare besides the conduits and an empty desk. There are no tools that could aid us, and even if there were, we couldn't get to them. I tug for the thousandth time at my handcuffs, but they aren't going anywhere. Nothing moves when I try to push from my mind alone. *I should have trained more with Renata. I should have read more books on telekinesis. I should have....*

Leo watches me with interest for a second, and then his face lights up. "My mom almost lost her wedding ring in the cold once!" he shouts.

I give him the most annoyed look I can muster. "I'm not sure why that matters right now."

He spins on his knees to face me. "Do you know what my Exceptional gift is?"

"No?" I shrug my shoulders, feeling guilty. I should have asked Grier about this at some point. Maybe this is why she hates me. Leo smiles, and I want to slap him. Why is he smiling right now?

He answers my unasked question. "Temperature change. A few winters ago, we went skiing, and my mom almost lost her wedding ring. Slipped right off her finger, even though it fit just fine at home in L.A. Sometimes, when it gets really hot there, her fingers even swell, but in the cold…" He pauses.

"They shrink!" My answer is tinted with hope.

He smiles. "I can drop the temperature in this room, and maybe if I drop it enough…"

"I can pull my wrists out. Even if you can just get it really slick, I might be able to pull it through!" I finish. I turn so that my handcuffs are closer to him. Leo lets out a long breath. "If you can get my hands free, Leo, we won't need to worry about yours at all."

"Okay." Leo sits up on his knees, closing his eyes to concentrate. He looks like he's praying. "I've never done it this fast, but…here it goes." As I watch him, I begin to feel the temperature dropping rapidly. It goes from balmy and hot beneath the sparking lines of electricity to pleasantly warm, and then a few moments later, to the edge of cold. My skin tightens as a cold front seems to rise from within him and sweeps past me, encircling our space, growing a degree colder each few seconds.

Colder and colder still, like going deeper into a cave. Leo's lips are turning the color of a ripe plum, and my own teeth start chattering as the temperature plummets. After a few minutes, the electricity starts acting weird as well; and I remember something vaguely about conductivity decreasing when temperature does. *I really should pay attention in class.* The room gets colder still, and I can feel the freezing brush of metal against my wrist.

"Now," Leo pleads, as the temperature continues to plummet. He falls forward with a cry. It's hurting him; he is gritting his teeth, and his spine is shaking violently. I want to stop him from going too far, but I won't. Not when my sister's life is at stake. Not when the life of everyone at this school is at stake. *I will let him freeze if that means saving her.* I pull against the sharp metal of the handcuffs, turning my wrist left and right against the metal, attempting to slide them through.

"More!" I order Leo, and he gives a shudder, but it becomes colder still. As the temperature drops, I can see my breath, and in the corner of the room, ice is crusting over the side of the door. My skin feels like ice. I pull and twist at the handcuffs and it feels like my hands are being ripped from my body. I feel warm blood drip down my hand. Leo is lying on his side, convulsing. His lips are blue. *Shit.* A whimper escapes my lips and I strain against the restraints. *Come on, Valora. Come on.* I hear Renata's voice in my head, pushing me, further and further.

I let out a scream, and it feels like my wrist is breaking, but it's sliding and the metal is up to mid-hand and then....my hand slides free. I whip around to send a wave of power over him, blowing the cold air beyond his body. "Leo!" I bend over him and shake his shoulders. "Leo! Stop!"

After a second, the intense cold lessens and he gives me an exhausted smile. I watch gratefully as the color returns to his face. "You're free," he says, through blue lips.

"We are getting out of here. Come on."

I rip the duct tape off my feet and then use the power in my palms to pull apart Leo's handcuffs, and the one dangling from my wrist. They fall to the floor with a clink. Leo kneels beside me, blowing on his freezing hands.

The electricity overhead continues to surround us in a complex web that keeps us low to the ground. "Can you move them? The currents?" he asks

I focus on pushing the electrical currents outward with my palms, but nothing happens except for a few spare sparks landing on the floor in front of us. "I don't think so. The molecules are different; I can't grab or move them."

"Be careful; push too hard and you could draw them to yourself. Let's not have that happen."

One of the black pillars catches my eye. "I bet I can move one of those, but what if I change the map of the current and it hits us?"

Leo sits forward. "You're not going to. Give me a second." He thinks for a moment, resting his fingers against his lips. "Okay. Let's hope all my geometry lessons weren't for nothing." Slowly but steadily, at Leo's careful direction, I move the conduits, inches at a time. "That one a few inches to the right. And this one, bring it up towards us about three feet. Then behind us, push that one sideways." It's intensive, meticulous work to move the heavy pillars dancing with electricity, but our patience pays off when I move the last pillar to the right of the door: all of a sudden, a shape takes place, and lines of dancing sparks now make a straight line towards the door.

"Yes!" We high-five even though it hurts my palm and sprint for the door, which is locked from the outside. I raise my hand to blast it off its hinges, but Leo stops me. "I have a feeling you are going to need to save your power for later." He's not wrong, so I watch as he batters his body against the door. We explode into an abandoned hallway, somewhere underneath the basement of Proctor Moor.

"Where are we?" Leo breathes.

I pause for a moment and lift my nose. I know this smell, this sweaty aroma of teenage lust. "We're near the Mat," I answer.

We run down the dark hallway toward a double door that leads us to a stairway. At the top of the stairs, the doors open into the weight room.

"I had no idea this was here," Leo whispers. "But then again, it's not like the gym is a place I enjoy visiting."

"You don't take her to the Mat?" We are weaving our way through the dusky gym now, moving as fast as we can.

"Why would anyone take anyone EVER to the Mat? It's

disgusting. Also, I would never take Grier there because I actually like her."

I pause, searching for the right words. "I'm glad you do. I'm guilty of not seeing the best in my sister, but I can tell that you do."

Leo smiles. "Thanks. And Grier loves you, even if she doesn't know how to show it. I think having a sister who's always about to die has made her numb."

Grier loves you. I didn't know how badly I needed to hear those words until now. I wipe my eyes and pray that my sister is okay, wherever she is. We have so much to tell each other.

Leo and I explode out of the stairwell into the hallways at Proctor Moor. "Okay, what now?" he asks.

I don't even look back at him. "We can do more good if we split up. Go find Renata and tell her to sound the alarm. All the students need to be aware, all the staff. If Erys is coming, it can't be a surprise." I turn to go, but he grabs my hand.

"Please," he says with a deep fear in his eyes. "Please don't let Grier die."

"I won't." A brief, heavy silence follows as we both consider that I can't promise it.

"Where are you going?" he asks.

I look him square in the face. "I need to suit up."

He cracks a small grin. "Valora, that's the most badass thing you've ever said."

27

GRIER

ALLEN'S IRON GRIP ON MY ARM REMAINS AS HE LEADS ME TOWARD the side entrance to the Proctor Moor gardens.

"Keep up, Grier. We aren't out for a stroll," he snaps.

I wince in pain as his grip tightens. As we reach the doors, one opens, and two younger students whose faces I vaguely recognize enter with baskets of produce from the winter greenhouse. Upon seeing us, they smile. "Hey, Grier!" one of them, a willowy girl with braces and a sandy blonde ponytail, greets me. "Hey, Mr. Ferguson." She smiles at me, and I try desperately to will her to move on, and quickly.

"Hi, ladies!" Allen's voice is jovial, his hand still clamped onto my arm. He extends a hand toward the ponytail girl, patting her on the shoulder, then letting his hand linger. I watch in horror as she jolts, her eyes rolling back into her head as the basket of broccoli and winter squash tumbles to the floor. She drops like a dead weight as her friend recoils and drops her own basket. Before she can scream, and without breaking his grip on me, Allen lunges for her and catches her by the wrist. It's over in a heartbeat, and she crumples to the ground in a heap. Allen yanks me around the bodies and scattered vegetables and pulls me out the door.

I look back; thankfully they are breathing. "Why? Why did you do that? You monster!" I finally manage to scream at him, my voice full of rage.

"Grier, please. Stop it. I don't have time for your hysterics. They were in the way. I couldn't always do that, you know. Concentrate the electric shock to just one hand." He's conversational, his tone terrifyingly nonchalant. "It was my second gift. Useless. Static electricity at best. But then Erys found me. She helped me realize there was far more to my gifts than I ever could have imagined.. I'm powerful. Like you." He chuckles. "Look at the things we've accomplished, Grier! And here we are, on the cusp of something really spectacular."

The temperature outside is crisp and my cheeks sting as Allen pulls me over the stone bridge spanning Proctor Moor's moat, the wind whipping through my thin sweater. We pass the statue of Everett Proctor, lines of electricity sparking behind us with each step Allen takes.

"Where are you taking me?" I demand, my strong tone unmatched with the terrified beating of my heart.

"Outlook Point. Ever been there? Stellar leaf-peeping spot, I'm told. Keep up, Grier."

I have been there, once. Outlook Point stands just inside of Proctor Moor's property line. Once used as a fire lookout tower, its legs hold it high above the treeline, affording incredible views of Proctor Moor's entire sprawling grounds. In the fall, school donors are treated to elegant banquets in the renovated tower, sipping local wine and dining on local delicacies while admiring the autumnal colors from above. Our school is ridiculous, I think, but I want to stay here. I want to live to hate it another day and then another. It's imperfect, but it's home.

I look up at Allen, at the hard face that I barely recognize as

I stumble over a rock. "You really lack any of the physical grace your sister has, don't you?" he sneers.

Valora. My sister. I can't stop myself from recalling our last conversation, our fight. If she dies, if I die, one of the last things I said to her was, "You have nothing." Tears are streaming down my face, cold and wet. *She has to know that isn't true. Please let her know that isn't true.*

As we reach the treeline a hundred or so yards from the property line, a tall, bulky man clad in black and camouflage steps out toward us. He's easily half a foot taller than Allen and is far more muscular. He's armed, a rifle on his back and a handgun at his hip, and he holds out an enormous hand to stop us. "Mr. Ferguson, I'm afraid I can't let you go into these woods." His voice is firm, grave, and leaves no question that he means what he says. He's speaking to Allen, but looking at me, eyeing my tear-stained face. His gaze stops at Allen's hand wrapped around my forearm, then flickers to my captor's face. The armed man's eyes narrow. "Sir." He steps forward, one meaty hand hovering near the weapon on his belt. "What is— "

He never finishes the sentence. Allen shoots an arc of electricity through him so quickly, I almost don't see it happen. The bolt is much bigger than the one he used on the other students, and when the man drops to the ground with a heavy thud, smoke rises from his blackened neck. I feel bile rising in my throat, and I retch.

"Oh, for heaven's sake, Grier," Allen scoffs, rolling his eyes at me. He pulls me closer to the man's body and leans over, unfastening the handgun from the man's holster and tucking it into his own waistband. "That'll come in handy. Just in case electrocution gets a little dull," he winks at me and grins, a sickeningly cavalier gesture that makes my stomach churn again.

Silently I stumble along with him as he pulls me through the trees, over ground where the last hint of snow hasn't quite melted yet, my sneakers growing more sodden by the minute.

We reach the base of Outlook Point. Four metal legs stretch high above the treetops, and a spiral staircase in the center leads to the top. Allen lets go of me and shoves me toward the structure.

"Get going. The stairs will be slippery. Don't be stupid and fall. Don't be even stupider and try something, or I will kill them."

Trembling, I grip the metal handrails of the spiral staircase and force myself to focus only on the steps in front of me. If I look anywhere else, I will vomit or pass out. If I do either of those things, everyone I love will die. I climb slowly, treading carefully on the narrow metal stairs. The handrail is freezing, and my fingers begin to go numb. At the top, I crawl onto the platform, then lean against the metal wall, shaking as Allen comes up right behind me. "Get up," he commands, and a flash of anger burns through me.

"Wait!" I growl, trying to catch my breath in the cold air. "Or don't and go ahead and kill me, but then what are you going to do up here all by yourself?"

He's stunned into momentary silence, and for a second, I wonder how much I'm going to regret that. Then he chuckles. "There's a little spirit. I like it."

He crosses his arms and stares at me with an air of benevolence as he waits for me to stagger to my feet, then follows me to the wide glass door centered along one wall of the tower. It's unlocked, and Allen shoves me into the tower room. The space is entirely open, encased on all sides by floor-to-ceiling windows.

"There." Allen points toward the lake in the distance. It's barely thawed this early in the spring. "Those boulders along the bank, where the river meets the shore."

An outcropping of boulders juts out along the shoreline on one side, providing a high place popular for cannonballs into the deep lake waters in the summertime. The river feeds into it.

"Where the two waters meet," he mumbles to himself, manic. I stare at the boulders, unsure of what Allen wants me to look at, and then I see her.

In the distance, I see a small, black shrouded figure with something writhing just above its head. My breath catches in my throat.

Erys.

I gasp involuntarily, my knees threatening to give out. Allen chuckles softly behind me, placing his hands on my shoulders and leaning close to me, whispering into my ear, his breath warm on my cheek. "That's right. There she is. Waiting for us. Waiting for you, Grier, the real Chosen One, a chosen one who will change the world. She needs to get to the school in order to get to your sister. We're using you to get to her, a concept I'm sure you're familiar with."

I grit my teeth and grip the railing, anger sending tiny portals sparking from my fingertips.

"Here's the plan, so listen carefully. It's simple." He turns me so I'm facing him, and when I look away, he gently takes my face in his hands so I have no choice. "Grier," his voice is a low purr. "Do you know your sister actually thought my ultimate goal was sleeping with you?" My skin crawls, and I stiffen as he slides one arm around my waist and draws me closer. "Can you imagine?" he murmurs, tucking a stray lock of hair behind my ear almost tenderly. He's so close, I can feel his breath on my face as he gazes down at me. My heart is thudding in my chest and I'm certain I'll vomit. "If that's what I'd wanted, that's what I'd have gotten a long time ago. I wouldn't have needed to go to such extravagant lengths."

"You're disgusting," I hiss.

He laughs, throwing his head back. "And you were desperate. Just like you are now. Desperate girls are easy to manipulate," he spits. "So here's what's going to happen. You're going to open a portal where she is standing. She's going to step inside. Then you're going to open the other end of the portal there." He drags me around the corner of the tower deck to where we can see the school in its vast clearing. "Right in front of the outer doors. Not on the grass or the greater grounds. There." He points to where warm lights shimmer behind windows; where students are laughing and eating and living, unaware their lives are about to change forever.

I blink, momentarily speechless. "I don't know if I can," I stammer honestly.

"You don't have a choice! You fail, or you refuse, and I will kill you. Put her anywhere but where I told you, and I'll kill everyone you care about." He holds up a small, flat device the size of a deck of cards. "One click and the electric net will close over your sister and Leo. So Grier, think long and hard about what you are about to do."

If I fail, everyone dies. If I succeed... I choke back a sob. If I succeed, everyone might die anyway. But I have no choice. I won't condemn my sister to die without a fight. Valora maybe has a chance, and then so would everyone else. It buys us time. *Valora.* I feel the strange, tugging sensation in my heart again at her name. "Fine."

Allen watches silently as I face the boulders at the edge of the lake and reach out toward them with my palm. Heart pounding, I grit my teeth and concentrate. At this distance, with an adult human, I don't even know if I can. *But I have to.* My palm burns, and fire spreads up my arm and into my shoulder. My entire body shakes as the portal forms, shimmering blue light at the base of the boulders. Just as I'm sure I can't hold it open a second longer, the narrow black figure steps into it. I curl my fingers and cry out in pain as the portal closes with a crack that echoes out across the lake. An immediate black cloud settles over my mind, sharp-edged and rotten. I press my hands over my ears, trying to hold back the lilting voice I hear inside my mind, a terrible whisper that rakes fetid claws across my mind. *Grier...*

"That's it," Allen encourages me in the same tone he used when I spent my time delighting over my newfound ability to portal arrows.

I'm shaking and clinging to the railing as he shoves me to where I have a clear view of Proctor Moor. The voice in my head grows louder, and suddenly I'm desperate to get her out. *Poor little Grier...* As quick as I can, I raise my arm, taking aim at the courtyard so far in the distance. Then I take a breath. *Please forgive me,* I pray silently. *Forgive me, Valora. I'm sorry.*

Pain rips through my body, and my hand feels like it's being flayed open while the portal appears in the distance. I can't look. I squeeze my eyes shut and scream in pain just as Allen breathes, "She's in."

I drop to the deck, drenched in cold sweat and exhausted, but he yanks me back to my feet. "Not so fast," he snarls. "Open another portal."

"Why?" I pant, unable to make sense of what he wants.

"I need to be there with her." He's a man possessed.

I shake my head. "I can't. I'm not...I can't." Out of the corner of my eye, I see one of the mounted telescopes that attaches to the railing on the other side of the platform. It's big, and it looks like it weighs a hundred pounds. In the background, I can hear Allen still talking. *Why is he always talking?*

"Grier," he is saying, as though speaking to a very small child. "If I'm not there in the next few seconds because you drop me elsewhere, Erys will know why, and any wild ideas you may have had will backfire to the tune of suffering for everyone you love." He stands back and looks at me expectantly. Ignoring the ache in my arms, I brace myself. The pain is no less agonizing this time, but the portal opens in front of me.

"Fine," I snarl.

Allen gives me a curt nod. "Don't forget what I said. Best of luck to you," he sneers, stepping forward and vanishing. My heart clutches, but I race to the other side of the platform and take my position. I can feel him in my mind, his presence like a cold, menacing shadow. Once I'm ready, I raise my hand. I've been working all this time on putting things in very specific places; arrows over crowds, furniture stacked on top of each other, bugs in moats. And now, I funnel all of my rage into one final burst of energy and carefully lay the portal open. Allen steps out right in front of me, looking bewildered. "Grier, I thought I said – "

But I grab the telescope and swing it with as much strength as I can muster and watch as it cracks him directly in the face. He falls down with a hard thud, his head slamming against the platform. He's breathing, but there is a lot of blood across his face, and he doesn't even move as I yank the video controller out of his hand. I look at the screen and a breath of relief escapes my lips. They aren't there anymore: Valora and Leo have escaped somehow.

An uncontrollable exhaustion from portaling two people sweeps over me, and I collapse again on the deck, barely able to keep my eyes open. That's when I hear a series of sharp snaps below me, forcing me to sit up. Through the metal bars of the observation deck, I see the tops of the trees below me shaking, and the tower itself trembles with the sound of heavy footsteps. Not normal footsteps:: heavy slogging, slithering, the crunch of many feet, the buzz of wings.

Erys has brought her monsters.

28

VALORA

My heart clutches nervously as I look around my room for probably the last time. I look over the quilt my grandmother made me on the bed, the pictures of myself and Julian that I never bothered to take down ,the teddy bear that I can't seem to part with. Then, Grier's bed, her record player, her worn backpack and well-loved books. I close my eyes. I don't know where she is at the moment, but if we make it through this night alive, I am going to tell my sister I love her. Better yet, I'm going to show her.

I pull off my clothes and reach into my closet. I am about to face the woman that killed my grandmother and hundreds – maybe thousands – of others over the years, and I am not going to be wearing a Proctor Moor sweatshirt and leggings to do it. I pull out my black uniform and check it for goodies. Yes, there they are all here: the laser-edged daggers, steel-toed boots, the fingerless black leather gloves with cooling pads embedded in the palms, and finally my fireproof cape.

Maybe I'm not the Chosen One, and I'm probably going to die tonight, *but I am going to look cool as fuck doing it.* Outside the door in the hallway the alarm sounds: "This is not a drill. This is not a drill."

I run out of my dorm, sprinting my way past the posters that bear my face and head down into the atrium, toward the front doors to the school. As I race through crowds of students, they part for me like waters once again, true fear etched on their faces.

"Valora!" I hear Renata calling my name, her voice full of terror. I follow it to the main part of the hall, where clusters of staff are gathered at the bamboo forest. Renata's face crumples when she sees me. "Oh god, I thought...I thought maybe..."

She pulls me into a hug, and I think for a moment about just how much this woman has done for me. How much she loves me. She leads me around to the massive front doors of the school, past a throng of teachers discussing frantically what best to do with the students. To the left of the large metal doors is a staircase, one that has always been sectioned off, but now Renata unlatches the chain and we climb a narrow, winding staircase up two flights. She pushes open a small wooden door and we are outside. Curiously, I step into the wind. We are above the main entrance to the school, on a narrow balcony that sits above the grandiose wooden sign proclaiming "Welcome to Proctor Moor!" The wind whips around us, and my cape snaps behind me.

"Are you ready?" Renata whispers as we look up over the grounds for any sign of her.

I shake my head. "No."

"Me either." She turns to me and I notice how old she suddenly seems. Her eyes are dark, and wrinkles pull at the corners of her eyes. She takes my hand. "Valora Rigmore. I have known your name since the day you were born, and I have loved you just as long. Whatever you may believe, I need you to know this: I know in my heart that you are the Chosen One. I know that you can defeat this great evil. I believe in you. Your heart beats faster and stronger than Erys's because hers is dark and rotted with jealousy. Her hatred makes her weak." She puts both hands on my shoulders and looks me squarely in the face. "Kill her and then come back to me."

I turn back to the balcony. There is a flash of blue light in the distance, out toward the furthest outbuildings of the property. I squint. It's coming from Outlook Point, where visitors to Proctor Moor can take in the fall foliage. It grows larger, a swirling blue and white light that grows from a bright speck into something quite large, like some sort of celestial rip. "What is that?" Renata leans forward and raises the glasses hanging on her necklace onto her nose.

"That," I say softly, "is Grier."

The portal grows large and I can feel it filling the air with a strange, alien energy. Then it disappears with a crack.

"Get ready," whispers Renata. "I had Leo call the authorities, but...." She trails off as the understanding passes between us without words. Soldiers with guns and helicopters aren't going to be much help against a telekinetic. They're going to try, though. Suddenly a blast of air comes from the courtyard in front of the school, the same place I fought the Mistspawn six months ago. I feel the horrible truth before I see it.

She's here.

Up close, the portal is incredible: a mosaic of white and blue light streaking in a circular motion. It's not of this world, and the sheer beauty of it renders me speechless, along with the strange realization that my sister is doing this. It's amazing, this power. I'm still in awe of it when the face in my nightmares appears through the rip in the air. The portal snaps shut with a crack, and I swear that I hear my sister scream from somewhere far away. The sound pierces my heart, and from across the trees in the distance, I feel a strange tug between her heart and mine. I feel her distress, that she thinks she has betrayed the world to save us.

Of course. Mr. Ferguson used us as leverage to get Grier to open the portal. To bring *her.*

Now Erys steps out of the blue light. She's wearing a long wool black coat, the bottom of it wet and trailing slime. Her dark blue dress underneath is frayed at the hem and when she raises her hands, I see that she has snakes coiled around both wrists. The skin around her eyes is dark grey, though her face is pale and sharp. Just above her head floats a creature of nightmares: body shaped like a two-foot sphere, with no discernible features. Two dozen small smooth tentacles emerge from its body and they float around her, not subject to gravity in any way. This is the Baleful, the first monster that clung to her. Where she moves, it moves, attached to the air above her head by some sort of invisible bond. The tentacles float forward and back with each step, like hair under water.

Her face is wild and unstable as she looks up at the school, and then she sees us. I barely have time to react before she throws up her hands toward us. The stone balcony explodes underneath our feet and Renata and I both go tumbling toward the ground in a cascade of stone and rebar. I'm not fast enough to catch us, so instead I bring the ground toward us, tearing up a large chunk of concrete so that we can safely ride it to the ground. It's still impossibly hard, and my feet ache upon the landing. Renata skids off and hits her head hard on the concrete.

Erys claps her hands with glee and the creature bounces with the impact of each clap. "There's Valora Rigmore! This is going to be so fun!"

I have barely climbed to my feet when she blows my body sideways, sending me skidding fifty yards past her, onto the wide gangplank that leads to the school. There is a twenty-foot drop into the moat below, and I am barely able to grip the edge before I go over, my body spinning in mid-air. The cooling pads in my gloves make it hard to hold on, and I grip harder, not wanting to fall into the moat below which is suddenly roiling with hungry creatures.

Erys walks slowly toward Renata as I struggle to hold on, the cooling pads on my palms making it nearly impossible for me to gain traction without slipping into the foul water below, teeming with hungry creatures. This wasn't a fight. I never even got a chance. She raises one hand and I watch in horror as she drags my barely conscious mentor up beside her, Renata's body floating beside her like a ragdoll.

"Stop!" I scream, trying to hold on as best I can. "Don't hurt her...don't..."

Erys smiles cruelly as her eyes turn to Renata. "Ah yes, Everett's lover, at long last we have a proper introduction! I have you and your little knife to thank for the scar that never quite healed as it should have. My brother had many skeletons in his closet, but none as passionate as this one."

Renata faces Erys with not even an ounce of fear on her face, her eyes half open. "He was ten times the Proctor you'll ever be, proper upbringing or not. You will never match him, no matter how long you hunt for his acclaim."

"Yet he is dead, and I am not, and you will always be a widow. Just without the honor." A nasty, wide smile passes over her face. "I'm about to do you a favor - arranging a meeting with your lover and his wife! Now you will finally have a chance to explain yourself."

Erys raises her hands and begins to bend Renata in half. I am crying her name, trying to hold on, tears streaming down my face, unable to stop her and save myself at the same time. I watch with horror as Erys snaps her palms together one final time, I watch as she breaks my mentor's back right in front of me, and the scream I let out echoes through Proctor Moor. *I would rather face the monsters of the deep than this.* I let go of the ledge, but I don't fall. Erys reaches out for me, her telekinetic power holding me in the air, but she's a second too late. I throw out my hand as I'm falling and send a wave of power her direction to counteract it. I see it blow her backwards as my body starts to fall.

Just before the dark waters of the moat swallow me whole, I see Erys step over Renata's broken body. When the water closes over my head, I fight to keep from gagging at the stench of it. I immediately feel the pull of the current below me, feel my legs sinking down into the black mud at the bottom of the moat, awakening the creatures that feed off whatever hellish bacteria live down here. I push off the bottom and try to swim for the surface, but two long slithering creatures that I can't see have latched themselves around my ankles. I've never tried to use my powers underwater before, but I press down with both hands and imagine the creatures being blasted apart. It works and I see chunks of their bodies float past me.

From under the water, I hear a terrifying, muffled sound; the sound of something large lurching towards me, the swish of a tail, the sound of a belly dragging over wet moss. *I have to get out of here.* I throw my palms downwards and push against the water. I've never tried this before, and I suspect it looks less like Superman than I would have liked, but somehow it blows me up and out of the moat before I splash down again. I swim to the side, gratefully gulping in air as I claw myself up and out of the water and roll onto the bank. I sputter water out of my mouth and let out a wail. I can't tell the water from my tears as I let out a great heaving sob.

Renata. The sound of her back breaking will never leave me. *I have failed her. I am going to fail everyone.*

Far above me I hear Erys battle against the metal reinforced doors. I curl my fists and stand, black water dripping down my face as I look out past the courtyard and into the forest that surrounds the school. The trees are swaying back and forth, and I see dark shapes creeping across the lawn. The monsters have arrived.

I'm just about to turn when I see it: another flash of blue light. A portal. My shoulders sag forward in relief. Grier is alive, at least for now. I feel that same odd magnetic pull toward where she is that I felt before, surprising and potent. Perhaps it's what I should have felt for her all these years, but now it's too late.

Above me, the sounds of screaming students fills the air while in front me my sister tries to fight something off. *I can't save both.* I hear the sound of my own breathing, feel the beat of my heart thundering in my chest. I close my mind, and think of my family. Think of my mother's smile and my dad's jokes and the glint of sunlight on my sister's hair. I think of my Nan perched on a tree and Renata, lying motionless only a few feet away from me. *I'm sorry Grier.* The guilt that rips through my chest is real, but I sprint towards the school.

E rys has not yet breached the school. The doors are buckling as she stands in front of them, fighting them with a tremendous amount of energy coming from her palms. Other Exceptionals are trying to use their gifts to deter her and it's admirable, but it's not working: she easily bats away a small tendril of water that arches her way, doesn't even look annoyed when a tiny thunder cloud hovers over her, and when my history teacher opens his mouth to let out a scream that can freeze people in their tracks, Erys wrests control of his neck and snaps it. He falls to the ground. I recoil.

To my relief, I hear a telltale thumping sound from above me and I look up to see four Black Hawk helicopters on the horizon. The reinforcements are here. They won't stop her, but they might delay her. I barely have time to focus before Erys whirls around.. The Baleful reaches out its arms above her, echoing her movements, and I wonder for the first time how their powers are connected. Does it amplify her telekinesis?

Her eyes narrow in focus as the helicopters edge closer, their sound vibrating my teeth. As she's distracted, I leap over the edge of the moat and sprint to where Renata is lying, half covered with a piece of gnarled steel. I easily bend it up and off of her. "Valora," she croaks, and I can see that she doesn't have much time left. Her eyes are glassy and there is a spot of blood at the corner of her mouth.

Gently, I cradle her broken body against my own and run for the door, chaos reigning behind me. I hear the rattle of machine guns as the helicopters try to take out Erys, but we're close enough that the ground under us is exploding in a shower of pebbles as bullets tear past me. I turn and kneel over Renata, and put my hands out in front of us, creating a shield of power that pushes bullets aside. They fall like rain around us. I spare a glance back and watch as Erys steps forward. After a moment of what looks like wrestling the air, she waves her hands violently to the right and I watch with horror as one Black Hawk helicopter plows into another, their blades tangling up in each other's bodies as they pitch forward toward the school. I look away as they land in a massive explosion of fire and metal on the north side of the grounds. The helicopters soar close overhead and then circle around for another go. Erys raises her hands again. I scoop up Renata in my arms and make a beeline for the door. I hear Agnes's shouts from the windows above. "It's Valora! Open it!"

A small reinforced door inside the larger door opens and we are able to duck inside. Two staff members grab Renata out of my arms and place her on the ground and begin first aid. Leo runs over to me. "Where is she?" His face is frantic.

"Out there!" I point toward the door. We hear the helicopters again, and the sounds of gunfire, the shouts of Marines and then a huge fiery explosion that rattles the windows of the school and sends glass shattering. "Go back to your dorms!" I scream at the students, but they aren't listening. The doors buckle once and again, and I stand and face them as the rest of the students back away.

"Valora!" It's Renata. Our literature teacher is holding her as best she can, propping her up. "Come here." I hold up my hands, ready to defend these stupid students until my last breath. Which will be any minute now. "Valora! Come here! I order it." I pause and kneel next to her. Renata is growing weaker every minute. I bend over and put my ear next to her lips, cradling her head ever so gently, appreciating the way her hair is always wild, the way she smells like basil and tea. She whispers words to me and I recoil.

"No. NO!" What she is suggesting is unthinkable.

Her stern faces shows no mercy. "You will do this, Valora. Listen to me this one last time. This is the only way." Her eyes flutter. "It is the only way." I kneel beside her, tears dripping down my face.

"You can't ask me to do this."

"I am. And you will listen to your mentor. For once." s She laugh a little and my face crumples before I let out an ugly sob. "I am so proud. You must know."

I shake my head, cries filling my throat. "Please, please don't ask me this." Agnes sits beside us and takes Renata's hand in her own before placing it against my face. I press my cheek back against it.

"Give this meaning," Renata instructs me, nodding to the chaos around us. "I'm going either way."

Finally, I lean back and surrender. Agnes steps back with wide eyes, and I nod at her reluctantly. "Get in a line!" she screams at the students. "Line up!"

The students scurry forward, relieved to be able to do something to help. They understand very quickly what is happening and some of them start crying. Leo joins Agnes, and they run up and down the line of students, telling them to join hands, checking their connection. Slowly, a line forms that wraps all through the atrium and up and down the stairwells as the entire staff and student body of Proctor Moor becomes one.

A hole punches through the door as the last helicopter is slammed against it, and suddenly the smoking blade of a helicopter tears through the front of our school. I look up to see Cicely, watching me with tears on her face. Her hair is as white as snow. Leo is last in line. He takes Cicely's palm in one hand and then reaches out for Renata, connecting them all. I look up at the line of students as the front door begins to bend with a terrible screech and then look at Renata's as her hand reaches for my own.

I remember the first time she showed me her gift; I was seven years old, and she took the energy from a single light bulb and passed it over my skin; she the conduit, the channeler. It felt warm and happy, and after that I moved a heavy stone, something that had been impossible before. She had picked me up even though using her power had exhausted her and told me that someday I wouldn't need her energy to do such things.

She was wrong.

"Don't ask me to take this from you," I whimper one last time, but she smiles through her pain.

"I'm not asking," she says plainly, before closing her eyes. The door buckles inward, and the burning helicopter is pushed through the metal and goes roaring into the atrium. A shower of burning ash and metal barrels towards the line, but they hold. *My peers, they hold.* Renata's lip trembles and I look at her face one last time. Then I take her hand and everything goes burning white as the energy from hundreds of students pours into me through my mentor's body.

29

GRIER

THE GROUND BELOW ME QUAKES AS I GINGERLY MAKE MY WAY TO the staircase. I have no idea what I'm up against. Monsters: Biology and Behavior was an elective I took two years ago, and I doubt even then I would have been able to identify the hordes of terrible creatures slithering and crawling their way through the forest below me. I wish Leo were here. Leo would know. When I see him again, I'm never going to let him go.

I'm nearing the ground when I hear an intense buzzing above me. A black blur whizzes past my face and I instinctively swat at it. It reels and buzzes at me again, hovering a few feet above my face. The strange insect, hummingbird-sized, fat, and black-fuzzed, examines me in an eerily human-like manner, almost as if it's considering whether or not I'm worth its effort.

A Noxious Semp, I realize, recognizing the poisonous mosquito-like creature once responsible for paralyzing an entire resort of families enjoying a summer holiday in the Adirondacks. One bite, and I'll never make it back to Proctor Moor. It dives, and I smack it as hard as I can, knocking it against the stair railing and onto a step several feet below me. It twitches and flops, and before it can take to the air again, I jump over the railing and crush it under my heel. With a satisfying crunch, it's gone, obliterated into an oozing, greenish-purple smear on the metal staircase.

I stay close against the stairs and survey the forest around me. I seem to have found a window between waves of horrible creatures, and I'm not waiting around for more of them. Then something happens: the exhaustion I'd felt just moments earlier is replaced by a rush of adrenaline so intense I feel as though it might push me out of my own skin. It crackles over my skin and through my veins, giving me power, giving me strength. I don't know what it is or where it comes from, but I'll take it. It's not like I have time to ponder it. I scramble to my feet and take off running in the direction of the school, my senses on high alert. I dodge around trees, avoiding boulders and fallen branches, my feet occasionally slipping on crusty patches of dirty snow the sun hasn't reached yet. Then ten yards in front of me, the earth begins to churn, spraying dirt and bits of dead leaves into the air.

Keep running, I scream at myself, giving the roiling ground a wide berth. It's nearly behind me when I'm knocked off my feet by another explosion of dirt and leaves. I slam into the trunk of a nearby tree, hitting it hard enough with my cheek that I'm temporarily dazed as I hit the ground. I scramble backwards, crablike, as the earth before me opens and dozens, then hundreds of writhing legs slither out. I stare in horror at the creature rising in front of me: its body, nearly six feet long, is covered in milky white translucent armor-like plates, its blackish blue innards visible below. The entire underside of its body is studded with round, gaping mouths, blood red and fanged, and hundreds of claw-tipped legs wriggle out from its body. Fanged Chilopoda, I think – I remember Leo talking about them as we'd watched a tiny centipede scurry along an outer wall of Proctor Moor. To my left, another slithers from the first hole, struggling to free itself from a tangle of fallen branches. Oh my God. It's huge.

I leap to my feet and run, narrowly dodging clawed legs as the first monster heaves its body toward me, skittering quickly across the ground. I dodge behind a tree when another erupts in front of me. *I can't run. I have to fight.*

I throw my hand out from behind the tree and channel every ounce of energy I have toward the creature. It scuttles forward just as my brilliant portal appears, and it's swallowed whole. Behind me, the other two are slithering toward me through the trees. A wave of strength courses through me and with a loud crack, I send the portal flying towards them, dropping the first Chilopoda onto the other two. They turn on each other, a writhing, stabbing mass of legs and gnashing, horrible mouths. I hear their screams as I run.

In the skies above me, I hear heavy, rhythmic chopping, and I glance up to see the underbellies of half a dozen military helicopters heading toward the school. *Maybe it's not too late.* Behind me, another droning sound grows louder. I stop against a tree trunk and turn to see a swarm of Noxious Semps coming directly toward me. Without thinking, I aim in front of them, and they disappear into my portal. It suddenly strikes me that I have no idea where to send flying creatures that'll inevitably make their way back to me, but I aim at the ground, projecting my mind deep underneath the soil under a fallen tree. Then I release them. To my surprise, it works. It'll at least buy me time.

There's a sharp stitch in my side and the freezing air burns my lungs as I race for the treeline. In the distance, where the forest meets the cleared grounds of Proctor Moor, automatic gunfire rings out from the circling helicopters. A giant explosion lights up the forest around me, and when I look around, I feel pure horror: the monsters are everywhere. I'm so tired, and my limbs are already shaking from what I've done, and that's when something strange happens: a burst of energy, strange energy that burns like a hot white light barrels towards me from the direction of the school. I don't understand it, but I feel it wrap its way around my body, snaking over my hands, then plunging deep into my chest, surrounding my heart. I'm not afraid, because somehow I know that this power comes from Valora. It feels like her: sharp and crackling as it makes its way in. It stings like her words. It is fierce and alive. And I am suddenly filled with this fathomless strength that pulls me towards my sister.

From behind comes a deep, earth-shaking rumble so loud it nearly drowns out the military choppers. I pump my legs faster than I ever thought possible and don't look back, determined to make it to the clearing. I burst out from the forest and glance over my shoulder. At least half a dozen Rache, hideous beasts with humped, fur-covered backs and scaly, rat-like tails, are bearing down on me. They howl and yip, a maniacal sound akin to wild laughter. Their beady eyes glow, and their mouths drip foamy saliva.

I veer to one side with my mind racing, and then I turn and stand my ground. I can't outrun them; I'll have to take them one or two at a time. I portal two, flinging them across the wide expanse of the school grounds. The portal opens a good twenty feet in the air and drops them with a sickening thud on the hard ground below. I'm able to dispose of two more the same way, leaving their bodies broken and struggling in the distance, when one of the remaining two charges me from behind and knocks me flat. With a howl of laughter, it spins out in front of me, screaming and snapping as the other takes its aim. I duck and roll, flinging one hand out and portaling the charging Rache near its dying companions. I barely have caught my breath when the last beast charges, and this time I'm not fast enough. It knocks the wind out of me, and I lay on my back, gasping for air. It closes in on me, the foul stench of death from its foaming jaws washing over me as it scream-laughs again.

Desperate, I launch myself at it just as it charges again, and that's enough to startle it and knock it off course, the momentum sending it rolling across the grass. This gives me enough time to throw my arm out toward it as it scrambles to its feet, sending it right into a portal to be disposed of like the rest. I drop it over the moat.

Gasping and bleeding, I stagger to my feet and stare at the scene in front of me with disbelief. Hell has come to Proctor Moor. The grounds before me are strewn with the charred, smoking wreckage of helicopters, and the front doors of the school have been caved in. I hear more helicopters behind me, along with the cries of more monsters. I hear screaming coming from inside the school.

Where is Valora? I feel a stabbing pain in one foot and glance down to find the grey canvas torn, the top of my foot cut and bleeding. The shoe is destroyed and is only going to slow me down, so I grit my teeth and kick both of them off before running toward the melee.

I reach the closest bridge over the moat and survey the churning water in front of me. The side of the bridge has been smashed, and concrete chunks the size of my head are scattered everywhere. I start to cross the bridge, hands held out at the ready, eyes wide. I'm about to reach the halfway point when something leaps out of the water below: a ghostly white fish the size of a Great Dane, its scale-less skin pale and rubbery. It lands dead-center on the bridge behind me with a wet plop, mouth gaping. Its gills flare dark red and it makes a sucking sound as its cloudy black eyes roll wildly. I let out a cry as the fish crawls after me at an alarming pace, pulling itself along ghoulishly with two long, bony arms. I run faster, aiming my portal at the creature and releasing it out over the treetops of the forest.

On the other side of the moat, I can see Erys, fire in the background, Baleful writhing over her head. I'm moving backward now, trapped between creatures coming up from all sides and Erys. I dispatch another swarm of Noxious Semp, then dodge two Chilopoda breaking through the earth. I'm moving faster than I ever have. Something else is driving me, some strange tether to Valora, unworldly and powerful. Maybe it's my desperation. Maybe it's love or envy, but whatever it is, it's strong.

I'm hit from behind, knocked flat again, and I hear the hideous cackle of at least three more Rache. *RUN,* I scream at myself.

Staggering to my feet, I tear toward the school, leaping over another grotesquely pale fish creature. It's trampled under the scaly feet of the Rache, who leave it spattered across the dead winter grass as they pursue me. I'm able to portal one of them far off into the sky above the forest, but I feel the hot, stinking breath of the others at my back. A blinding pain shoots through my left ankle as one of them manages to grab hold of my leg. I scream and tumble toward the ground before turning over and kick the beast as hard as I can, sending it rolling into the other one. I send a surge of energy through my hands and the two Rache tumble into my portal, where I fling them into a mess of tangled Chilopoda.

A gust of wind nearly knocks me to the ground again as I make it to the courtyard, and as I stumble forward, I realize it wasn't a gust of wind at all. Twenty yards in front of me, folding its enormous steely-grey feathered wings, stands a creature whose figure is startlingly human-like. It glares at me with ember-like eyes set deep in its decidedly mannish face. Above its head rise twisted black horns. Its wings flex again and I notice its hands, tipped with long, sharp claws.

GREAT. Now there's a bird dude with big-ass sword claws, I think, blinking. The creature and I stare at each other, and I'm waiting for it to make a move toward me so I can open a portal when I'm hit from behind again. Above me I see enormous, moth-like white wings beating overhead, battering me as I try to stand. Something scrapes my shoulder, and out of the corner of my eye I see a Chilopoda slither by, weaving between enormous, fat, fanged worms that have begun to burrow up from under the cobblestones. I'm on my knees, arms out, desperately opening and closing portals, but each time one monster is gone, two more seem to take its place. The ground bursts open before me and I watch in silent horror as an Onyxcobra, larger than the one that hunted Valora, slithers out of the ground.

My hands ache, and portals are opening and closing all around me, but there are too many. I know I'm finally overcome. I lean back and watch as they descend all around me, their mouths and eyes hungry as they move closer.

I close my eyes and reach for my sister. *I'm so sorry, Valora.*

30

VALORA

FOR A SECOND, I CAN'T SEE ANYTHING, BECAUSE THE JOLT OF energy from Renata is so strong that it blinds me. When I finally open my eyes, I turn my hands over in amazement, watching the power lick over my palms. What is coursing through me is foreign and new; it doesn't feel like my own power, which is as familiar as the blood in my veins. This is a gasoline mixed with fire pouring out of my pores. This is a nuclear reactor spilling inside of me. I burn like wildfire. My enhanced power from Renata flows out of my palms like a waterfall, invisible and strong. I drop her hand and fall to my knees in front of her. Her skin is ashen, her lips black, but the expression on her face is one of peace. She knew I would take it all from her. She is dead.

Outside, I can hear chaos; the cries of monsters, the shouts of Marines and a then a scream that I recognize: Grier's. There are bullets and maniacal laughter and the stench of smoke. I watch in silence as the flame from the Black Hawk begins licking up the side of the front door.

I can't let Proctor Moor burn. Erys is coming in either way.

"Get out of here!" I scream at the students, and they slowly back away, but none of them leave. They are all watching me, waiting. I raise my hands and give a small push forward. The doors explode outward, taking the helicopter with them. The hole I have blown in the school is maybe thirty feet high and wide. I look at my hands.

"Holy crap!" Agnes steps away from the crowd, her eyes wide with amazement as she looks at me. She waves to the door. "What are you waiting for? Go kick her ass, Valora!" Something awakens in me at her utter display of faith.

I turn and sprint away, passing through the gaping hole that I left in the entrance to Proctor Moor. I race into the courtyard, where Erys...isn't. I pivot as I search for her, but something else catches my eye: Grier, at the center of the courtyard, literally surrounded by monsters. She's throwing portals back and forth with incredible speed, but it's not enough. She stumbles as they close in: Fanged Chilopoda are crawling toward her on the ground, while Crextees buzz around her head, yanking at her arms.. An Onyxcobra slithers in a circle around of these night-marish creatures, its head weaving back and forth as it hunts. Grier is on the ground now, scooting backwards as a Cloven Rangibeest aims its moss-covered antlers at her in front of her face, its peaked beak snapping.

I don't even think as I'm sprinting towards her. I'm screaming her name and my hands are moving out in front of me like they have a purpose of their own. In my mind, I hear Renata's voice. *"This is what you've trained for."* Then, I explode.

The Onyxcobra sees me coming and darts toward me first, fangs at the ready, but when it goes to strike, I grab it mid-air and hold it there, my hand outstretched. The power that is flowing through me is incredible. Then I rip the bottom half of his jaw loose. The snake screams and thrashes its tail, which takes out about a dozen monsters and throws the circle around Grier into chaos. I throw my palms out and the Swampworms lift off the ground one after another and fly into the air, their bodies thrashing. Once they are up, I bring my hands down in a swift, hard motion and they are crushed into the ground.

The Rangibeest backs up and then charges at Grier. I reach out, but Grier is faster. A portal explodes in front of the Beest and swallows it. She turns weakly and raises her hand high in the air, and I watch as the Beest emerges and falls to its death. My hands are still moving in front of me, almost so fast I can barely see them, and I watch the monsters around her turn to shreds: I rip the wings from the Crextees and crush Noxious Semps with a curl of my fist. Overhead Mantharas sweep and dive, and I send them careening into each other. I ram the Siberian Snowhorn into the ground, their horns trapping them for a moment while I rip their hearts from their chests.

A Brachyphod scuttles up beside me and lashes out of with one of his claws, catching me in the leg. I let out a shout as the sharp hooks dig into my skin, and I bring my hands down hard, pinning his crab-like neon blue legs against his own body. I send him screeching into the sky.

There's a shout behind me and I spin around, ready to kill, but it's Pike. He's running towards me with huge plumes of flame flickering on his palms. I don't even ask his permission before I grab his flame with my own energy and hurl it toward the monsters, a stream of fire and death. Pike stands still as I wield his flame like a whip, watching it set fire to every creature it touches. I spin and send it low, catching all sorts of demonic little creatures running amok over the field: poisonous crabs trying to tangle my ankles, and Harebits, monsters that look like bunnies but open their mouths to unveil barbed tentacles.

When I turn, a team of Marines is running up behind me, and bullets are sprayed widely across the green. They stream past, firing through the line of monsters as I rip them apart. The sky is filled with fire as I work my way farther into the courtyard, the blood of monsters raining from the skies. My hands never stop moving. I throw them up toward Grier, producing an arc of power that passes over her and amazed at what happens. The monsters that are almost on her are sent sprawling backward. I move forward, dropping to my knees and spinning my hands out in front of me, ripping Kilati – walking skeletons with bird beaks – in half, and with a burst of power send Chilopoda hurtling away from me. Pike finishes off anything that gets away with a healthy blast of flame.

I send the daggers from my boot straight for a pack of Rache that stalk about the outside of the perimeter. I watch Oshimai, hideous land-crawling fish, grab a Marine and take him down, trying to get their mouths over his arms and legs. I separate their heads from their bodies, one by one, until he is laying surrounded by four headless monsters like some kind of macabre sacrifice. It's all gross. *I don't give a shit.*

I'm moving so fast that I don't have time to think, don't have time to feel. The energy is pouring from me in great waves. Another surge of creatures emerges from the woods, and for some variety I reach behind me and grab the pieces of rock, glass, and metal that fill the destroyed courtyard and fling them toward the onslaught of monsters. They whiz past my head, blowing my hair in their wake. The newest wave is destroyed, crushed, impaled. A line of Marines marches toward the line of the trees, shooting everything in its path.

Anger flares in my chest. These strange, dark creatures are dying all around me, but they shouldn't have to. They should be living out their lives in shadow, hunting in the dark. Instead they are here, getting torn apart because Erys commanded them to kill us. A Harebit runs up to me and tries to ensnare my ankle with its long tentacle mouth. I send it flying with a soccer kick. I'm now almost to Grier, who's trying to catch a Siberian Snowhorn that keeps charging her. Finally, she whirls a portal to the right of her and then moves right in front of it. The ram leaps and Grier dodges left and sends the ram screaming into her portal. She deposits it over the moat.

I open my mouth to shout her name, but I hear commotion behind me and whirl around to see a Mantharas grab Pike by the shoulders and lift him straight into the air. I rip its wings in half. The Mantharas dips and lets out a howl as it plummets to the ground. Pike is falling, streams of fire trailing him like a shooting star. I catch him mid fall, my energy gently cradling his body and dropping him roughly onto the ground.

"Great catch!" he yells over the chaos and runs off to burn some more Kilati. If I manage to live through this day, I am going to ask him on a date. It's decided. I lift up two more Rangibeests and throw them into the side of Proctor Moor, and then I'm running for my sister, tears blurring my eyes with each step closer.

My heart is crying: *Grier, Grier, Grier.*

"Valora!" I'm almost there - but a bolt of electricity cuts between us, and I come to a violent stop in front of it. Out of the crowd of monsters, Allen walks forward confidently, electricity pouring from his flexed fingers in a jagged net around us. I watch as he electrocutes a Rangibeest who passes by just for the enjoyment of it. The air smells of burning flesh.

"Hello, girls!" I look over at Grier, who is trapped between two currents, her eyes wide as the sparking light dances past her face. His face is covered with dried blood and there is lump rising on his forehead. "I feel like I owe both of you an apology. Grier, I should have never doubted you! Knocking me with the telescope, clever girl. But still, you portaled Erys in beautifully, with nary a scratch." He glances toward me. "Oh, did you know, Valora, that Grier brought the woman who wants to kill you right to your doorstep? You'll have her to thank when she tears you into pieces, just like poor Mr. Proctor."

"I had no choice!" Grier whispers, and I know that it's true.

I turn to Allen. "You are done separating us; done pitting us against each other."

"I never had to do that," he snaps irritably. "You two did that just fine on your own." His eyes glitter menacingly. "I had to do very little to make the Rigmore sisters collapse. A single question was all that was needed: which one of you is the Chosen One? Hmmm..." I watch him angrily, but I'm more interested in what Grier is doing inside his web of electricity. Her hands are moving carefully in a large circular shape, tracing a portal that appears at the edge of the courtyard. I see a large black tail slither into the portal and disappear.

She flinches and turns pale, but instead of collapsing she stands and faces Allen. "You think that you used me. You think that I was so insecure and weak I would let you use my powers for evil and then lay down and die."

"You're about to do just that," Allen tells her matter-of-factly. "Lay down and die."

Grier's eyes narrow and I see that beneath her soft exterior there is a raging fire. A will to live. I don't even recognize her. "I don't think so, Mr. Ferguson." She whirls her hand once, right to the side of her and then leaps away as an Onyxcobra, missing half its jaw, explodes out of the portal right on top of Allen. It's as big as a city bus, and Allen is the first thing that it sees. It rears up and strikes. Allen is caught off guard and throws out his currents in front of him, sending lines of electricity over the snake, which writhes in electrified agony.

Grier and I run toward the school, bolts of white hot current chasing us across the grass and igniting the manicured bushes and trees. A spark catches Grier's heel and she pitches to the ground, shaking. Allen is moving towards us now, a net of crackling light trailing behind him. And while I can't move the currents, I can move him.

"Face him!" I scream.

I face Allen with my hands out, pull his legs out from under him, dragging him along the ground. Lines of electricity reach for me, but they are too late: Grier has made a portal in front of me, and it swallows his current. She throws her arm out violently and the portal moves over him, swallowing him before he even has a chance to understand what happened. She quickly closes it. I lean toward her. I don't understand fully how her gift works - not now, but I will – but when I look at her, I'm alarmed at the sparks of electricity in her eyes, as if Allen is passing *through* her. She clutches her chest and stumbles forward. I can tell this pains her, whatever it is.

"I know just where he needs to go. Can you do something about that?" she screams, pointing to the glass-and-stone building to the right, where a Kilati is snacking on the lavish landscaping. I understand her immediately, and hell yes, I can. I focus all my power on the building and release, channeling everything that Renata gave me into one steady stream. I think about the individual stones that make up the building, the panes of glass, the steel beams between them. And then I tear the entire thing apart.

With the entire structure of the pool house missing, all that remains is our lovely Olympic-sized pool, perfect for water polo and killing henchmen. I turn to my sister and marvel at her mind, the way she concentrates on the portal resting just above the surface of the water. She has streaks of white electricity appearing at the corners of her eyes now, like tiny lightning bolts sparking from her lashes. He's using his powers inside the portal.

"Get him out of there!" I shriek as I raise my hands. Grier nods and turns.

"Goodbye, Allen," he whispers quietly. "And thank you." My incredible sister moves her hand in a quick, brutal circle. Allen emerges above the pool in a blaze of electric light and I push my hands down, using my power to shove him into the water.

We watch as his body dances in frantic, unnatural movements as his own gift destroys him, his body flailing long after he's gone. Finally, he stops moving and all that is left of him is a floating corpse, facedown. A trail of blood flows from his ears, staining the water. Shots of electricity continue to sputter from the tips of his fingers like a malfunctioning computer. Grier turns and retches, and I feel an overwhelming sense of relief that she is still, well, Grier. My relief is short-lived, though, as every inch of my skin becomes aware of *her* presence. The same dark dread that I've always felt in my heart, that invasive, creeping fear for my future whispers in my mind... My eyes fall on the remainder of the school, and I stop breathing.

All the students are gathered outside on the courtyard, but they are eerily still, their eyes on us as they are surrounded by monsters on every side. Rising above them with her, arms outstretched and the Baleful floating above her head, is Erys.

31

VALORA AND GRIER

VALORA -

My hands are shaking as I raise them to face Erys. Beside
me, I can hear Grier's labored breathing. My mind is racing.
Any collateral damage will kill the students. I can fight her, but
I must move either the students or her, and I certainly can't do
both. The power burst from Renata is weakening. *This is it.*

Erys speaks softly, but I hear her as if she is whispering
right in my ear. "Come and play, little Chosen One." News helicopters are circling overhead now and one of them dips low for
a shot. I blink in surprise, but that second takes me out of the
moment and it's a mistake. Erys has a clear shot at me and I feel
a sudden violent yanking in my chest.

At first I think I'm having a heart attack, but then I realize
what is happening. Erys is trying to yank my heart out. I
quickly push all my own power against hers and the rending
stops, but then Grier lets out a cry and drops to her knees,
clutching at her own chest. I shift the wall of air so that it's
protecting Grier's heart, but as soon as I do, the ripping on my
own returns. I kneel to the ground as we both start screaming. I
crawl toward my twin, sure this is how we die: all of Proctor

Moor will watch the Rigmore girls lose their hearts together. My poor parents.

Tears are running down my blood-splattered face as I reach out for my sister, who is now lying on the ground, trying her best to keep her own heart beating in her chest. She reaches out for me, and I grab her hand, pulling her close enough to wrap my arms around her. My sister, close to me at last, in a way that we have never been outside of the....

I gasp, a memory overwhelming me in the midst of chaos. I am seven years old, and there is a knock at the door. When I open it, there is a beautiful black woman in a navy suit standing nervously on our doormat. When she sees my face she smiles.

"I know you. You're a Rigmore girl."

"Yes, ma'am!" I say shyly, tucking my hands behind me.

"Who is it?" my father asks from the living room. He comes around the corner and nervousness transforms his face. "Can I help you?"

He gently pushes me behind him and I peek out from behind his legs. The woman steps forward, clearly determined. "Mr. Rigmore, sir, my name is Carla, and I was Thackeray Chadwick's assistant. I have something important I need to tell you."

This gives my father a moment of pause, but he still leans over her, struggling to stay calm. "Are you one of those skeptics that says the prophecy doesn't matter? That it's not real. Well, I can tell you the prophecy is very real. Valora has already shown signs of the gift."

Carla nervously smooths her collar.

"Oh, I believe that the prophecy is real, which is why I am here all the way from London, sir. When Thackeray died, he said something else, something he couldn't get out because he was choking. I think he was saying…"

"We're not interested. You need to leave." Dad shuts the door and locks it. I'm frozen, unsure what to do with myself. My doll drops to the floor. From outside the door, I can still hear Carla yelling as she starts banging on the door. "Mr. Rigmore, listen to me, please!"

I am terrified at this very adult confrontation.

"Don't be afraid," my father says, kneeling as he softly takes my chin in his hand. "You are going to save the world someday. You are the Chosen One, Valora." Then he takes my hand and leads me away, leaving Carla yelling behind our front door..

"The prophecy wasn't finished, Mr. Rigmore, please! You have to listen to me!"

Just before he pulls me into his office, I wrench my hand out of my father's and sprint back down the hallway to grab my doll. She's lying in a thin ray of sunlight, filtered through the open mailbox in the door. When I bend down to grab her, and I see Carla's bright eyes watching me through the open slit.

Then she whispers words to me that I don't understand.

You aren't enough.

Instead of responding, I turn and walk away, leaving my doll behind. I see Grier watching

I won't play with it ever again. I see Carla's face outside the window, yelling because my father won't listen to her. I watch as the mailbox slot opens and I hear Carla's voice on the other side, whispering to me as I bend over to pick my doll.

"You probably won't remember this, Valora, but the prophecy is wrong. It was the last thing Thackeray tried to say to me as he was dying, but he couldn't get it out, so it couldn't be changed." I hear her take a deep breath.

"I believe what he was trying to say was not the Chosen One, *but the Chosen Womb.*"

G rier-
　　As my sister grabs me and we cling to one another, something strange and powerful bursts through and flows

between my sister and me. It's a cry, a signal pulled from the depths of our hearts that reaches across the chasm between us. It is like a beacon, a bond that I didn't know existed, a bond that I always wanted. The signal opens us up, clearing the way so that our hearts reach out for each other and there, in the empty place, we find each other. The gaping void where sisterhood should have been is rapidly filling, strong love pouring in like a flash flood. I look at Valora's face, and I see that she is feeling the same thing, and I wonder how that is possible, but then I understand that a deep truth is revealing itself to us, surely as a book falls open in my hands, and then I see it.

I am not the Chosen One. She is not the Chosen One.

"We are the Chosen Ones."

We say it together, staring for maybe the first time ever right into each other's eyes, our hands placed on each other's hearts, protecting what's there. The words rip something open between us that has been sealed over since birth. It has always kept us apart, like a wound that could never heal. My eyes are full of tears and Valora's are too as I reach out and grasp her face. Our foreheads meet as we lean into one another.

"Valora. It's us. Together."

She nods. "Oh my God. Thackeray's assistant came to the house once, I think she tried to tell me."

Behind us, I hear the screams of students and the wild laughter of Erys.

"How?" Valora asks. "How do we do this? Fight her? Grier..." She shakes her head. "I can't beat her." I can feel the truth passing from her to me, this gate finally blown open in desperation.

"I know," I whisper, and for just a moment, I close my eyes, running through all the things I know about our powers, and then the answer is there, as it always has been, waiting for me to discover it. I clutch her hand. "We are meant to do this together. The Chosen Ones." Once I think about it, it's so clear.

Valora is a weapon; honed and sharp...but I am the hand that wields it. I am wise and calculated, where she is reckless and fierce. I have the focus and she has the bravery. My portal isn't meant to move monsters. *It's meant to move my sister.*

I look over at Erys, who is drifting silently toward us over the students' heads. The Baleful lets its sharp tentacles drape over the faces of terrified students as their quiet sobs fill the courtyard.

"We can do this," I whisper to my sister. "You fight, and I'll move you where you need to go." She stares at me for a moment, bewildered, but then I watch her eyes widen. Maybe it's because she understands, but I see something else in them: trust, and a strange reassurance that pulses through our hearts, finally beating as one. She believes in me. *She sees me.*

Valora-

Erys is slowly walking toward us, hands outstretched, and instead of attacking, I do something utterly insane: I prepare to step into Grier's portal that she draws for me. It whirls open in front of me and I take a deep breath as I leap into it without thinking. I look back at Grier as it closes, and then it's like being hurtled through a wormhole of swirling blue light and hazy gray and then I'm being deposited on the other side of the courtyard. It happens in seconds; it's distorting and strange and my stomach turns, but I don't have time for nausea.

Erys is still facing where I had been a moment before, and I have a second to use to my advantage. I run up at her from behind and I hold my hands down as I do it. As I move I tear up everything around me; rocks, plants, dirt, stones, gravel, metal, and glass whirl behind me in a vortex of angry death. It gathers steam as I run, and then with everything I have in me, I throw it all at Erys and the monsters beside her. Then with a sweep of my hand, I send the students backward, away from my rain of chaos. The blow catches her off guard; she doesn't have time to block the onslaught and so all the debris smashes directly into her, sending her screaming against the school walls.

"RUN, YOU IDIOTS!" I scream at my classmates. They scatter. The Baleful above her head lashes its tentacles out at me, but just as Erys spins to face me, the blue light whirls around me again and then I'm back in Grier's portal. This time it spits me out on the grass, farther away from the courtyard. I try not to dry heave on the grass. This is going to take some getting used to.

Back in front of the school, Erys lets out a shout and long metal pylons come flying my way so fast I barely have time to drop to the ground as they soar over my head. My body is jerked up like a rag doll, and then Erys is pulling me toward the snapping jaws of a half-dead Oshimai. I try to release her hold, but I'm not strong enough. The creature's mouth brushes the top of my hair just as a portal opens beneath me. The swirling happens again and then I'm above Erys, dropped about five feet above where she is floating, and I think *seriously Grier?*

But then I see that I'm falling directly above the Baleful, and I don't have these fancy laser-edged knives for nothing. I pull them both out of my boots and plunge them directly into its head as I fall. It lets out a terrible screech and there are tentacles lashing all around me as I stab it again and again as we fall towards the ground, but I never hit.

Instead, I'm ferried through the portal back out to the grass, where Erys cannot go. I crawl forward a few feet, my bloody hands leaving prints behind. My body aches and I can feel Renata's power reserve seeping out of me. Erys is screaming as the Baleful writhes in her bloodied hands. I look over at Grier and she gives me a thumbs up, but our joy is short lived.

Erys lets out a terrible sound and I watch in horror as I helicopter blade comes whirling my way, too fast for me to move, but then it's a whirl of blue light and I'm standing safely outside the doors of the school. I see Erys make the connection of what's happening just before she goes for Grier. Something about the Baleful was connected to her power, and instead of lashing out with telekinesis, she is flying toward Grier as monsters advance from every side. My hands move fast, throwing monsters left and right, but I'm not fast enough and Erys is almost on my sister. *She's about to die.* Grier is trying to open a portal in front of her, but it's hard when monsters are crawling up her legs and grabbing her shoulders. I sink to my knees and pull off my gloves, and raise my hands. I feel my gift coursing through my veins and I focus it all, pulling the dregs of my power into a singular burst, and I send it out toward Grier.

It's farther than I've ever projected my power, and when it releases, it's so strong that I *see it* leave my hands like a shimmering wave as it passes over the ruins of the courtyard. Monsters go flying backward into the trees. I watch the blast hit Erys square in the chest as she raises her arms to kill my sister, and I watch it blow her backward – but no more than a few feet. It's not strong enough to kill her, but it is enough to push her into Grier's portal, the one she opened right as I sent the blast. The portal closes around Erys, and I think we've won. Then I see Erys's hand shoots out of the whirling blue and suddenly my sister's body is jerked up off the ground. I watch in utter horror as Erys sucks Grier into the portal with her. Then I'm alone.

My scream rattles the stones at Proctor Moor.

G rier -
I thought we had her, I thought we had won. I watched my sister with wonder, calling up a power that is somehow both of her and subordinate to her and I knew in that

second that I would never forget that moment, seeing the power flow out of her. I watched as Valora pushed it out from herself, face covered with the blood of a hundred monsters and still fighting. In that second, I saw her for who she truly is: Valora Rigmore, the most powerful Exceptional to ever live. I open the portal, and Erys disappears into it. *That's my sister, everyone,* I think, but then my body is jerked backward like a puppet on a string, a tether that's connected underneath my ribs.

Suddenly I'm being dragged, bony fingers closing around my wrist as I'm pulled into my own portal. My body begins thrashing as my brain races; Allen and I talked about this once, the possibility of me going inside my own portal, but we both agreed that that would cause some catastrophic paradox or possibly end the world with negative energy. Also, there was a high possibility that I would just die. And maybe that's what has happened here.

I feel the swirling blackness, like being underwater, a tremendous rush of air, and then there it is: bright blue light. I'm almost sure that I have died when my feet hit the ground. No, not the ground, but something like it. Everything around me is physical without being real. The air around us feels unbearably still and oppressive, yet seems to be filled with a heavy fog. There are no walls, no floors or ceilings, no up or down. There is just...everything. When I make my portal, all I see is a blue swirling light, but I see now that I was wrong; it's not just blue. It's a trillion different shades of blue, and they swirl together slowly, like paints mixing in a can. Behind them is a whirling, feverish light source, and when it meets the blue, it's dazzling. It's the most beautiful thing I've ever seen, and I'm tempted to stay forever just so I can watch. It's like being inside a star, only a star made of every good part of me. My hand trembles as I reach out and touch the light: the swirling colors explode into a thousand tiny sparks. They kiss my skin with a cool breath.

"You must be Grier." Erys's tone is calm and terrifying.

I turn around to find her facing me, watching me intently with a neutral expression on her face. Her bloodshot eyes glitter, and while I know I should be panicking or fighting to escape, I find myself instead watching her, waiting to see what she does next.

"Hello," I respond evenly, keeping the tremor from my voice. Behind her, the entire world swirls with liquid light.

She steps closer. "You know, I have to admit I didn't expect you to live this long. It seems Allen greatly underestimated you. He always underestimated everyone. That's the problem with narcissists. They're far too busy with their own foolish delusions of invincibility that they assume they're smarter than everyone else. He turned you into a lion but then forgot to lock the cage."

"We killed him," I mutter, remaining still, trying to keep my breathing steady.

She chuckles, a hollow, unnatural sound. "Oh, I know. I saw. I would say that I'm sad, but I'm not. He had begun to be a liability, and his worship of me was exhausting. Allen was just one more swamp creature looking for love and purpose. He served me well, but now his time is up."

She leans in and scrapes one filthy, blackened nail down my cheek. . I shudder involuntarily, and she throws back her head and laughs, her tiny white teeth so strange in their ordinariness. She steps forward.

"Have I frightened you, Grier? Don't tell me all those fairy-tales painting your arrogant sister as hero have you scared."

I still say nothing, but I flinch at the mention of Valora.

"Ah, it seems I've struck a nerve. Can't say I blame you. I know all about that, you know. You've spent your entire life overlooked, haven't you? Valora the Chosen One. Valora the beautiful one. Valora the popular one. And who are you? The afterthought, the spare. Nobody cared what you wanted, what you felt." She sighs, shrugging her narrow shoulders.. "It doesn't have to be that way. You can change it, Grier. We can change it. Together." She gestures around her.

"Let's leave here and give this world a real show. Give those waiting cameras what they really want: a spectacular end to the Chosen One, and then you and I..." She smiles, and it's so genuine that my hair stands on end. "You and I together will be unstoppable. In one year, we can have people worshipping us as queens."

She leans away and watches me for a reaction, and it dawns on me: *she doesn't know.* Erys still believes Valora is the sole Chosen One. She doesn't know that we were born to defeat her together. I fight to keep my expression from betraying anything and remain silent. She paces around me, lines of dewy light swirling around her as she moves. Her movement causes the swirling fog to billow and plume my direction, but I give it a stern look and it dissipates, and that's when I understand: I control what happens in my portal. It is beholden to me the way Valora's power is to her. I am safe here.

"I can offer you everything you didn't think you could have as the sister of the Chosen One," Erys hisses in my ear. *Like exile and horrible creatures?* I think, but stay quiet, my heart pounding.

"Look," she appeals to me. "You have all this power. More than your sister can ever hope to have. I know you know what it's like to live in the shadow of supposed greatness. I do. I spent what should've been the best years of my life, miserable and shoved aside, all because of Everett." She spits his name out as though it's poison.

"He was nothing compared to me, compared to what I could do, but did anyone even bother learning my name? Did anyone even bother acknowledging my existence? No. Not until it was too late, and even though I got him out of my way, now they speak of him as though he died some sort of martyr. Don't make the same mistake I did, Grier. Don't spend years waiting in her shadow. Let me kill Valora and you can take what is yours."

I say nothing. Her black eyes begin to blaze, and she lunges towards me.

"Don't waste my time, you foolish child! Answer me!" Somewhere outside the portal, I hear my sister screaming from a world away. As Erys reaches for me, I look at her and cock my head sideways. Her body freezes in mid air.

"No," she murmurs. "No, no, no." She turns on me again with one hand raised and unleashes what should have been instantaneous death. But it isn't. It's nothing here. Erys is powerless here while I'm in here with her. I feel one corner of my mouth turn up slightly as she paces like a caged animal, muttering to herself and shaking out her hands.

"This is mine." At the sound of my voice, she stops short and stares at me with desperate eyes. "You're powerless when I'm here because this portal is *mine*," I tell her. "I control it. It's my power, and you can't touch it. It's not a weapon; it's a world." *And I am God here.*

For a moment, I'm afraid she's going to fly into a rage again, but she approaches me slowly.

I stare at her, long and hard, calculating my next move, and then step back. "You're wrong, by the way." My voice is clear and steady. "It isn't Valora."

"What do you mean?" Erys sneers. "If she isn't the Chosen One, then who is? You?" She laughs. "Allen made that up. You don't mean to tell me you believed anything that idiot said, do you?"

I gaze levelly at her. "It isn't me. It's both of us. Together. You may have hated your brother, but I *love* my sister, even if I want to scream at her sometimes. We were made to defeat you, and we're going to."

Her mouth twists into an ugly knot, and she begins to shake. She lunges for me, and I know the time is now. In my mind, I see long fingers of the grey fog closing around her body, and then it happens. She is bound inside my portal. I take one last look at her, struggling against them, and I stretch my hand out.

"Goodnight, Erys," I say, before squeezing my eyes closed. I feel a rush of cool air pass through my body, and a strange tugging sensation at the back of my mind and then I'm swirling through the blue light again.

"Oh my god, Grier!" Valora is standing over me, her blood-spattered face creased with concern.

"I'm okay. I'm okay!" I assure her. "I'm here."

She helps me to my feet, and I'm hit with a wave of intense pain, both ears ringing as though my head is a clanging bell. "Grier, what's happening?"

She's ripping me apart is what's happening. I feel Erys in my mind, pulling me downward, fighting me. If I'm not in the portal, then she isn't bound. And she's unleashing hell.

"She's in my head. She's still there. I'm still holding her there!" I grit my teeth and grab my head with a cry of pain.

"Grier, your fingers," Valora gasps, and I look down to see the nail beds turning black, the darkness branching upward through my fingers as though it's coursing through my capillaries. "Get her out of your head!"

"I can't bring her back here. I can't. She'll kill us!"

"We can fight her together. We can, I know it," Valora is pleading now, clinging to my hands as the darkness spreads through me. I double over in pain, and when I open my eyes,

I'm looking right at the blown rock of Everett Proctor's head. My eyes widen. I understand just what we have to do.

"We don't have to fight her. We just have to put her over there."

Valora's gaze follows where I'm pointing, to the vast, rolling grounds of Proctor Moor, just past the concrete.

"Hurry," she says. Valora takes one of my hands in hers and holds it tightly. "We'll only have a second." I'm weakened, and my vision is fading into darkness, but I stretch out my palm one final time, closing my eyes and feeling the current flow through me. I hear the crackling of a whorl beginning to form, and then Valora gasps. I open my eyes just in time to see the portal widen.

For a moment, it whirls only feet above the ground, and then Erys appears, flailing wildly. Her power hits us and throws us backward, but Valora is ready. With everything in her, she pulls her arms downwards. I know, because I'm holding them too. With Valora's downward pull, we manage to make one of Erys's toes brush the ground. The ground infused with the chemical created by Everett Proctor.

We both take a breath; waiting, watching. At first I think nothing will happen, but then Erys freezes. Her eyes turn blood red and black liquid begins to pour from her ears as her fingers seem to liquefy in front of us. Her mouth opens in a silent scream as her skin begins to boil. Her feet dissipate and her body hits the ground. And then Erys combusts into a dark red mist, coating the grass for ten feet in all directions.

My sister and I stare, hand in hand, and for a moment, neither of us speaks. Then Valora opens her mouth to say something, and instead vomits at my feet.

. . .

Valora-

In case you were wondering, seeing someone get vaporized is super gross. As Erys's blood covers us like a mist I vomit, purging Erys from my life, purging all the death I have seen and delivered today. I hear shouts from behind me as Marines, staff members, and photographers surround us. Agnes wraps her arms around both Grier and I and squeezes us so hard that I feel anchored for just a moment. The flashes of cameras are blinding, followed by staff and students shouting questions at us. Above the clamor rises the cheering of the students of Proctor Moor, but I can't even deal and neither can Grier, and so I look at her wearily and she nods. Apparently, we are able to communicate without words now. Agnes holds back the press as we walk slowly back to the school, leaning on each other. As we walk past what used to be the doors of the school, I see Renata's body covered with a white sheet, and I am reminded of her final, brave moment. My greatest gift wasn't my power. It was her belief in me.

My entire body is exhausted beyond measure and by the way Grier's shoulders sag I can tell that she only has a few more minutes until she is going to pass out in spectacular fashion. Just before we go inside, I look back at the carnage left behind: bodies of monsters strewn across the grounds in a sea of blood, the courtyard now a pile of stone, rubble, and glass. The smoking skeletons of military helicopters flicker against the stars. And on the grass, a dark circle that used to be Erys.

"We should help." Grier mutters weakly, but I cup her face and turn it toward me, managing an honest smile at my sister for maybe the first time ever.

"You are a Chosen One," I whisper. "And Chosen Ones don't have to clean up."

Together we weave our way through throngs of cheering students until we finally reach our room, blessedly untouched in the still-standing Rigmore Wing. We don't even have enough energy to change so we both sink into my bed, covered in the blood and guts of monsters and doused in our own sweat, but for some reason it's never been sweeter. I curl up onto my side and Grier curls behind me and after a second's hesitation, flings an arm over me. We haven't cuddled like this since we were little girls, when we were free of the burdens laid at my feet. They are no more. It's over.

Soon, the outside world will descend on us. Parents, press, military, maybe the President even, who knows, but right now it's just us. With a sigh of relief 16 years in the making, I lay my head back against my sister's face and am calmed by the sound of her heavy breathing.

She is here. I am here.

The cheering outside acts like lullaby.

EPILOGUE - LEO

One Year Later

They are arguing again.

"Did you wear my shirt yesterday?"

"No, why?"

"I'm pretty sure that's my shirt in your hamper. Dark green, probably a little too big on you?"

Valora shakes her head with a sly, foxy smile. "I have no idea what you are talking about."

"Seriously, I was going to wear that tomorrow."

"Seriously Grier, I'm sure you'll live." She gestures to Grier's new, enormous closet.

"Fine, but you need to wash it. Soon." My girlfriend sighs good-naturedly and begins packing her stuff into a duffel bag. "What time is the chopper landing to take us to the plane?" she asks me after a minute, her eyes meeting mine with a twinkle. It's pretty fun being her handler, but then again, I can't imagine a time when I won't enjoy handling Grier.

I flip open my tablet, all business. "It lands in approximately seven minutes."

Valora tosses her long hair out of her eyes as she pulls on her boots, laden with dangerous goodies. "Where are we going again?"

I flip shut the tablet. "The smallest of the Hawaiian islands. There is a medium sized Lavasoji wreaking havoc on the local villages. There is also a dangerous cult that has grown to worship its existence that we'll have to deal with."

Valora rolls her eyes. "Of course there is. Can we at least visit a beach after?"

"No, this is work." I sigh, but then she raises her eyebrows at me and I know it's not a request.

"I'll see what I can do." They both smile.

Since the total vaporization of Erys, the monsters have kept coming. They aren't being controlled by anyone, but she did leave them with an insatiable taste for human flesh and destruction. A final parting gift. Just like her brother, Everett Proctor, Erys saved the best for last. It's bad, but it's manageable, and when both the Chosen Ones are in play...well, let's say the monsters hardly stand a chance. It's over within minutes.

And lives forever in infamy on the internet.

I watch Grier as she laces up her own boots: hers are brown, and her own uniform fits her perfectly. Where Valora's are sleek, black, and primed for combat, Grier's are comfortable, something she can move in. She wears green leggings and a navy blouse with cats all over it. She pulls her hair up in a messy bun, and God, I'm butter. I slide over to her and kiss her, feeling her soft body against mine.

"Uggghhhh..." I hear Valora groaning at us, and ignore her, just like we always do. When I pull away, I watch the blush rise up Grier's cheeks. I lean my forehead against hers.

"I love you," I murmur.

She nods in return. "Same." It's what we say.

I step back and circle my fingers. "Alright, let's wrap it up!"

Valora is applying lipstick in the mirror. "This isn't a beauty pageant, Valora."

She looks over at me, always exasperated. "I'll keep that mind, Leo."

We have this conversation at least once a month; she's the annoying sister I never wanted. I clear my throat. Now it's time to be their official handler. It was part of their stipulation: that their handlers had to be students their own age. No more adults telling them what to do, no more secrets. And for the most part, Agnes and I don't tell them what to do. They know best about their gifts. They know best how to handle the monsters. But scheduling themselves and handling logistics is a different matter, and Agnes and I...we've got that.

In the distance we hear the whipping blades of our helicopter, which carries the girls' own personal squadron of Marines. Valora looks out the window in anticipation. "Meet you out there, Leo?"

I nod and take my leave, but I stop just outside the door to watch my favorite ritual. Valora and Grier turn toward each other, and I watch them speak quiet, loving words to one another: promises to protect, promises to listen when the other needs decompressing. There is a bond here, yes; whatever bonded them in the womb is now flowing freely between them, but it's mostly that they have worked at their relationship, day after day, fight after fight. I have watched as these sisters have crawled their way toward one another over years of baggage until they are where they are now: as close as twins can be.

Their foreheads meet, and then, without warning, they start giggling at the intensity of it all. They may be the Chosen Ones, but they are still teenage girls. Grier says something that makes Valora groan and then there is a circle of blue light that traces around them. Grier is barely moving her hand; in fact, she's very close to being able to make the portal with no physical effort at all. The portal glows and whirls. I never tire of looking at it, so wild and strange in both its beauty and control. It's so very Grier. Valora raises her hand and their bags lift off the bed and land solidly next to their feet.

"Ready?" asks Grier, and Valora nods. She reaches down and takes her sister's hand and the portal swallows them both. I run through the school, students stepping back to let me through. I swiftly make my way out to the front of the school and jog into the newly built courtyard, packed with students lolling about on the grass, where Agnes stands to greet the girls and the helicopter. Everyone watches the helicopter when it lands, not with panic but with the casual curiosity of people who see this all the time. There is a crack, and Grier's portal opens next to Agnes and the helicopter. The Chosen Ones step out. Agnes bursts out laughing, and I chuckle and shake my head. *God, they are so lazy sometimes.* Last week I caught them using it to steal donuts from the school kitchen. Pink frosted ones; they were good.

A young Marine steps out of the helicopter and helps Valora up, while totally forgetting to help Grier. She looks back at me with total exasperation and I shrug. Pike can't help it. Even now that he's left Proctor Moor for this special team of Marines, Pike still sees only Valora and no one else. I'm 80% sure they are secretly dating.

I'm running across the lawn as Grier beckons me over. "Leo, come on!"

I climb clumsily onto the helicopter, wave to Agnes, and find my seat as she signals the pilot that we're cleared for take-off. I sit next to our gruff commander who barks a few words at me before going silent. I pull out my tablet. "Okay! Let's go over this now before we get to the plane. The Lavasoji, roughly the size of a football field, originated from the volcanic..." I continue talking, but the girls aren't listening, and that's okay. Their power doesn't come from knowledge; it's more for their team's sake. They lean against each other, resting in their friendship, identical half-smiles plastered across their faces

I smile. The Chosen Ones have finally chosen each other.

The violent cut of the blades fade into background noise as the Rigmore sisters soar out over the Connecticut hills, sleepy after a long winter.

I settle in for the ride.

THE END

ACKNOWLEDGMENTS

Erin wishes to thank:

Travis, my best friend and forever partner in crime. You always believe in me, even when I forget to believe in myself.

Mom and dad, for loving and encouraging me always.

My late grandmothers, Maxine and Lois, who gave me new worlds in the form of books and told me I could do anything.

Mrs. Nevetta Sieg and Mrs. Alice Rohde, my fourth and sixth grade teachers, for encouraging an awkward little girl with a wild imagination. You saw potential, and you nurtured it in your classrooms. I am forever grateful for you.

My mom village, for carrying me and encouraging me as a person, a writer, and a mom; Kristin Bork and Kelly Curran, this only child's lifelong sister-friends.

Early readers for honest and encouraging feedback, and for helping this story grow.

Dr. Katie Hanson for being a tireless cheerleader and never batting an eye when we picked her pathologist brain with bizarre questions like, "So what happens to a body when somebody's electrocuted, anyway?"

Colleen Oakes, who said I should write a book with her and

meant it. What an adventure we've had. Thank you for your confidence in me, for your patience and wisdom. Look what we did!

Colleen wishes to thank:

Ryan, for always believing in me, and not blinking an eye when I want to take calculated risks and not so calculated ones. You love me for who I am in every changing minute.

Tricia McCulley, for being the best listener I've ever met and the best mom I've ever known.

Dad, for the spark. For Denise, thanks for calming the spark when it gets too bright.

Cynthia, for laugher. This book is about sisters, and I have the best one. You understand my silly heart in a way that no one else does, and I would be lost without you.

Erin, who was totally on board with this insane idea from day one. It wasn't easy, but it was beautiful, and I believe that Valora and Grier breathed as much life into us as we did into them. I'm forever grateful that it brought us closer through endless emails and one sweaty weekend spent in a St. Louis café.

For the friends who hold steady when the world is spinning, who bring wine and cheese and much needed road trips: Katie Hall, Nicole London, Kimberly Stein, Elizabeth Wagner, Jonathan and Adrienne Kern, Brianna Shrum, Amanda Sanders, Cassandra Splittgerber, James and Jackie Fernandez.

For those who support my books and my writing through hell and high water, but especially Christopher Stewart, who has made it his job to pass along my books and the staff at Anythink WF.

For my readers: I love you. I write many things, none the same, and I appreciate your flexibility as I create and stay loyal to the strange literary beatings of my heart.

ALSO BY COLLEEN OAKES

CPSIA information can be obtained
at www.ICGtesting.com
Printed in the USA
LVHW090818230920
666664LV00023B/23/J